The Hanging Man
& OTHER WESTERN STORIES
By Bill Pronzini

T0361609

STARK HOUSE

Stark House Press • Eureka California

THE HANGING MAN & OTHER WESTERN STORIES

Published by Stark House Press
1315 H Street
Eureka, CA 95501, USA
griffinskye3@sbcglobal.net
www.starkhousepress.com

ISBN: 979-8-88601-106-7

Cover and text design by Mark Shepard, shepgraphics.com

First Stark House Press Edition: December 2024

THE HANGING MAN

Bill Pronzini has been writing westerns throughout his long and varied career, and this volume collects the author's best.

Here are stories peopled by such familiar figures as lawmen, ranchers, cowhands, gamblers, detectives, newspapermen, gunfighters and timberjacks; and by such less utilized characters as stable hands, ferry tenders, writers, bartenders, saddle makers, tramp printers, confidence men, traveling dentists, moonshiners and patent medicine drummers.

Here are stories set in small, imaginary Montana towns and ranches to actual locales such as the California Mother Lode, the Sacramento River delta, and the Oregon wilderness.

Here are stories that run the gamut from dark character studies to stories of action, mystery and adventure to lighthearted tall tales.

"Burglarproof" features John Quincannon, the male half of the 1890s firm of Carpenter and Quincannon, Professional Detective Services. "McIntosh's Chute" tells of the hardships faced by a deep woods logging gang and the fitting vengeance they enact on its tyrannical leader.

"Crucifixion River" is a collaborative novella set in and around a delta slough ferry crossing, and earned Pronzini and his wife Marcia Muller a 2008 Western Writers of America Spur Award for the best short fiction published the previous year. A new story, "A Cruel and Deadly Winter," shares a dying man's thoughts as he contemplates the life he leaves behind.

And then there's "The Hanging Man"…

TABLE OF CONTENTS

ACKNOWLEDGMENTS

AUTHOR'S PREFACE

The Western story is a uniquely American art form, not only embraced by American enthusiasts but by citizens of many foreign countries. There have been a vast number of fictionalized accounts of the great westward expansion of the 19th and early 20th centuries – literary novels, dime novels, pulp and "slick" magazine stories, comic books, films, episodic TV shows. Many were factually based to one degree or another, but the preponderance created and popularized Western myth.

The stories collected here are the best of my short contributions to the genre. (I've also published several Western novels.) They encompass an array of characters, settings, and themes, and are peopled by such familiar figures as lawmen, ranchers, cowhands, gamblers, detectives, newspapermen, gunfighters, and timberjacks, and by such little used Westerners as stable hands, ferry tenders, writers, bartenders, saddle makers, tramp printers, confidence men, traveling dentists, moonshiners, and patent medicine drummers. Settings extend from small, imaginary Montana towns and ranches to actual locales such as the California Mother Lode, the Sacramento River delta, and the Oregon wilderness.

In scope they run the gamut from dark character studies to stories of action, mystery and adventure to lighthearted tall tales. "Burglarproof" features John Quincannon, the male half of the 1890s firm of Carpenter and Quincannon, Professional Detective Services, who considers himself "the most celebrated sleuth west of the Mississippi River." The hardships faced by a deep woods logging gang, the fitting vengeance they enact on its tyrannical leader, and "the damnedest sight a man ever set eyes on" is the stuff of "McIntosh's Chute." A collaborative novella set in and around a delta slough ferry crossing, "Crucifixion River," earned my wife Marcia Muller and me a 2008 Western Writers of America Spur Award for the best short fiction published the previous year.

Some critics would have us believe that the traditional Western story is limited to conventional plots, stock characters, and simplistic themes. This is patently not the case. The Western tale can be many things; the 17 stories gathered here demonstrate a fraction of its wide range of possibilities.

—Petaluma, CA
November 2023

The Hanging Man

& OTHER WESTERN STORIES

By Bill Pronzini

THE HANGING MAN

It was Sam McCullough who found the hanging man, down on the river bank behind his livery stable.

Straightaway he went looking for Ed Bozeman and me, being as we were the local sheriff's deputies. Tule River didn't have any full time law officers back then, in the late 1890s; just volunteers like Boze and me to keep the peace, and a fat-bottomed sheriff who came through from the county seat two or three days a month to look things over and to stuff himself on pig's knuckles at the Germany Café.

Time was just past sunup, on one of those frosty mornings Northern California gets in late November, and Sam found Boze already to work inside his mercantile. But they had to come fetch me out of my house, where I was just sitting down to breakfast. I never did open up my place of business—Miller's Feed and Grain—until 8:30 of a weekday morning.

I had some trouble believing it when Sam first told about the hanging man. He said, "Well, how in hell do you think I felt." He always has been an excitable sort and he was frothed up for fair just then. "I like to had a hemorrhage when I saw him hanging there on that black oak. Damnedest sight a man ever stumbled on."

"You say he's a stranger?"

"Stranger to me. Never seen him before."

"You make sure he's dead?"

Sam made a snorting noise. "I ain't even going to answer that. You just come along and see for yourself."

I got my coat, told my wife Ginny to ring up Doc Petersen on Mr. Bell's invention, and then hustled out with Sam and Boze. It was mighty cold that morning; the sky was clear and brittle-looking, like blue-painted glass, and the sun had the look of a two-day-old egg yolk above the tule marshes east of the river. When we came in alongside the stable I saw that there was silvery frost all over the grass on the river bank. You could hear it crunch when you walked on it.

The hanging man had frost on him, too. He was strung up on a fat old oak between the stable and the river, opposite a high board fence that separated Sam's property from Joel Pennywell's fixit shop next door. Dressed mostly in black, he was—black denims, black hoots, a black cutaway coat that had seen better days. He had black hair, too, long and kind of matted. And a black tongue pushed out at one corner of a black-mottled face. All that black was streaked in silver, and there was silver on the rope that stretched between his neck and the thick limb above. He was the damnedest sight a man ever stumbled on, all right. Frozen up there, silver and black, glistening in the cold sunlight, like something cast up from the Pit.

We stood looking at him for a time, not saying anything. There was a thin wind off the river and I could feel it prickling up the hair on my neck. But it didn't stir that hanging man, nor any part of him or his clothing.

Boze cleared his throat, and he did it loud enough to make me jump. He asked me, "You know him, Carl?"

"No," I said. "You?"

"No. Drifter, you think?"

"Got the look of one."

Which he did. He'd been in his thirties, smallish, with a clean-shaven fox face and pointy ears. His clothes were shabby, shirt cuffs frayed, button missing off his cutaway coat. We got us a fair number of drifters in Tule River, up from San Francisco or over from the mining country after their luck and their money ran out—men looking for farm work or such other jobs as they could find. Or sometimes looking for trouble. Boze and I had caught one just two weeks before and locked him up for chicken stealing.

"What I want to know," Sam said, "is what in the name of hell he's doing *here?*"

Boze shrugged and rubbed at his bald spot, like he always does when he's fuddled. He was the same age as me, thirty-four, but he'd been losing his hair for the past ten years. He said, "Appears he's been hanging a while. When'd you close up last evening, Sam?"

"Six, like always."

"Anybody come around afterwards?"

"No."

"Could've happened any time after six, then. It's kind of a lonely spot back here after dark. I reckon there's not much chance anybody saw what happened."

"Joel Pennywell, maybe," I said. "He stays open late some nights."

"We can ask him."

Sam said, "But why'd anybody string him up like that?"

"Maybe he wasn't strung up. Maybe he hung himself."

"Suicide?"

"It's been known to happen," Boze said.

Doc Petersen showed up just then, and a couple of other townsfolk with him; word was starting to get around. Doc, who was sixty and dyspeptic, squinted up at the hanging man, grunted, and said,

"Strangulation."

"Doc?"

"Strangulation. Man strangled to death. You can see that from the way his tongue's out. Neck's not broken; you can see that too."

"Does that mean he could've killed himself?"

"All it means," Doc said, "is that he didn't jump off a high branch or get jerked hard enough off a horse to break his neck."

"Wasn't a horse involved anyway," I said. "There'd be shoe marks in the area; ground was soft enough last night, before the freeze. Boot marks here and there, but that's all."

"I don't know anything about that," Doc said. "All I know is, that gent up there died of strangulation. You want me to tell you anything else, you'll have to cut him down first."

Sam and Boze went to the stable to fetch a ladder. While they were gone I paced around some, to see if there was anything to find in the vicinity. And I did find something, about a dozen feet from the oak where the boot tracks were heaviest in the grass. It was a circlet of bronze, about three inches in diameter, and when I picked it up, I saw that it was one of those Presidential Medals the government used to issue at the Philadelphia Mint. On one side it had a likeness of Benjamin Harrison, along with his name and the date of his inauguration, 1889, and on the other were a tomahawk, a peace pipe, and a pair of clasped hands.

There weren't many such medals in California; mostly they'd been supplied to Army officers in other parts of the West, who handed them out to Indians after peace treaties were signed. But this one struck a chord in my memory: I recollected having seen it or one like it some months back. The only thing was, I couldn't quite remember where.

Before I could think any more on it, Boze and Sam came back with the ladder, a plank board, and a horse blanket. Neither of them seemed inclined to do the job at hand, so I climbed up myself and sawed through that half-frozen rope with my pocket knife. It wasn't good work; my mouth was dry when it was done. When we had him down we covered him up and laid him on the plank. Then we carried him out to Doc's wagon and took him to the Spencer Funeral Home.

After Doc and Obe Spencer stripped the body, Boze and I went through the dead man's clothing. There was no identification of any kind; if he'd been carrying any before he died, somebody had filched it. No wallet or purse, either. All he had in his pockets was the stub of a lead pencil, a half-used book of matches, a short-six seegar, a nearly empty Bull Durham sack, three wheatstraw papers, a two-bit piece, an old Spanish real coin, and a dog-eared and stained copy of a Beadle dime novel called *Captain Dick Talbot, King of the Road; Or, The Black-Hoods of Shasta.*

"Drifter, all right," Boze said when we were done. "Wouldn't you say, Carl?"

"Sure seems that way."

"But even drifters have more belongings than this. Shaving gear, extra clothes—at least that much."

"You'd think so," I said. "Might be he had a carpetbag or the like and it's hidden somewhere along the river bank."

"Either that or it was stolen. But we can go take a look when Doc gets through studying on the body."

I fished out the bronze medal I'd found in the grass earlier and showed it to him. "Picked this up while you and Sam were getting the ladder," I said. "Belonged to the hanging man, maybe."

"Maybe. But it seems familiar, somehow. I can't quite place where I've seen one like it."

Boze turned the medal over in his hand. "Doesn't ring any bells for me," he said.

"Well, you don't see many around here, and the one I recollect was also a Benjamin Harrison. Could be coincidence, I suppose. Must be if that fella died by his own hand."

"If he did."

"Boze, you think it *was* suicide?"

"I'm hoping it was," he said, but he didn't sound any more convinced than I was. "I don't like the thought of a murderer running around loose in Tule River."

"That makes two of us," I said.

Doc didn't have much to tell us when he came out. The hanging man had been shot once a long time ago—he had bullet scars on his right shoulder and back—and one foot was missing a pair of toes. There was also a fresh bruise on the left side of his head, above the ear.

Boze asked, "Is it a big bruise, Doc?"

"Big enough."

"Could somebody have hit him hard enough to knock him out?"

"And then hung him afterward? Well, it could've happened that way. His neck's full of rope burns and lacerations, the way it would be if somebody hauled him up over that tree limb."

"Can you reckon how long he's been dead?"

"Last night some time. Best I can do."

Boze and I headed back to the livery stable. The town had come awake by this time. There were plenty of people on the boardwalks and Main Street was crowded with horses and farm wagons; any day now I expected to see somebody with one of those newfangled motor cars. The hanging man was getting plenty of lip service, on Main Street and among the crowd that had gathered back of the stable to gawk at the black oak and trample the grass.

Nothing much goes on in a small town like Tule River, and such as a hanging was bound to stir up folks' imaginations. There hadn't been a killing in the area in four or five years. And damned little mystery since the town was founded back in the days when General Vallejo owned most of the land hereabouts and it was the Mexican flag, not the Stars and Stripes, that flew over California.

None of the crowd had found anything in the way of evidence on the river bank; they would have told us if they had. None of them knew anything about the hanging man, either. That included Joel Pennywell, who had come over from his fixit shop next door. He'd closed up around 6:30 last night, he said, and gone straight on home.

After a time Boze and I moved down to the river's edge and commenced a search among the tule grass and trees that grew along there. The day had warmed some; the wind was down and the sun had melted off the last of the frost. A few of the others joined in with us, eager and boisterous, like it was an Easter egg hunt. It was too soon for the full impact of what had happened to settle in on most folks; it hadn't occurred to them yet that maybe they ought to be concerned.

A few minutes before ten o'clock, while we were combing the west-side bank up near the Main Street Basin, and still not finding anything, the Whipple youngster came running to tell us that Roberto Ortega and Sam McCullough wanted to see us at the livery stable. Roberto owned a dairy ranch just south of town and claimed to be a descendant of a Spanish conquistador. He was also an honest man, which was why he was in town that morning. He'd found a saddled horse grazing on his pastureland and figured it for a runaway from Sam's livery, so he'd brought it in. But Sam had never seen the animal, an old swaybacked roan, until Roberto showed up with it. Nor had he ever seen the battered carpetbag that was tied behind the cantle of the cheap Mexican saddle.

It figured to be the drifter's horse and carpetbag, sure enough. But whether the drifter had turned the animal loose himself, or somebody else had, we had no way of knowing. As for the carpetbag, it didn't tell us any more about the hanging man than the contents of his pockets. Inside it were some extra clothes, an old Colt Dragoon revolver, shaving tackle, a woman's garter, and nothing at all that might identify the owner.

Sam took the horse, and Boze and I took the carpetbag over to Obe Spencer's to put with the rest of the hanging man's belongings. On the way we held a conference. Fact was, a pair of grain barges were due upriver from San Francisco at eleven, for loading and return. I had three men working for me, but none of them handled the paperwork; I was going to have to spend some time at the feed mill that day, whether I wanted to or not. Which is how it is when you have part-time deputies who are also full-time businessmen. It was a fact of small-town life we'd had to learn to live with.

We worked it out so that Boze would continue making inquiries while I went to work at the mill. Then we'd switch off at one o'clock so he could give his wife Ellie, who was minding the mercantile, some help with customers and with the drummers who always flocked around with Christmas wares right after Thanksgiving.

We also decided that if neither of us turned up any new information by five o'clock—or even if we did—we would ring up the country seat and make a full report to the sheriff. Not that Joe Perkins would be able to find out anything we couldn't. He was a fat-cat political appointee, and about all he knew how to find was pig's knuckles and beer. But we were bound to do it by the oath of office we'd taken.

We split up at the funeral parlor and I went straight to the mill. My foreman, Gene Kleinschmidt, had opened up; I'd given him a set of keys and he knew to go ahead and unlock the place if I wasn't around. The barges came in twenty minutes after I did, and I had to hustle to get the paperwork ready that they would be carrying back down to San Francisco—bills of lading, requisitions for goods from three different companies.

I finished up a little past noon and went out onto the dock to watch the loading. One of the bargemen was talking to Gene. And while he was doing it, he kept flipping something up and down in his hand—a small gold nugget. It was the kind of thing folks made into a watch fob, or kept as a good-luck charm.

And that was how I remembered where I'd seen the Benjamin Harrison Presidential Medal. Eight months or so back a newcomer to the area, a man named Jubal Parsons, had come in to buy some sacks of chicken feed. When he'd reached into his pocket to pay the bill he had accidentally come out with the medal. "Good-luck charm," he said, and let me glance at it before putting it away again.

Back inside my office I sat down and thought about Jubal Parsons. He was a tenant farmer—had taken over a small farm owned by the Siler brothers out near Willow Creek about nine months ago. Big fellow, over six feet tall, and upwards of 220 pounds. Married to a blonde woman named Greta, a few years younger than him and pretty as they come. Too pretty, some said; a few of the womenfolk, Ellie Bozeman included, thought she had the look and mannerisms of a tramp.

Parsons came into Tule River two or three times a month to trade for supplies, but you seldom saw the wife. Neither of them went to church on Sunday, nor to any of the social events at the Odd Fellows Hall. Parsons kept to himself mostly, didn't seem to have any friends or any particular vices. Always civil, at least to me, but taciturn and kind of broody-looking. Not the sort of fellow you find yourself liking much.

But did the medal I'd found belong to him? And if it did, had he hung the drifter? And if he had, what was his motive?

I was still puzzling on that when Boze showed up. He was a half hour early, and he had Floyd Jones with him. Floyd looked some like Santa Claus—fat and jolly and white-haired—and he liked it when you told him so. He was the night bartender at the Elkhorn Bar and Grill.

Boze said, "Got some news, Carl. Floyd here saw the hanging man last night. Recognized the body over to Obe Spencer's just now."

Floyd bobbed his head up and down. "He came into the Elkhorn about eight o'clock, asking for work."

I said, "How long did he stay?"

"Half hour, maybe. Told him we already had a swamper and he spent five minutes trying to convince me he'd do a better job of cleaning up. Then he gave it up when he come to see I wasn't listening, and bought a beer and nursed it over by the stove. Seemed he didn't much relish going back into the cold."

"He say anything else to you?"

"Not that I can recall."

"Didn't give his name, either," Boze said. "But there's something else. Tell him, Floyd."

"Well, there was another fella came in just after the drifter," Floyd said. "Ordered a beer and sat watching him. Never took his eyes off that drifter once. I wouldn't have noticed except for that and because we were near empty. Cold kept most everybody to home last night."

"You know this second man?" I asked.

"Sure do. Local farmer. Newcomer to the area, only been around for—"

"Jubal Parsons?"

Floyd blinked at me. "Now how in thunder did you know that?"

"Lucky guess. Parsons leave right after the drifter?"

"He did. Not more than ten seconds afterward."

"You see which direction they went?"

"Downstreet, I think. Toward Sam McCullough's livery."

I thanked Floyd for his help and shooed him on his way. When he was gone Boze asked me, "Just how did you know it was Jubal Parsons?"

"I finally remembered where I'd seen that Presidential Medal I found. Parsons showed it when he was here one day several months ago. Said it was his good-luck charm."

Boze rubbed at his bald spot. "That and Floyd's testimony make a pretty good case against him, don't they?"

"They do. Reckon I'll go out and have a talk with him."

"We'll both go," Boze said. "Ellie can mind the store the rest of the day. This is more important. Besides, if Parsons is a killer, it'll be safer if there are two of us."

I didn't argue; a hero is something I never was nor wanted to be. We left the mill and went and picked up Boze's buckboard from behind the mercantile. On the way out of town we stopped by his house and mine long enough to fetch our rifles. Then we headed west on Willow Creek Road.

It was a long cool ride out to Jubal Parsons' tenant farm, through a lot of rich farmland and stands of willows and evergreens. Neither of us said much. There wasn't much to say. But I was tensed up and I could see that Boze was, too.

A rutted trail hooked up to the farm from Willow Creek Road, and Boze jounced the buckboard along there some past three o'clock. It was pretty modest acreage. Just a few fields of corn and alfalfa, with a cluster of ramshackle buildings set near where Willow Creek cut through the northwest corner. There was a one-room farmhouse, a chicken coop, a barn, a couple of lean-tos, and a pole corral. That was all except for a small windmill—a Fairbanks, Morse Eclipse—that the Siler brothers had put up because the creek was dry more than half the year.

When we came in sight of the buildings I could tell that Jubal Parsons had done work on the place. The farmhouse had a fresh coat of whitewash, as did the chicken coop, and the barn had a new roof.

There was nobody in the farmyard, just half a dozen squawking leghorns, when we pulled in and Boze drew rein. But as soon as we stepped down, the front door of the house opened and Greta Parsons came out on the porch. She was wearing a calico dress and high-button shoes, but her head was bare; that butter-yellow hair of hers hung down to her hips, glistening like the bargeman's gold nugget in the sun. She was some pretty woman, for a fact. It made your throat thicken up just to look at her, and funny ideas start to stir around in your head. If ever there was a woman to tempt a man to sin, I thought, it was this one.

Boze stayed near the buckboard, with his rifle held loose in one hand, while I went over to the porch steps and took off my hat. "I'm Carl Miller, Missus Parsons," I said. "That's Ed Bozeman back there. We're from Tule River. Maybe you remember seeing us?"

"Yes, Mr. Miller. I remember you."

"We'd like a few words with your husband. Would he be somewhere nearby?"

"He's in the barn," she said. There was something odd about her voice—a kind of dullness, as if she was fatigued. She moved that way, too, loose and jerky. She didn't seem to notice Boze's rifle, or to care if she did.

I said, "Do you want to call him out for us?"

"No, you go on in. It's all right."

I nodded to her and rejoined Boze, and we walked on over to the barn. Alongside it was a McCormick & Deering binder-harvester, and further down, under a lean-to, was an old buggy with its storm curtains buttoned up. A big gray horse stood in the corral, nuzzling a pile of hay. The smell of dust and earth and manure was ripe on the cool air.

The barn doors were shut. 1 opened one half, stood aside from the opening, and called out, "Mister Parsons? You in there?"

No answer.

I looked at Boze. He said, "We'll go in together," and I nodded. Then we shouldered up and I pulled the other door half open. And we went inside.

It was shadowed in there, even with the doors open; those parts of the interior I could make out were empty. I eased away from Boze, toward where the corn crib was. There was sweat on me; I wished I'd taken my own rifle out of the buckboard.

"Mister Parsons?"

Still no answer. I would have tried a third time, but right then Boze said, "Never mind, Carl," in a way that made me turn around and face him.

He was a dozen paces away, staring down at something under the hayloft. I frowned and moved over to him. Then I saw too, and my mouth came open and there was a slithery feeling on my back.

Jubal Parsons was lying there dead on the sod floor, with blood all over his shirtfront and the side of his face. He'd been shot. There was a .45-70 Springfield rifle beside the body, and when Boze bent down and struck a match, you could see the black-powder marks mixed up with the blood.

"My God," I said, soft.

"Shot twice," Boze said. "Head and chest."

"Twice rules out suicide."

"Yeah," he said.

We traded looks in the dim light. Then we turned and crossed back to the doors. When we came out Mrs. Parsons was sitting on the front steps of the house, looking past the windmill at the alfalfa fields. We went over and stopped in front of her. The sun was at our backs, and the way we stood put her in our shadow. That was what made her look up; she hadn't seen us coming, or heard us crossing the yard.

She said, "Did you find him?"

"We found him," Boze said. He took out his badge and showed it to her.

"We're county sheriff's deputies, Missus Parsons. You'd best tell us what happened in there."

"I shot him," she said. Matter-of-fact, like she was telling you the time of day. "This morning, just after breakfast. Ever since I've wanted to hitch up the buggy and drive in and tell about it, but I couldn't seem to find the courage. It took all the courage I had to fire the rifle."

"But why'd you do a thing like that?"

"Because of what he did in Tule River last night."

"You mean the hanging man?"

"Yes. Jubal killed him."

"Did he tell you that?"

"Yes. Not long before I shot him."

"Why did he do it—hang that fellow?"

"He was crazy jealous, that's why."

I asked her, "Who was the dead man?"

"I don't know."

"You mean to say he was a stranger?"

"Yes," she said. "I only saw him once. Yesterday afternoon. He rode in looking for work. I told him we didn't have any, that we were tenant farmers, but he wouldn't leave. He kept following me around, saying things. He thought I was alone here—a woman alone."

"Did he—make trouble for you?"

"Just with words. He kept saying things, ugly things. Men like that—I don't know why, but they think I'm a woman of easy virtue. It has always been that way, no matter where we've lived."

"What did you do?" Boze asked.

"Ignored him at first. Then I begged him to go away. I told him my husband was wild jealous, but he didn't believe me. I thought I was alone too, you see; I thought Jubal had gone off to work in the fields."

"But he hadn't?"

"Oh, he had. But he came back while the drifter was here and he overheard part of what was said."

"Did he show himself to the man?"

"No. He would have if matters had gone beyond words, but that didn't happen. After a while he got tired of tormenting me and went away. The drifter, I mean."

"Then what happened?"

"Jubal saddled his horse and followed him. He followed that man into Tule River and when he caught up with him he knocked him on the head and he hung him."

Boze and I traded another look. I said what both of us were thinking: "Just for deviling you? He hung a man for that?"

"I told you, Jubal was crazy jealous. You didn't know him. You just—you don't know how he was. He said that if a man thought evil, and spoke evil, it was the same as doing evil. He said if a man was wicked, he deserved to be hung for his wickedness and the world would be a better place for his leaving it."

She paused, and then made a gesture with one hand at her bosom. It was a meaningless kind of gesture, but you could see where a man might take it the wrong way. Might take *her* the wrong way, just like she'd said. And not just a man, either; women, too. Everybody that didn't keep their minds open and went rooting around after sin in other folks.

"Besides," she went on, "he worshipped the ground I stand on. He truly did, you know. He couldn't bear the thought of anyone sullying me."

I cleared my throat. The sweat on me had dried and I felt cold now. "Did you hate him, Missus Parsons?"

"Yes, I hated him. Oh, yes. I feared him, too—for a long time I feared him more than anything else. He was so big. And so strong-willed. I used to tremble sometimes, just to look at him."

"Was he cruel to you?" Boze asked. "Did he hurt you?"

"He was and he did. But not the way you mean; he didn't beat me, or once lay a hand to me the whole nine years we were married. It was his vengeance that hurt me. I couldn't stand it, I couldn't take any more of it."

She looked away from us again, out over the alfalfa fields—and a long ways beyond them, at something only she could see. "No roots," she said, "that was part of it, too. No roots. Moving here, moving there, always moving—three states and five homesteads in less than ten years. And the fear. And the waiting. This was the last time, I couldn't take it ever again. Not one more minute of his jealousy, his cruelty . . . *his* wickedness."

"Ma'am, you're not making sense—"

"But I am," she said. "Don't you see? He was Jubal Parsons, the Hanging Man."

I started to say something, but she shifted position on the steps just then—and when she did that her face came out of shadow and into the sunlight, and I saw in her eyes a kind of terrible knowledge. It put a chill on my neck like the night wind does when it blows across a graveyard.

"That drifter in Tule River wasn't the first man Jubal hung on account of me," she said. "Not even the first in California. That drifter was the Hanging Man's sixth."

MARKERS

Jack Bohannon and I had been best friends for close to a year, ever since he'd hired on at the Two Bar Cross, but if it hadn't been for a summer squall that came up while the two of us were riding fence, I'd never have found out about who and what he was. Or about the markers.

We'd been out two weeks, working the range southeast of Eagle Mountain. The fences down along there were in middling fair shape, considering the winter we'd had; Bohannon and I sported calluses from the wire cutters and stretchers, but truth to tell, we hadn't been exactly overworking ourselves. Just kind of moving along at an easy pace. The weather had been fine—cool crisp mornings, warm afternoons, sky scrubbed clean of clouds on most days—and it made you feel good just to be there in all that sweet-smelling open space.

As it happened, we were about two miles east of the Eagle Mountain line shack when the squall came up. Came up fast, too, along about three o'clock in the afternoon, the way a summer storm does sometimes in Wyoming Territory. We'd been planning to spend a night at the line shack anyway, to replenish our supplies, so as soon as the sky turned cloudy dark we lit a shuck straight for it. The rain started before we were halfway there, and by the time we raised the shack, the downpour was such that you couldn't see a dozen rods in front of you. We were both soaked in spite of our slickers; rain like that has a way of slanting in under any slicker that was ever made.

The shack was just a one-room sod building with walls coated in ashes-and-clay and a whipsawed wood floor. All that was in it was a pair of bunks, a table and two chairs, a larder, and a big stone fireplace. First things we did when we came inside, after sheltering the horses for the night in the lean-to out back, were to build a fire on the hearth and raid the larder. Then, while we dried off, we brewed up some coffee and cooked a pot of beans and salt pork. It was full dark by then and that storm was kicking up a hell of a fuss; you could see lightning blazes outside the single window, and hear thunder grumbling in the distance and the wind moaning in the chimney flue.

When we finished supper Bohannon pulled a chair over in front of the fire, and I sat on one of the bunks, and we took out the makings. Neither of us said much at first. We didn't have to talk to enjoy each other's company; we'd spent a fair lot of time together in the past year—working the ranch, fishing and hunting, a little mild carousing in Saddle River—

and we had an easy kind of friendship. Bohannon had never spoken much about himself, his background, his people, but that was all right by me. Way I figured it, every man was entitled to as much privacy as he wanted.

But that storm made us both restless; it was the kind of night a man sooner or later feels like talking. And puts him in a mood to share confidences, too. Inside a half hour we were swapping stories, mostly about places we'd been and things we'd done and seen.

That was how we came to the subject of markers—grave markers, first off—with me the one who brought it up. I was telling about the time I'd spent a year prospecting for gold in the California Mother Lode, before I came back home to Wyoming Territory and turned to ranch work, and I recollected the grave I'd happened on one afternoon in a rocky meadow south of Sonora. A mound of rocks, it was, with a wooden marker anchored at the north end. And on the marker was an epitaph scratched out with a knife.

"I don't know who done it," I said, "or how come that grave was out where it was, but that marker sure did make me curious. Still does. What it said was, 'Last resting place of I. R. Lyon. Lived and died according to his name.'"

I'd told that story a time or two before and it had always brought a chuckle, if not a horse laugh. But Bohannon didn't chuckle. Didn't say anything, either. He just sat looking into the fire, not moving, a quirly drifting smoke from one corner of his mouth. He appeared to be studying on something inside his head.

I said, "Well, *I* thought it was a mighty unusual marker, anyhow."

Bohannon still didn't say anything. Another ten seconds or so passed before he stirred—took a last drag off his quirly and tossed it into the fire.

"I saw an unusual marker myself once," he said then, quiet. His voice sounded different than I'd ever heard it.

"Where was that?"

"Nevada. Graveyard in Virginia City, about five years ago."

"What'd it say?"

"Said 'Here lies Adam Bricker. Died of hunger in Virginia City, August 1882.'"

"Hell. How could a man die of hunger in a town?"

"That's what I wanted to know. So I asked around to find out."

"Did you?"

"I did," Bohannon said. "According to the local law, Adam Bricker'd been killed in a fight over a woman. Stabbed by the woman's husband, man named Greenbaugh. Supposed to've been self-defense."

"If Bricker was stabbed, how could he have died of hunger?"

"Greenbaugh put that marker on Bricker's grave. His idea of humor, I reckon. Hunger Bricker died of wasn't hunger for food, it was hunger for the woman. Or so Greenbaugh claimed."

"Wasn't it the truth?"

"Folks I talked to didn't think so," Bohannon said. "Story was, Bricker admired Greenbaugh's wife and courted her some; she and Greenbaugh weren't living together and there was talk of a divorce. Nobody thought he trifled with her, though. That wasn't Bricker's way. Folks said the real reason Greenbaugh killed him was because of money Bricker owed him. Bricker's claim was that he'd been cheated out of it, so he refused to pay when Greenbaugh called in his marker. They had an argument, there was pushing and shoving, and when Bricker drew a gun and tried to shoot him, Greenbaugh used his knife. That was his story, at least. Only witness just happened to be a friend of his."

"Who was this Greenbaugh?"

"Gambler," Bohannon said. "Fancy man. Word was he'd cheated other men at cards, and debauched a woman or two—that was why his wife left him—but nobody ever accused him to his face except Adam Bricker. Town left him pretty much alone."

"Sounds like a prize son of a bitch," I said.

"He was."

"Men like that never get what's coming to them, seems like."

"This one did."

"You mean somebody cashed in his chips for him?"

"That's right," Bohannon said. "Me."

I leaned forward a little. He was looking into the fire, with his head cocked to one side, like he was listening for another rumble of thunder. It seemed too quiet in there, of a sudden, so I cleared my throat and smacked a hand against my thigh.

I said, "How'd it happen? He cheat you at cards?"

"He didn't have the chance."

"Then how . . . ?"

Bohannon was silent again. One of the burning logs slid off the grate and made a sharp cracking sound; the noise seemed to jerk him into talking again. He said, "There was a vacant lot a few doors down from the saloon where he spent most of his time. I waited in there one night, late, and when he came along, on his way to his room at one of the hotels, I stepped out and put my gun up to his head. And I shot him."

"My God," I said. "You mean you *murdered* him?"

"You could call it that."

"But damn it, man, why?"

"He owed me a debt. So I called in his marker."

"What debt?"

"Adam Bricker's life."

"I don't see—"

"I didn't tell you how I happened to be in Virginia City. Or how I happened to visit the graveyard. The reason was Adam Bricker. Word reached me that he was dead, but not how it happened, and I went there to find out."

"Why? What was Bricker to you?"

"My brother," he said. "My real name is Jack Bricker."

I got up off the bunk and went to the table and turned the lamp up a little. Then I got out my sack of Bull Durham, commenced to build another smoke. Bohannon didn't look at me; he was still staring into the fire.

When I had my quirly lit I said, "What'd you do after you shot Greenbaugh?"

"Got on my horse and rode out of there."

"You figure the law knows you did it?"

"Maybe. But the law doesn't worry me much."

"Then how come you changed your name? How come you traveled all the way up here from Nevada?"

"Greenbaugh had a brother, too," he said. "Just like Adam had me. He was living in Virginia City at the time and he knows I shot Greenbaugh. I've heard more than once that he's looking for me—been looking ever since it happened."

"So he can shoot you like you shot his brother?"

"That's right. I owe him a debt, Harv, same as Greenbaugh owed me one. One of these days he's going to find me, and when he does he'll call in his marker, same as I did mine."

"Maybe he won't find you," I said. "Maybe he's stopped looking by this time."

"He hasn't stopped looking. He'll never stop looking. He's a hardcase like his brother was."

"That don't mean he'll ever cross your trail—"

"No. But he will. It's just a matter of time."

"What makes you so all-fired sure?"

"A feeling I got," he said. "Had it ever since I heard he was after me."

"Guilt," I said, quiet.

"Maybe. I'm not a killer, not truly, and I've had some bad nights over Greenbaugh. But it's more than that. It's something I know is going to happen, like knowing the rain will stop tonight or tomorrow and we'll have clear weather again. Maybe because there are too many markers involved, if you take my meaning—the grave kind and the debt kind. One of these days I'll be dead because I owe a marker."

Neither of us had anything more to say that night. Bohannon—I couldn't seem to think of him as Bricker—got up from in front of the fire and climbed into his bunk, and when I finished my smoke I did the same. What he'd told me kept rattling around inside my head. It was some while before I finally got to sleep.

I woke up right after dawn, like I always do—and there was Bohannon, with his saddlebags packed and his bedroll under one arm, halfway to the door. Beyond him, through the window, I could see pale gray light and enough of the sky to make out broken clouds; the storm had passed.

"What the hell, Bohannon?"

"Time for me to move on," he said.

"Just like that? Without notice to anybody?"

"I reckon it's best that way," he said. "A year in one place is long enough—maybe too long. I was fixing to leave anyway, after you and me finished riding fence. That's why I went ahead and told you about my brother and Greenbaugh and the markers. Wouldn't have if I'd been thinking on staying."

I swung my feet off the bunk and reached for my Levi's. "It don't make any difference to me," I said. "Knowing what you done, I mean."

"Sure it does, Harv. Hell, why lie to each other about it?"

"All right. But where'll you go?"

He shrugged. "Don't know. Somewhere. Best if you don't know, best if I don't myself."

"Listen, Bohannon—"

"Nothing to listen to." He came over and put out his hand, and I took it, and there was the kind of feeling inside me I'd had as a button when a friend died of the whooping cough. "Been good knowing you, Harv," he said. "I hope you don't come across a marker someday with my name on it." And he was gone before I finished buttoning up my pants.

From the window I watched him saddle his horse. I didn't go outside to say a final word to him—there wasn't anything more to say; he'd been right about that—and he didn't look back when he rode out. I never saw him again.

But that's not the whole story, not by any means.

Two years went by without me hearing anything at all about Bohannon. Then Curly Polk, who'd worked with the two of us on the Two Bar Cross and then gone down to Texas for a while, drifted back our way for the spring roundup, and he brought word that Bohannon was dead. Shot six weeks earlier, in the Pecos River town of Santa Rosa, New Mexico. But it hadn't been anybody named Greenbaugh who pulled the trigger on him. It had been a local cowpuncher, liquored up, spoiling for trouble; and it had happened over a spilled drink that Bohannon had refused to pay for. The only reason Curly found out about it was that he happened to pass through Santa Rosa on the very day they hung the puncher for his crime.

It shook me some when Curly told about it. Not because Bohannon was dead—too much time had passed for that—but because of the circumstances of his death. He'd believed, and believed hard, that someday he'd pay for killing Greenbaugh; that there were too many markers in his life and someday he'd die on account of one he owed. Well, he'd been wrong. And yet the strange thing, the pure crazy thing, was that he'd also been right.

The name of the puncher who'd shot him was Sam Marker.

HERO

The mob boiled upstreet from Saloon Row toward the jailhouse. Some of the men in front carried lanterns and torches made out of rag-wrapped sticks soaked in coal oil; Micah could see the flickering light against the black night sky, the wild quivering shadows. But he couldn't see the men themselves, the hooded and masked leaders, from back here where he was at the rear of the pack. He couldn't see Ike Dall neither. Ike Dall was the one who had the hang rope already shaped out into a noose.

Men surged around Micah, yelling, waving arms and clubs and sixguns. He just couldn't keep up on account of his damn game leg. He kept getting jostled, once almost knocked down. Back there at Hardesty's Gambling Hall he'd been right in the thick of it. He'd been the center of attention, by grab. Now they'd forgot all about him and here he was clumping along on his bad leg, not able to see much, getting bumped and pushed with every dragging step. He could feel the excitement, smell the sweat and the heat and the hunger, but he wasn't a part of it no more.

It wasn't right. Hell damn boy, it just wasn't right. Weren't for him, none of this would be happening. Biggest damn thing ever in Cricklewood, Montana, and all on account of him. He was a hero, wasn't he? Back there at Hardesty's, they'd all said so. Back there at Hardesty's, he'd talked and they'd listened to every word—Ike Dall and Lee Wynkoop and Mack Clausen, all of them, everybody who was somebody in and around Cricklewood. Stood him right up there next to the bar, bought him drinks, looked at him with respect, and listened to every word he said.

"Micah seen it, didn't you, Micah? What that drifter done?"

"Sure I did. Told Marshal Thrall and I'm tellin' you. Weren't for me, he'd of got clean away."

"You're a hero, Micah. By God you are."

"Well, now. Well, I guess I am."

"Tell it again. Tell us how it was."

"Sure. Sure I will. I seen it all."

"What'd you see?"

"I seen that drifter, that Larrabee, hold up the Wells, Fargo stage. I seen him shoot Tom Porter twice, shoot Tom Porter dead as anybody ever was."

"How'd you come to be out by the Helena road?"

"Mr. Coombs sent me out from the livery, to tell Harv Perkins the singletree on his wagon was fixed a day early. I took the shortcut along the river, like

I allus do when I'm headin' down the valley. Forded by Fisherman's Bend and went on through that stand of cottonwoods on the other side. That was where I was, in them trees, when I seen it happen."

"Larrabee had the stage stopped right there, did he?"

"Sure. Right there. Had his sixgun out and he was tellin' Tom to throw down the treasure box."

"And Tom throwed it down?"

"Sure he did. He throwed it right down."

"Never made to use his shotgun or his side gun?"

"No sir. Never made no play at all."

"So Larrabee shot him in cold blood."

"Cold blood—sure! Shot Tom twice. Right off the coach box the first time, then when Tom was lyin' there on the ground, rollin' around with that first bullet in him, Larrabee walked up to him cool as you please and put his sixgun agin Tom's head and done it to him proper. Blowed Tom's head half off. Blowed it half off and that's a fact."

"You all heard that. You heard what Micah seen that son of a bitch do to Tom Porter—a decent citizen, a man we all liked and was proud to call friend. I say we don't wait for the circuit judge. What if he lets Larrabee off light? I say we give that murderin' bastard what he deserves here and now, tonight. Now what do you say?"

"Hang him!"

"Stretch his dirty neck!"

"Hang him high!"

Oh, it had been fine back there at Hardesty's. Everybody looking at him the way they done, with respect. Calling him a hero. He'd been somebody then, not just poor crippled-up Micah Hays who done handy work and run errands and shoveled manure down at the Coombs Livery Barn. Oh, it had been fine! But now—now they'd forgot him again, left him behind, left him out of what was going to happen on *his* account. They were all moving upstreet to the jailhouse with their lanterns and their torches and their hunger, leaving him practically alone where he couldn't do or see a damn thing . . .

Micah stopped trying to run on his game leg and limped along slow, watching the mob, wanting to be a part of it but wanting more to see everything that happened after the mob got to the jailhouse. Then he thought: Why, I *can* see it all! Sure I can! I know just where I got to go.

He hobbled ahead to the alley alongside Burley's Feed and Grain, went down it to the staircase built up the side wall. The stairs led to a railed gallery overlooking the street, and to the offices of the town lawyer, Mr. Spivey, that had been built on top of the feed-store roof. Micah stumped up the stairs and went past the dark offices and on down to the far end of the gallery.

Hell damn boy! He sure *could* see from up here, clear as anybody could want. The mob was close to the jailhouse now; in the dancy light from the lanterns and torches, he could make out the hooded shape of Ike Dall with his hang-rope noose held high, the shapes of Lee Wynkoop and Mack Clausen and the others who were leading the pack. He could see that big old shade cottonwood off to one side of the jail, too, with its one gnarly limb that stretched out over the street. That was where they was going to hang the drifter. Ike Dall had said so, back there at Hardesty's. *"We don't have to take him far, by Christ. We'll string him up right there next to the jail."*

The front door of the jailhouse opened and out come Marshal Thrall and his deputy, Ben Dietrich. Micah leaned out over the railing, squinting, feeling the excitement scurry up and down inside his chest like a mouse on a wall. Marshal Thrall had a shotgun in his hands and Ben Dietrich held a rifle. The marshal commenced to yelling, but whatever it was got lost in the noise from the mob. Mob didn't slow down none, neither, when old Thrall started waving that Greener of his. Marshal wasn't going to shoot nobody, Ike Dall had said. *"Why, we're all Thrall's friends and neighbors. Ben Dietrich's, too. They ain't goin' to shoot up their friends and neighbors, are they? Just to stop the lynching of a murderin' son of a bitch like Larrabee?"*

No sir, they sure wasn't. That mob didn't slow down none at all. It surged right ahead, right on around Marshal Thrall and Ben Dietrich like floodwaters around a sandbar, and swallowed them both up and carried them right on into the jail-house.

A hell of a racket come from inside. Pretty soon the pack parted down the middle and Micah could see four or five men carrying that drifter up in the air, hands tied behind him, the same way you'd carry a side of butchered beef. Hell damn boy! Everybody was whooping it up, waving torches and lanterns and twirling light around in the dark like a bunch of kids with pinwheel sparklers. It put Micah in mind of an Independence Day celebration. By grab, that was just what it was like. Fireworks on the Fourth of July.

Well, they carried that murdering Larrabee on over to the shade cottonwood. He was screaming things, that drifter was—screaming the whole way. Micah couldn't hear most of it above the crowd noise, but he caught a few of the words. And one whole sentence: "I tell you, I didn't do it!"

"Why, sure you did," Micah said out loud. "Sure you did. I seen you do it, didn't I?"

Ike Dall threw his rope over the cottonwood's gnarly limb, caught the other end and give it to somebody, and then he put that noose around Larrabee's neck and drew it tight. Somebody else brung a saddle horse around, held him steady whilst they hoisted the drifter onto his back. That Larrabee was screaming like a woman now.

Micah leaned hard against the gallery railing. His mouth was dry, real dry; he couldn't even work up no spit to wet it. He'd never seen a lynching before. There'd been plenty in Montana Territory—more'n a dozen over in Beaverhead and Madison counties a few years back, when the vigilantes done for Henry Plummer and his gang of desperadoes—but never one in Cricklewood nor any of the other towns Micah had lived in.

The drifter screamed and screamed. Then Micah saw everybody back off some, away from the horse Larrabee was on, and Ike Dall raised his arm and brought it down smack on the cayuse's rump. Horse jumped ahead, frog-stepping. And Larrabee quit screaming and commenced to dancing in the air all loosey-goosey, like a puppet on the end of a string. Before long, though, the dancing slowed down and then it quit altogether. That's done him, Micah thought. And everybody in the mob knew it, too, because they all backed off some more and stood there in a half-circle, staring up at the drifter hanging still and straight in the smoky light.

Micah stared too. He leaned against the railing and stared and stared, and kept on staring long after the mob started to break up.

Hell damn boy, he thought over and over. Hell damn boy, if that sure wasn't something to see!

It took the best part of a week for the town to get back to normal. There was plenty more excitement during that week—county law coming in, representatives from the territorial governor's office in Helena, newspaper people, all kinds of curious strangers. For Micah it was kind of like the lynching went on and on, a week-long celebration like none other he'd ever been part of. Folks kept asking him questions, interviewing him for newspapers, buying him drinks, shaking his hand and clapping his back and calling him a hero the way the men had done that night at Hardesty's. Oh, it was fine. It was almost as fine as when he'd been the center of attention before the lynch mob got started.

But then it all come to an end. The law and the newspaper people and the strangers went away; Cricklewood settled down to what it had been before the big event, and Micah settled back into his humdrum job at the Coombs Livery Barn and his nights on the straw bunk in one corner of the loft. He did his handy work, ran errands, shoveled manure—and the townsfolk and ranchers and cowhands stopped buying him drinks, stopped shaking his hand and clapping his back and calling him hero, stopped paying much attention to him at all. It was the same as before, like he was nobody, like he didn't hardly even exist. Mack Clausen snubbed him on the street no more than two weeks after the lynching. The one time he tried to get Ike Dall to talk with him about that night, how it had felt putting the noose around Larrabee's neck, Ike wouldn't have none of it. Why, Ike claimed he hadn't even been there that night, hadn't been part of the mob—said that lie right to Micah's face!

Four weeks passed. Five. Micah did his handy work and ran errands and shoveled manure and now nobody even *mentioned* that night no more, not to him and not to each other. Like it never happened. Like they was ashamed of it or something.

Micah was feeling low the hot Saturday morning he come down the loft ladder and started toward the harness room like he always done first thing. But this wasn't like other mornings because a man was curled up sleeping in one of the stalls near the back doors. Big man, whiskers on his face, dust on his trail clothes. Micah had never seen him before.

Mr. Coombs was up at the other end of the barn, forking hay for the two roan saddle horses he kept for rent. Micah went on up there and said, "Morning, Mr. Coombs."

"Well, Micah. Down late again, eh?"

". . . I reckon so."

"Getting to be a habit lately," Mr. Coombs said. "I don't like it, Micah. See that you start coming down on time from now on, hear?"

"Yes, sir. Mr. Coombs, who's that sleepin' in the back stall?"

"Just some drifter. He didn't say his name."

"Drifter?"

"Came in half-drunk last night, paid me four bits to let him sleep in here. Not the first time I've rented out a stall to a human animal and it won't be the last."

Mr. Coombs turned and started forking some more hay. Micah went away toward the harness room, then stopped after ten paces and stood quiet for a space. And then, moving slow, he hobbled over to where the fire ax hung and pulled it down and limped back behind Mr. Coombs and swung the axe up and shut his eyes and swung the ax down. When he opened his eyes again Mr. Coombs was lying there with the back of his head cleaved open and blood and brains spilled out like pulp out of a split melon.

Hell damn boy, Micah thought.

Then he dropped the ax and run to the front doors and threw them open and run out onto Main Street yelling at the top of his voice, "Murder! It's murder! Some damn drifter killed Mr. Coombs! Split his head wide open with a fire ax. I seen him do it, I seen it, I seen the whole thing!"

McINTOSH'S CHUTE

It was right after supper and we were all settled around the cookfire, smoking, none of us saying much because it was well along in the roundup and we were all dog-tired from the long days of riding and chousing cows out of brush-clogged coulees. I wasn't doing anything except taking in the night—warm Montana fall night, sky all hazed with stars, no moon to speak of. Then, of a sudden, something come streaking across all that velvet-black and silver from east to west: a ball of smoky red-orange with a long fiery tail. Everybody stirred around and commenced to gawping and pointing. But not for long. Quick as it had come, the thing was gone beyond the broken sawteeth of the Rockies.

There was a hush. Then young Poley said, "What in hell was that?" He was just eighteen and big for his britches in more ways than one. But that heavenly fireball had taken him down to an awed whisper.

"Comet," Cass Buckram said.

"That fire-tail . . . whooee!" Poley said. "I never seen nothing like it. Comet, eh? Well, it's the damnedest sight a man ever set eyes on."

"Damnedest sight a *button* ever set eyes on, maybe."

"I ain't a button!"

"You are from where I sit," Cass said. "Big shiny man-sized button with your threads still dangling."

Everybody laughed except Poley. Being as he was the youngest on the roundup crew, he'd taken his share of ragging since we'd left the Box 8 and he was about fed up with it. He said, "Well, what do *you* know about it, oldtimer?"

That didn't faze Cass. He was close to sixty, though you'd never know it to look at him or watch him when he worked cattle or at anything else, but age didn't mean much to him. He was of a philosophical turn of mind. You were what you were and no sense in pretending otherwise— that was how he looked at it.

In his younger days he'd been an adventuresome gent. Worked at jobs most of us wouldn't have tried in places we'd never even hoped to visit. Oil rigger in Texas and Oklahoma, logger in Oregon, fur trapper in the Canadian Barrens, prospector in the Yukon during the '98 Rush, cowhand in half a dozen states and territories. He'd packed more living into the past forty-odd years than a whole regiment of men, and he didn't mind talking about his experiences. No, he sure didn't mind. First time I met him, I'd taken him for a blowhard. Plenty took him that way in the beginning, on account of his windy nature. But the stories he told were true, or at least every one had a core of truth in it. He had too many facts and a whole warbag full of mementoes and photographs and such to back 'em up.

All you had to do was prime him a little—and without knowing it, young Poley had primed him just now. But that was all right with the rest of us. Cass had honed his storytelling skills over the years; one of his yarns was always worthwhile entertainment.

He said to the kid, "I saw more strange things before I was twenty than you'll ever see."

"Cowflop."

"Correct word is bullshit," Cass said, solemn, and everybody laughed again. "But neither one is accurate."

"I suppose you seen something stranger and more spectacular than that there comet."

"Twice as strange and three times as spectacular."

"Cowflop."

"Fact. Ninth wonder of the world, in its way."

"Well? What was it?"

"McIntosh and his chute."

"Chute? What chute? Who was McIntosh?"

"Keep your lip buttoned, button, and I'll tell you. I'll tell you about *the* damnedest sight I or any other man ever laid eyes on."

Happened more than twenty years ago [Cass went on], in southern Oregon in the early nineties. I'd had my fill of fur-trapping in the Barrens and developed a hankering to see what timber work was like, so I'd come on down into Oregon and hooked on with a logging outfit near Coos Bay. But for the first six months I was just a bullcook, not a timberjack. Low-down work, bullcooking—cleaning up after the jacks, making up their bunks, cutting firewood, helping out in the kitchen. Without experience, that's the only kind of job you can get in a decent logging camp. Boss finally put me on one of the yarding crews, but even then there was no thrill in the work and the wages were low. So I was ready for a change of venue when word filtered in that a man named Saginaw Tom McIntosh was hiring for his camp on Black Mountain.

McIntosh was from Michigan and had made a pile logging in the North Woods. What had brought him west to Oregon was the opportunity to buy better than 25,000 acres of virgin timberland on Black Mountain. He'd rebuilt an old dam on the Klamath River nearby that had been washed out by high water, built a sawmill and a millpond below the dam, and then started a settlement there that he named after himself.

And once he had a camp operating on the mountain, first thing he did was construct a chute, or skidway, down to the river.

Word of McIntosh's chute spread just as fast and far as word that he was hiring timber beasts at princely wages. It was supposed to be an engineering marvel, unlike any other logging chute ever built. Some scoffed when they were told about it; claimed it was just one of those tall stories that get flung around among Northwest loggers, like the one about Paul Bunyan and Babe the blue ox. Me, I was willing to give Saginaw Tom McIntosh the benefit of the doubt. I figured that if he was half the man he was talked of being, he could accomplish just about anything he set his mind to.

He had two kinds of reputation. First, as a demon logger—a man who could get timber cut faster and turned into board lumber quicker than any other boss jack. And second, as a ruthless cold-hearted son of a bitch who bullied his men, worked them like animals, and wasn't above using fists, peaveys, calks, and any other handy weapon if the need arose. Rumor had it that he—

What's that, boy? No, I ain't going to say any more about that chute just yet. I'll get to it in good time. You just keep your pants on and let me tell this my own way.

Well, rumor had it that McIntosh was offering top dollar because it was the only way he could get jacks to work steady for him. That and his reputation didn't bother me one way or another. I'd dealt with hardcases before, and have since. So I determined to see what Saginaw Tom and his chute and Black Mountain were all about.

I quit the Coos Bay outfit and traveled down to McIntosh's settlement on the Klamath. Turned out to be bigger than I'd expected. The sawmill was twice the size of the one up at Coos Bay, and there was a blacksmith shop, a box factory, a hotel and half a dozen boardinghouses, two big stores, a school, two churches, and a lodge hall. McIntosh may have been a son of a bitch, but he sure did know how to get maximum production and how to provide for his men and their families.

I hired on at the mill, and the next day a crew chief named Lars Nilson drove me and another new man, a youngster called Johnny Cline, upriver to the Black Mountain camp. Long, hot trip in the back of a buckboard, up steep grades and past gold-mining claims strung along the rough-water river. Nilson told us there was bad blood between McIntosh and those miners. They got gold out of the sand by trapping silt in wing dams, and they didn't like it when McIntosh's river drivers built holding cribs along the banks or herded long chains of logs downstream to the cribs and then on to the mill. There hadn't been any trouble yet, but it could erupt at any time; feelings were running high on both sides.

Heat and flies and hornets deviled us all the way up into scrub timber: lodgepole, jack, and yellow pine. The bigger trees—white sugar pine— grew higher up, and what fine old trees they were. Clean-growing, hardly any underbrush. Huge trunks that rose up straight from brace roots close to four feet broad, and no branches on 'em until thirty to forty feet above the ground. Every lumberman's dream, the cut-log timber on that mountain.

McIntosh was taking full advantage of it, too. His camp was twice the size of most—two enormous bunkhouses, a cook-shack, a barn and blacksmith shop, clusters of sheds and shanties and heavy wagons, corrals full of work horses and oxen. Close to a hundred men, altogether. And better than two dozen big wheels, stinger-tongue and slip-tongue both—

What's a big wheel? Just that, boy—wheels ten and twelve feet high, some made of wood and some of iron, each pair connected by an axle that had a chain and a long tongue poking back from the middle. Four-horse team drew each one. Man on the wheel crew dug a shallow trench under one or two logs, depending on their size; loader pushed the chain through it under the logs and secured it to the axle; driver lunged his team ahead and the tongue slid forward and yanked on the chain to lift the front end of the logs off the ground. Harder the horses pulled, the higher the logs hung. When the team came to a stop, the logs dropped and dragged. Only trouble was, sometimes they didn't drop and drag just right—didn't act as a brake like they were supposed to—and the wheel horses got their hind legs smashed. Much safer and faster to use a steam lokey to get cut logs out of the woods, but laying narrow gauge track takes time and so does ordering a lokey and having it packed in sections up the side of a wilderness mountain. McIntosh figured to have his track laid and a lokey operating by the following spring. Meanwhile, it was the big wheels and the teams of horses and oxen and men that had to do the heavy work.

Now then. The chute—McIntosh's chute.

First I seen of it was across the breadth of the camp, at the edge of a steep drop-off: the chute head, a big two-level platform built of logs. Cut logs were stacked on the top level as they came off the big wheels, by jacks crowhopping over the deck with cant hooks. On the lower level other jacks looped a cable around the foremost log, and a donkey engine wound up the cable and hauled the log forward into a trough built at the outer edge of the platform. You follow me so far?

Well, that was all I could see until Nilson took Johnny Cline and me over close to the chute head. From the edge of the drop-off you had a miles-wide view—long snaky stretches of the Klamath, timberland all the way south to the California border. But it wasn't the vista that had my attention; it was the chute itself. An engineering marvel, all right, that near took my breath away.

McIntosh and his crew had cut a channel in the rocky hillside straight on down to the river bank, and lined the sides and bottom with flat-hewn logs—big ones at the sides and smaller ones on the bottom, all worn glass-smooth. Midway along was a kind of trestle that spanned an outcrop and acted as a speed-brake. Nothing legendary about that chute: it was the longest built up to that time, maybe the longest ever. More than twenty-six hundred feet of timber had gone into the construction, top to bottom.

While I was gawking down at it, somebody shouted, "Clear back!" and right away Nilson herded Johnny Cline and me onto a hummock to one side. At the chute head a chain of logs was lined and ready, held back by an iron bar wedged into the rock. Far down below one of the river crew showed a white flag, and as soon as he did the chute tender yanked the iron bar aside and the first log shuddered through and down.

After a hundred feet or so, it began to pick up speed. You could hear it squealing against the sides and bottom of the trough. By the time it went over the trestle and into the lower part of the chute, it was a blur. Took just eighteen seconds for it to drop more than eight hundred feet to the river, and when it hit the splash was bigger than a barn and the fan of water drenched trees on both banks

"Hell!" young Poley interrupted. "I don't believe none of that. You're funning us, Cass."

"Be damned if I am. What don't you believe?"

"None of it. Chute twenty-six hundred feet of timber, logs shooting down over eight hundred feet in less than twenty seconds, splashes bigger than a barn . . ."

"Well, it's the gospel truth. So's the rest of it. Sides and bottom a third of the way down were burned black from the friction—black as coal. On cold mornings you could see smoke from the logs going down: that's how fast they traveled. Went even faster when there was frost, so the river crew had to drive spikes in the chute's bottom end to slow 'em up. Even so, sometimes a log would hit the river with enough force to split it in half, clean, like it'd gone through a buzz saw. But I expect you don't believe none of that, either."

Poley grunted. "Not hardly."

I said, "Well, *I* believe it, Cass. Man can do just about anything he sets his mind to, like you said, if he wants it bad enough. That chute must of been something. I can sure see why it was the damnedest thing you ever saw."

"No, it wasn't," Cass said.

"What? But you said—"

"No, I didn't. McIntosh's chute was a wonder but not the damnedest thing I ever saw."

"Then what *is?*" Poley demanded.

"If I wasn't interrupted every few minutes, you'd of found out by now." Cass glared at him. "You going to be quiet and let me get to it or you intend to keep flapping your gums so this here story takes all night?"

Poley wasn't cowed, but he did button his lip. And surprised us all— maybe even himself—by keeping it buttoned for the time being.

I thought I might get put on one of the wheel crews [Cass resumed], but I'd made the mistake of telling Nilson I'd worked a yarding crew up at Coos Bay, so a yarding crew was where I got put on Black Mountain. Working as a choke-setter in the slash out back of the camp—man that sets heavy cable chokers around the end of a log that's fallen down a hillside or into a ravine so the log can be hauled out by means of a donkey engine. Hard, sweaty, dangerous work in the best of camps, and McIntosh's was anything but the best. The rumors had been right about that, too. We worked long hours for our pay, seven days a week. And if a man dropped from sheer exhaustion, he was expected to get up under his own power—and was docked for the time he spent lying down.

Johnny Cline got put on the same crew, as a whistle-punk on the donkey, and him and me took up friendly. He was a Californian, from down near San Francisco; young and feisty and too smart-ass for his own good . . . some like you, Poley. But decent enough, underneath. His brother was a logger somewhere in Canada, and he'd determined to try his hand too. He was about as green as me, but you could see that logging was in his blood in a way that it wasn't in mine. I knew I'd be moving on to other things one day; he knew he'd be a logger till the day he died.

I got along with Nilson and most of the other timber beasts, but Saginaw Tom McIntosh was another matter. If anything, he was worse than his reputation—mean clear through, with about as much decency as a vulture on a fence post waiting for something to die. Giant of a man, face weathered the color of heartwood, droopy yellow mustache stained with juice from the quids of Spearhead tobacco he always kept stowed in one cheek, eyes like pale fire that gave you the feeling you'd been burned whenever they touched you. Stalked around camp in worn cruisers, stagged corduroy pants, and steel-calked boots, yelling out orders, knocking men down with his fists if they didn't ask how high when he hollered jump. Ran that camp the way a hardass warden runs a prison.

Everybody hated him, including me and Johnny Cline before long. But most of the jacks feared him, too, which was how he kept them in line.

He drove all his crews hard, demanding that a dozen turns of logs go down his chute every day to feed the saws working twenty-four hours at the mill. Cut lumber was fetching more than a hundred dollars per thousand feet at the time and he wanted to keep production at a fever pitch before the heavy winter rains set in. There was plenty of grumbling among the men, and tempers were short, but nobody quit the camp. Pay was too good, even with all the abuse that went along with it.

I'd been at the Back Mountain camp three weeks when the real trouble started. One of the gold miners down on the Klamath, man named Coogan, got drunk and decided to tear up a holding crib because he blamed McIntosh for ruining his claim. McIntosh flew into a rage when he heard about it. He ranted and raved for half a day about how he'd had enough of those goddamn miners. Then, when he'd worked himself up enough, he ordered a dozen jacks down on a night raid to bust up Coogan's wing dam and raise some hell with the other miners' claims. The jacks didn't want to do it but he bullied them into it with threats and promises of bonus money.

But the miners were expecting retaliation; had joined forces and were waiting when the jacks showed up. There was a riverbank brawl, mostly with fists and ax handles, but with a few shots fired too. Three timber stiffs were hurt bad enough so that they had to be carried back to camp and would be laid up for a while.

The county law came next day and threatened to close McIntosh down if there was any more trouble. That threw him into another fit. Kind of man he was, he took it out on the men in the raiding party.

"What kind of jack lets a gold-grubber beat him down?" he yelled at them. "You buggers ain't worth the name timberjack. If I didn't need your hands and backs, I'd send the lot of you packing. As is, I'm cutting your pay. And you three that can't work—you get no pay at all until you can hoist your peaveys and swing your axes."

One of the jacks challenged him. McIntosh kicked the man in the crotch, knocked him down, and then gave him a case of logger's smallpox: pinned his right arm to the ground with those steel calks of his. There were no other challenges. But in all those bearded faces you could see the hate that was building for McIntosh. You could feel it too; it was in the air, crackles of it like electricity in a storm.

Another week went by. There was no more trouble with the miners, but McIntosh drove his crews with a vengeance. Up to fifteen turns of logs down the chute each day. The big-wheel crews hauling until their horses were ready to drop; and two did drop dead in harness, while another two had to be destroyed when logs crushed their hind legs on the drag. Buckers and fallers working the slash from dawn to dark, so that the skirl of crosscuts and bucksaws and the thud of axes rolled like constant thunder across the face of Black Mountain.

Some men can stand that kind of killing pace without busting down one way or another, and some men can't. Johnny Cline was one of those who couldn't. He was hot-headed, like I said before, and ten times every day and twenty times every night he cursed McIntosh and damned his black soul. Then, one day when he'd had all he could swallow, he made the mistake of cursing and damning McIntosh to the boss logger's face.

The yarding crew we were on was deep in the slash, struggling to get logs out of a small valley. It was coming on dusk and we'd been at it for hours; we were all bone-tired. I set the choker around the end of yet another log, and the hook-tender signaled Johnny Cline, who stood behind him with one hand on the wire running to the whistle on the donkey engine. When Johnny pulled the wire and the short blast sounded, the cable snapped tight and the big log started to move, its nose plowing up dirt and crushing saplings in its path. But as it came up the slope it struck a sunken log, as sometimes happens, and shied off. The hook-tender signaled for slack, but Johnny didn't give it fast enough to keep the log from burying its nose in the roots of a fir stump.

McIntosh saw it. He'd come catfooting up and was ten feet from the donkey engine. He ran up to Johnny yelling, "You stupid goddamn greenhorn!" and gave him a shove that knocked the kid halfway down to where the log was stumped.

Johnny caught himself and scrambled back up the incline. I could see the hate afire in his eyes and I tried to get between him and McIntosh, but he brushed me aside. He put his face up close to the boss logger's, spat out a string of cuss words, and finished up with, "I've had all I'm gonna take from you, you son of a bitch." And then he swung with his right hand.

But all he hit was air. McIntosh had seen it coming; he stepped inside the punch and spat tobacco juice into Johnny's face. The squirt and spatter threw the kid off balance and blinded him at the same time—left him wide open for McIntosh to wade in with fists and knees.

McIntosh seemed to go berserk, as if all the rage and meanness had built to an explosion point inside him and Johnny's words had triggered it. Johnny Cline never had a chance. McIntosh beat him to the ground, kept on beating him even though me and some of the others fought to pull him off. And when he saw his chance he raised up one leg and he stomped the kid's face with his calks—drove those sharp steel spikes down into Johnny's face as if he was grinding a bug under his heel.

Johnny screamed once, went stiff, then lay still. Nilson and some others had come running up by then and it took six of us to drag McIntosh away before he could smallpox Johnny Cline a second time. He battled us for a few seconds, like a crazy man; then, all at once, the wildness went out of him. But he was no more human when it did. He tore himself loose, and without a word, without any concern for the boy he'd stomped, he stalked off through the slash.

Johnny Cline's face was a red ruin, pitted and torn by half a hundred steel points. I thought he was dead at first, but when I got down beside him I found a weak pulse. Four of us picked him up and carried him to our bunkhouse.

The bullcook and me cleaned the blood off him and doctored his wounds as best we could. But he was in a bad way. His right eye was gone, pierced by one of McIntosh's calks, and he was hurt inside, too, for he kept coughing up red foam. There just wasn't much we could do for him. The nearest doctor was thirty miles away; by the time somebody went and fetched him back, it would be too late. I reckon we all knew from the first that Johnny Cline would be dead by morning.

There was no more work for any of us that day. None of the jacks in our bunkhouse took any grub, either, nor slept much as the night wore on. We all just sat around in little groups with our lamps lit, talking low, smoking and drinking coffee or tea. Checking on Johnny now and then. Waiting.

He never regained consciousness. An hour before dawn the bullcook went to look at him and announced, "He's gone." The waiting was done. Yes, and so were Saginaw Tom McIntosh and the Black Mountain camp.

Nilson and the other crew chiefs had a meeting outside, between the two bunkhouses. The rest of us kept our places. When Nilson and the two others who bunked in our building came back in, it was plain enough from their expressions what had been decided. And plainer still when the three of them shouldered their peaveys. Loggers will take so much from a boss like Saginaw Tom McIntosh—only so much and no more. What he'd done to Johnny Cline was the next to last straw; Johnny dying was the final one.

At the door Nilson said, "We're on our way to cut down a rotted tree. Rest of you can stay or join us, as you see fit. But you'll all keep your mouths shut either way. Clear?"

Nobody had any objections. Nilson turned and went out with the other two chiefs.

Well, none of the men in our bunkhouse stayed, nor did anybody in the other one. We were all of the same mind. I thought I knew what would happen to McIntosh, but I was wrong. The crew heads weren't fixing to give him the same as he gave Johnny Cline. No, they had other plans. When a logging crew turns, it turns hard—and it gives no quarter.

The near-dawn dark was chill and damp, and I don't mind saying it put a shiver on my back. We all walked quiet through it to McIntosh's shanty—close to a hundred of us, so he heard us coming anyway. But not in time to get up a weapon. He fought with the same wildness he had earlier but he didn't have any more chance than he gave Johnny Cline. Nilson stunned him with his peavey. Then half a dozen men stuffed him into his clothes and his blood-stained boots and took him out.

Straight across the camp we went, with four of the crew heads carrying McIntosh by the arms and legs. He came around just before they got him to the edge of the drop-off. He realized what was going to happen to him, looked like, at about the same time I did.

He was struggling fierce, bellowing curses, when Nilson and the others pitched him into the chute.

He went down slow at first, the way one of the big logs always did. Clawing at the flat-hewn sides, trying to dig his calks into the glass-smooth bottom logs. Then he commenced to pick up speed, and his yells turned to banshee screams. Two hundred feet down the screaming stopped; he was just a blur by then. His clothes started to smoke from the friction, then burst into flame. When he went sailing over the trestle he was a lump of fire that lit up the dark . . . then a streak of fire as he shot down into the lower section . . . then a fireball with a tail longer and brighter than the one on that comet a while ago, so bright the river and the woods on both banks showed plain as day for two or three seconds before he smacked the river—smacked it and went out in a splash and steamy sizzle you could see and hear all the way up at the chute head.

"And that," Cass Buckram finished, "*that*, by God, was the damnedest sight I or any other man ever set eyes on—McIntosh going down McIntosh's chute, eight hundred feet straight into hell."

None of us argued with him. Not even Poley the button.

DECISION

The day was coming on dusk, the sky flame-streaked and the thick desert heat easing some, when I found the small hardscrabble ranch. It lay nestled within a broad ring of bluffs and cactus-strewn hillocks. Crouched beside a draw leading between two of the bluffs was a pole-and-'dobe cabin and two weathered outbuildings. Even from where I sat my steeldust high above, I could see that whoever lived there was not having an easy time of it. Heat had parched and withered the corn and other vegetables in the cultivated patch along one side, and the spare buildings looked to be crumbling, like the powdering bones of animals long dead.

There were no horses or other livestock in the open corral near the cabin, no sign of life anywhere. Except for the wisps of chimney smoke rising pale and steady, the place had the look of abandonment. It was the smoke that had drawn me off El Camino Real del Diablo some minutes earlier; that and the fact that both my waterbags were near empty.

Most days there seemed to be a fair amount of traffic on the Devil's Highway—the only good road between Tucson and Yuma, part of the Gila Trail that connected California with points east to Texas. Over the past week I'd come on pioneers, freighters, drifters, a Butterfield stagecoach, a company of soldiers on its way to Fort Yuma, groups of men looking for work on the rail line the Southern Pacific had begun building eastward from the Colorado River the previous year, 1878. But today, when I needed water and would have paid dear for it, the road had been deserted.

It was my own fault that I was low on water. I could have filled the bags when I passed through the town of Maricopa Wells last night, but I'd decided to keep on without stopping; it had been late enough so that even the saloons were closed, and I saw no need to go knocking on someone's door at that hour. It was my intention to buy water at the next way station for the Butterfield line, but when I got there, close to noon, the stationmaster had refused me. His main spring had gone bad, he said, and they had precious little for their own needs. He'd let me stay there for most of the afternoon, waiting in the shade by the corral; not a soul had passed by the time I rode on again at five o'clock. And I had seen no one since, either.

I hoped the people who lived down below had enough water to spare. If they didn't I would have to go back to the Devil's Highway and do some more waiting; neither the steeldust nor I was fit enough for moving on without water. I could see the ranch's well set under a plank lean-to in the dusty yard and I licked at my parched lips. Well, I had nothing to lose by riding down and asking.

I heeled the horse forward, sitting slack in the saddle. Even traveling mostly by night, and even though it was not yet the middle of May, a man dries out in the desert, wearies bone-deep.

But the desert also had a way of dulling the mind, which was just the reason why I had decided to ride alone instead of traveling by coach through these Arizona badlands. I didn't want company or conversation because they would only lead to questions and then sharpened memories I did not care to dwell on. Memories that needed to be buried, the way I had buried Emma four months and six days ago in the sun-webbed ground outside Lordsburg.

People I knew there, friends, said the pain would go away after a while. All you had to do was to keep on living the best you could and time would help you forget—forget how she'd collapsed one evening after a dozen hours' hard toil on our own hardscrabble land, and how I'd thought it was just the ague because she'd been complaining of chest pains, and that terrible time when I came back from town with the doctor and found her lying in our bed so still and small, not breathing, gone. Heart failure, the doctor said. Twenty-eight years old, prime of life, and her good heart had betrayed her. . . .

Maybe they were right, the friends who'd given their advice. But four months and six days of living the best I could hadn't eased the grief inside me, not with everything and everyone in Lordsburg reminding me of Emma. So a week ago I had sold the farm, packed a few changes of clothing and some personal belongings and a spare pistol into my saddlebags, and set out west into Arizona Territory. I had no idea where I was going or what I would do when the three hundred and eighty dollars I carried in my boot dwindled away. I had nothing and I wanted nothing except to drift through the long days and longer nights until life took on some meaning again, if it ever would.

The trail leading down to the ranch was steep and switch-backed in places, and it took me the better part of twenty minutes to get to where the buildings were. The harsh daylight had softened by then and the tops of the bluffs seemed to have turned a reddish-purple color; the sky looked flushed now, instead of brassy the way it did at midday.

I rode slowly toward the cabin, keeping my hands up and in plain sight. Desert settlers, being as isolated as they were, would likely be mistrustful of leaned-down, dust-caked strangers. When I reached the front yard I drew rein. It was quiet there and I still wasn't able to make out sound or movement at any of the buildings. Beyond the vegetable patch, a sagging utility shed stood with a padlock on its door; the only other structure was a long pole-sided shelter at the rear of the empty corral. In back of the shed, rows of pulque cactus stood like sentinels in the hot, dry earth.

I looked at the well, running my tongue through the dryness inside my mouth. Then I eased the steeldust half a rod closer to the cabin and called out, "Hello the house!"

Silence.

"Hello! Anybody home?"

There was more silence for a couple of seconds, and I was thinking of stepping down. But then a woman's voice said from inside, "What do you want here?" It was a young voice, husky, but dulled by something I couldn't identify. The door was closed and the front window was curtained in monk's cloth, but I sensed that the woman was standing by the window, watching me through the curtain folds.

"Don't be alarmed, ma'am," I said. "I was wondering if you could spare a little water. I'm near out."

She didn't answer. Silence settled again, and I began to get a vague feeling of something being wrong. It made me shift uncomfortably in the saddle.

"Ma'am?"

"I can't let you have much," she said finally.

"I'll pay for whatever you can spare."

"You won't need to pay."

"That's kind of you."

"You can step down if you like."

I put on a smile and swung off and slapped some of the fine powdery dust off my shirt and Levi's. The door opened a crack, but she didn't come out.

"My name is Jennifer Todd," she said from inside. "My husband and I own this ranch." She spoke the word "husband" as if it were a blasphemy.

"I'm Roy Boone," I said.

"Mister Boone." And she opened the door and moved out into the fading light.

My smile vanished; I stared at her with my mouth coming open. She was no more than twenty, hair the color of near-ripe corn and piled in loose braids on top of her head, eyes brown and soft and wide—pretty eyes. But it wasn't any of this that caused me to stare as I did. It was the blue-black bruises on both sides of her face, the deep cut above her right brow, the swollen, mottled surface of her upper lip and her right temple.

"Jesus God!" I said. "Who did that to you, Missus Todd?"

"My husband. This morning, just before he left for Maricopa Wells."

"But *why?*"

"He was hung over," she said. "Pulque hung over. Mase is mean when he's sober and meaner when he's drunk, but when he's bad hung over he's the devil's own child."

"He's done this to you before?"

"More times than I can count."

"Maybe I've got no right to say this, but why don't you leave him? Mrs. Todd, a man who'd do a thing like this to a woman wouldn't hesitate to kill her if he was riled enough."

"I tried to leave him," she said. "I tried it three times. He came after me each time and brought me back here and beat me half crazy. A work animal's got sense enough to obey if it's whipped enough times."

I could feel anger inside me. I was thinking of Emma again, the love we'd had, the tenderness. Some men never knew or understood feelings like that; some men gave only one kind of pain, never felt the other kind deep inside them. They never realized what they had with a good woman. Or cared. Men like that—

Impulsively I put the rest of the thought into words. "A man like that ought to be shot dead for what he's done to you."

Something flickered in her eyes and she said, "If I had a gun, Mister Boone, I expect I'd do just that thing—I'd shoot him, with no regrets. But there's only one rifle and one pistol, and Mase carries them with him during the day. At night he locks them up in the shed yonder."

It made me feel uneasy to hear a woman talking so casually about killing. I looked away from her, wondering if it was love or some other reason that made her marry this Mase Todd, somebody who kept her like a prisoner in a badlands valley, who beat her and tried to break her.

When I looked back at Mrs. Todd she smiled in a fleeting, humorless way. "I don't know what's the matter with me, telling you all my troubles. You've problems of your own, riding alone across the desert. Come inside. I've some stew on the fire and you can take an early supper with me if you like."

"Ma'am, I—"

"Mase won't be home until late tonight or tomorrow morning, if you're thinking of him."

"I wasn't, no. He doesn't worry me."

"You look tired and hungry," she said, "and we don't get many visitors out here. I've no one to talk to most days. I'd take it as a kindness if you'd accept."

I couldn't find a way to refuse her. I just nodded and let her show me inside the cabin.

It was filled with shadows and smelled of spiced jackrabbit stew and boiling coffee. The few pieces of furniture were handhewn, but whoever had made them—likely her husband—had done a poor, thoughtless job; none of the pieces looked as though it would last much longer. But the two rooms I saw were clean and straightened, and you could see that she'd done the best she could with what she had, that she'd tried to make a home out of it.

She lighted a mill lantern on the table to chase away some of the shadows. Then she said, "There's water in that basin by the hearth if you want to wash up. I'll fetch some drinking water from the well, and I'll see to your horse."

"You needn't bother yourself . . ."

"It's no bother."

She turned and went to the door, walking in a stiff, slow way but holding herself erect; her spirit wasn't broken yet. I watched her go out and shut the door behind her, and I thought: She's some woman. Most would be half-dead shells by now if they'd gone through what she has.

I crossed to the basin, washed with a cake of strong yellow soap. Mrs. Todd came back as I was drying off. She handed me a gourd of water, and while I drank from it she unhooked a heavy iron kettle from a spit rod suspended above a banked fire. She spooned stew onto tin plates, poured coffee, set out a pan of fresh corn bread.

We ate mostly in silence. Despite what she'd said about not having anyone to talk to, she seemed not to want conversation. But there was something I needed to say, and when I was done eating I got it said.

"Missus Todd, you've been more than hospitable to share your food and water with me. I can't help feeling there must be something I can do for you."

"No, Mister Boone. There's nothing you can do."

"Well, suppose I just stayed until your husband gets home, had a little talk with him—"

"That wouldn't be wise," she said. "If Mase comes home and finds a strange man, he wouldn't wait to ask who you are or why you're here. He'd make trouble for you, and afterward he'd make more trouble for me."

What could I do? It was her property, her life; this was business between her and her husband. If she'd asked for help, that would have been another matter. But she'd made her position clear. I had no right to force myself on her.

Outside, in the silky moon-washed purple of early evening, I thanked her again and tried to offer her money for the food and water. But she wouldn't have any of it. She was too proud to take payment for hospitality. She insisted that I fill my waterbags from the well before riding out, so I lowered the wooden bucket on the windlass and did that.

As I rode slowly out of the yard, I turned in the saddle to look back. She was still standing there by the well, looking after me, her hands down at her sides. In the silvery moonlight she had a forlorn, fixed appearance— as if she had somehow taken root in the desert soil.

An hour later I was once again on the Devil's Highway, headed west. And a mounting sense of uneasiness had come to ride with me. For the first time in four months and six days, it was someone other than Emma who was disturbing my thoughts; it was Jennifer Todd.

Like an echo in my mind, I heard some of the words she had spoken to me: *If I had a gun, Mister Boone, I expect I'd do just that thing—I'd shoot him, with no regrets. But there's only one rifle and one pistol, and Mase carries them with him during the day.*

I listened to the echo of those words, and I thought about the way she'd been watching me inside the cabin when I first rode in, the way she'd suddenly opened the door and come outside. Why had she come out at all? Beaten the way she was, most women would have stayed in the privacy of the cabin rather than allow a stranger to see them that way. And why had she talked so freely about her husband, about the kind of man he was?

Then I heard other words she'd spoken—*I'll fetch some drinking water from the well, and I'll see to your horse*—and I drew sharp rein, swung quickly out of the saddle. My fingers fumbled at the straps on the saddlebags, pulled them open, groped inside.

My spare sixgun was missing.

And along with it, three or four cartridges.

I stood there in the moonlight, leaning against the steel-dust's flank, and I knew exactly what she had begun planning when she saw me ride in, and what she was planning for when her husband came home from Maricopa Wells and tried to lay hand on her again. And yet, I couldn't raise anger for what she'd done. She had been driven to it. She had every right to protect herself.

But was it really self-defense? Or was it cold-blooded murder?

In the saddle again, I thought: I've got to stop her. Only then Emma came crowding into my thoughts again. Gone, now—gone too young. So many years never to be lived, so many things never to be done; the child we had tried so hard to have never to be born. There had been nothing I could do to save her. But there was something I could do for another suffering young woman on another hardscrabble ranch.

I made my decision.

I kept on riding west.

ALL THE LONG YEARS

I caught him some past noon on the second day, over on the west edge of my range near Little Creek.

Thing was, he wasn't much of a cow thief. He'd come onto my land in broad daylight, bold as brass, instead of nightherding and then doing his brand-burning elsewhere. And he'd built his fire in a shallow coulee, as if that would keep the smoke from drifting high and far. You could hear the bawling of the cows a long way off too.

I picketed my horse in some brush and eased up to the rim of the coulee and hunkered down behind a chokecherry to have a look at him. I wanted him to be a stranger, or one of the small dirt ranchers from out beyond the Knob. But you don't always get what you want in this life—hell, no, you don't—and I didn't this time. He wasn't a drifter and he wasn't a dirt rancher. He was just who I figured the brand-blotter to be: young Cal Dennison.

He had a running iron heating in the fire and he was squatting alongside, smoking a quirly while he waited. Close by were a lean-shanked orange dun cowpony and two of my Four Dot cows that he'd hobbled with piggin strings. The cows were both young brindle heifers, good breeding stock.

The tip of the running iron was starting to turn red. Cal Dennison rotated it once, finished his smoke, and went to drag one of the heifers over near the fire. When he set to work with that iron, he had his back to where I was. The smell of singed hair came up sharp on the warm afternoon breeze.

I stood and drew my Colt sixgun. Off on my left there was an easy path into the coulee. I moved there and made my way down, slow and careful. The bawling of the heifers covered what sounds I made. I stopped a dozen paces behind and to one side of him, close enough to see that he was almost done turning my Four Dot brand into a solid bar. If I gave him enough time he'd burn a "D" above the bar, the way he had with other of my cows over the past week or so. Then he'd do the other heifer and afterwards herd both over onto D-Bar graze, next to mine on the other side of Little Creek. D-Bar was Lyle Dennison's brand.

But I didn't give him enough time. I put the Colt's hammer on cock and said fast and loud, "You're caught, boy. Set still where you are."

He must have heard the snicking of the hammer because he was already moving by the time I got the words out. Cat-quick, he came all the way around with a look of wild surprise on his face.

"I said set still! You want to die, boy?"

Sight of the Colt and the tone of my voice, if not the words themselves, finally froze him on one knee with the running iron still in his hand. I could have emptied the Colt into him by the time he dropped the iron and drew his own sidearm, and he knew it. I watched him wet his mouth, get hold of himself; watched the wildness smooth out into an expression of sullen defiance.

"Bennett," he said, the way most men would say "Horseshit."

"Put the iron down. Slow."

He did it.

"Now your sixgun, even slower. Just two fingers." He did that too.

"Untie the heifer. Then go do the same with the other one." It took him a minute or so to get the piggin strings off the first heifer's legs. She scrambled up and went loping away down the coulee, still bawling. He got the second cow untied in quicker time, and while that one ran off he stood hipshot, glaring at me. I'd seen him in Cricklewood a few times but the Dennisons and the Bennetts had kept their distance the past twenty years; this was the first I'd had a good look at the boy up close. He'd be past nineteen now. Tall and sinewy and fair-skinned—the image of his ma, I thought. Same light brown curls and dark smoky eyes and proud stance. How long had Ellen Dennison been dead? Ten years? Eleven? Funny how time distorts your sense of its passage, how single years among all the long years blend and blur together until you can't tell one from another . . .

"Well?" young Cal said. "Now what?"

I didn't answer him. Instead I moved over to where he'd been by the fire and kicked his sidegun, an old Allen & Wheelock Navy .36, in among the branches of a wild rose bush.

He said angrily, "What'd you do that for? Them thorns'll scratch hell out of it."

"You won't be using it again."

"You going to shoot me, Bennett?"

"Mister Bennett to you."

"Go to hell, *Mister* Bennett."

"This was twenty years ago, I'd have already shot you."

"Well, it ain't twenty years ago."

"Rustling can still get you hung in this county."

"I ain't afraid of that. Or you, *Mister* Bennett."

"Then you're a damn fool in more ways than one."

He tried to work his mouth up into a sneer but he couldn't quite bring it off. He wasn't near so tough or fearless as he was trying to make out.

His gaze shifted away from me, roved up along the rim of the coulee. "Where's the rest of your crew?"

"There's just me. I don't need a crew to run down one punk brand-blotter. Only took me a day and a half."

He had nothing to say to that.

I said, "How many of my cows have you burned?"

"You're so goddamn smart, you figure it out."

"My riders say at least half a dozen."

"Two thousand," he said, smart-mouth.

"All right, then. Your pa know what you been up to?"

". . . No."

"I didn't think so. Whatever else Lyle Dennison is, he's not a brand-burner and a cow thief."

"I'll tell you what he is," the boy said. "He's twice the man you are."

"Maybe so. But you're not half the man either of us ever was."

That flared up his anger again. "You stole three thousand acres that belonged to him! You turned him into a broken-down dirt rancher!"

"No. That land belonged to me. Circuit judge said so in his open court—"

"You bought that judge! You bribed him! That's always been your way, *Mister* Bennett. Get what you want any way you can—lie and steal and cheat to get it. Ain't that right?"

There was another lie on my tongue, but it tasted bitter and I didn't say it. What did he know about how it was in the old days, a kid like him? Those three thousand acres were mine by right of first possession; my cattle were on free range before Lyle Dennison and others like him showed up in this valley. A man has to fight for what belongs to him, even if it means fighting dirty. If he doesn't, he loses it—and once it's gone, he'll never get it back. It's gone for good.

"That's what this brand-blotting business is all about?" I asked him. "Something that happened between your pa and me twenty years ago?"

"Damn right that's what it's all about. Way I figure it, I got as much right to steal your cattle as you had to steal my pa's land."

"Twenty years is a long time, boy. More years than you been on this earth."

"That don't change the way it was. Pa never would do nothing about it, he just give up. But not me. It's my fight now and I ain't giving up until it's settled, one way or another."

"Why is it your fight now?"

"Because it is."

"Something happen to your pa?"

"That's none of your look-out."

"You've made it my look-out. He didn't pass on, did he?"

". . . Might as well have."

"Sick, then? Some kind of ailment?"

The boy was silent for a time. But I could see it eating at him, the pain and the rage and the hate; he had to let it come out or bust from it. When he did let it come he threw the words at me as if they were knives. "He had a stroke last week. Crippled him. He can't hardly move, can't hardly talk, just lies there in his bed. You satisfied now? That make you happy?"

"No, boy, it doesn't. I'm sorry."

"Sorry? Christ—sorry! You son of a bitch—"

"That's enough. Go get your horse."

"What?"

"Get your horse. Lead him up to where mine is picketed."

"You takin' me to town?"

"We're going to the D-Bar. I want to see your pa."

"No!"

"You don't have a say in it. Do what I told you."

"Why? You aim to tell him about this?"

"Maybe. Maybe not."

"You do and it'll kill him."

"You should have thought of that before you came onto my land with that running iron."

"I won't go."

"You'll go," I said. "Sitting your saddle or tied across it with a bullet in your leg, either way."

He didn't move until I waggled the Colt at him. Then he spat hard into the grass and swung around and stomped over to where the orange dun was picketed.

Following him and the horse up to the coulee rim, I tried to figure what had put the notion to do this in my head. It wasn't just the brand-blotting. And it wasn't because I wanted to mortify the boy in front of Lyle, or that I wanted to pour salt in old wounds. Could be I would tell Lyle about the rustling but more likely 1 wouldn't. Maybe it was because Lyle Dennison and me had been friends once and now he was ailing, likely dying. Maybe it was that young Cal needed to be taught some kind of lesson. Or maybe it was just that there was a crazy need in me to touch the past again.

A man doesn't always know why he does a thing. Or need to know, for that matter. It's just something he has to do, so he goes ahead and does it. Let it go at that.

It was mid-afternoon when we came in sight of the D-Bar ranch buildings. They were grouped in a hollow where Little Creek ran, with the gaunt, snow-rimmed shapes of the Rockies rising up in the distance. I'd expected changes after so many years but none like the ones I saw as we topped the hill above the creek. The place appeared run-down, withered, as if nobody lived there any more. Gaps in the walls of the hip-roofed barn, missing rails in the corral fence, a rusty-wire chicken coop where the bunkhouse had once stood. The main house needed whitewash and new siding and a new roof. There had been flower beds and a vegetable garden once; now there were a few dried-up vines and bushes here and there, like scattered bones in a graveyard.

Cal said, "You like what you see, *Mister* Bennett?" and I come to realize he'd been watching me take it all in. It was the first he'd spoken since we had left my land.

"Why haven't you and your pa kept things up?"

"Why? Why in hell you think? He's old and I ain't got but two hands and there ain't but twenty-four hours in a day."

"Nobody working for you?"

"Not since anthrax took most of our cows two years ago."

"Anthrax took some of my cows too," I said.

"Sure it did. But then you went right out and bought some more, didn't you?"

We rode the rest of the way in a new silence. The boy leaned down and pulled the wooden pin that held the sagging gates shut, and we went on across the yard. Even the grass that grew here, even the big shade cottonwoods behind the house and the willows along the creek, seemed to have a dusty, lifeless look.

We drew rein at the tie rail near the house and got down. I said then, "I'll see him alone."

"Hell you will! You go waltzin' in there like you owned the place, he'll have another stroke—"

"You got no say in this, boy. I told you that."

"You can't just bust in on him!"

"I'll announce myself first."

"What about me? You expect me to just stand here and wait for you?"

"That's just what I expect. You won't run. And you won't try fighting me, neither, not with your pa lying in there."

We locked gazes; there was as much heat in it as a couple of maverick steers locking horns. But I was older and tougher and I had a sixgun besides, holstered though it was now and had been for most of the ride. Cal knew it as well as I did. It was what made him look away first, hating himself for doing it and hating me all the harder for backing him down.

He said thickly, "You goin' to tell him?"

"Still haven't made up my mind."

"He'll call you a liar if you do."

I said, "Stand here where you can hear me if I call you," and went on up the stairs to the screen door. He didn't try to follow me. When I turned to glance back at him he was rooted to the same spot with the hate shining out of his eyes like light shining out of a red-eye lantern.

I opened the screen door—the inside door was already open—and called, "Lyle? It's Sam Bennett. I've come to talk."

No answer.

"Sing out if you object to my coming in."

Still no answer.

I moved inside, let the screen door bang shut behind me. The day's warmth lay thick in the parlor. Dust, too—a thin layer of it on the floor and on the old, worn furniture. Ellen Dennison had been a neat, clean woman; she would have kept house the same way. But she was long gone. For ten or eleven years now it had been just Lyle and the boy.

"Lyle?"

My voice seemed to come bouncing back at me off the walls. I walked across the room, into a hall with three doors opening off of it. He was beyond the last of them, in the back bedroom. Lying in a four-poster with an old patchwork quilt draped over him. His eyes were wide open. One look at them that way and I knew he was dead.

One thin, veined hand lay palm up on the quilt. I went over and touched it, and it was cool and stiff. The stiffness was in his face and body too. Dead a while, since sometime this morning.

For a time I stood looking down at him. We were the same age, forty-six, but the years had ravaged him where they had only eroded me some. His hair was thin and gray-white, there were lines in his face as deep as cracks in sun-dried mud, and his hands were the hands of a man in his sixties. Death, for him, had come as something of a mercy.

A sadness built in me, seeing him up close like this, newly passed on. I'd never hated Lyle Dennison. He had been my friend once, and then he'd been my enemy, but I had never hated or even disliked him much. I'd hardly thought about him at all after the court fight. Hell, why should I? I'd claimed the three thousand acres and they were what counted. Land and money and power were the only things that counted.

That was the way I'd thought back then and most of my life, anyhow. It wasn't the way I thought now.

I leaned down to close Lyle's eyes. Then I made my way back through the house and out onto the porch. Cal was standing where I'd left him. The only thing he'd done was to take out the makings and build himself a smoke.

He said around the quirly, "That was some short talk."

"He's dead, Cal," I said.

"What?"

"Your pa is dead. Passed away this morning sometime, looks like."

"You're a goddamn liar!"

"Go in and see for yourself."

The cigarette dropped out of his mouth, hit the front of his hickory shirt and showered sparks on the way to the ground. He didn't notice. His face had gone bloodless. "You told him about me. You told him and he had another stroke—"

"He had another stroke, right enough. But he's been gone for hours. Go on, boy. See for yourself."

He bolted for the stairs. I got out of the way as he ran up and yanked open the screen door and bulled inside. When the door banged shut again I walked on down to the tie rail and made a cigarette of my own. But it tasted bad, like I was sucking in sulphur smoke; I threw it away after two drags. Then I just stood there and watched a hawk glide above the cottonwoods along the creek, and waited.

It was close to ten minutes before Cal came back out. By then he had himself under a tight rein, likely so I wouldn't see how much he was grieving. He came down to where I was and looked at me for a space, with the hate in his eyes banked now, smouldering.

He said, "Something I want to know."

"Ask it."

"If he'd been alive, would you of told him?"

"No," I said.

"How come?"

"This business is between you and me. You said as much yourself, back in the coulee."

He seemed to understand, or thought he did. He nodded once. "I'm goin' into town now, talk to the preacher and the undertaker. You can tell Sheriff Gaiters I'll be one place or the other when he wants me."

"What makes you think I'll be talking to Sheriff Gaiters?"

That surprised him some. "Mean you won't?"

"Not this time. But you stay off my land from now on. I catch you there again, or find out about any more brand-blotting, you'll pay and pay dear. You hear me?"

"I hear you," he said. "But you better hear something too, *Mister* Bennett. This don't change nothing. Nothing at all."

"I didn't expect it would."

"Just so you know. I ain't my pa's son. I ain't givin' up the way he did, never mind what you say or do."

He turned on his heel and walked over to the corral fence. Stood there with his back to me, gazing out at the mountains jutting sharp against the wide Montana sky, waiting for me to leave first.

I swung into leather, walked the horse slow across the yard. Cal moved his head to watch me. And I wondered again if I could shoot him, should it ever come down to that—kill him even in self-defense. Maybe, maybe not. You never know what you're capable of doing until the time comes for you to make a choice.

I wondered, too, if his ma had ever told Lyle about her and me. How I'd turned away from her in her time of need, because I was still wild and wanted no part of marriage and a family just then. How *her* choice, the only reasonable one open to her, had been to cast aside her pride and go straight to another man who did want to marry her. Not that it made a difference if she had told Lyle, for neither of them had ever told the boy. Nor would I, no matter what might happen between Cal and me. He had enough hate running through him as it was.

"I ain't my pa's son," the boy had said. But God help him, he was. In every way that counted he was just like his pa.

If a man doesn't fight for what belongs to him, he loses it. And once it's gone, he'll never get it back through all the long, empty years. It's gone for good. . . .

BURGLARPROOF

The four-car Sierra Railway train chuffed and wheezed into Jamestown just past noon, more than an hour behind schedule. Quincannon was in a grumpy mood when he alighted from the forward passenger coach, carpetbag in hand, and stood vibrating slightly from the constant jouncing and swaying. The overnight trip from San Francisco, by way of Stockton and Oakdale on the AT&SF, had been fraught with delays, the car had been overheated to ward off the early spring chill in the Mother Lode foothills, his head ached from all the soot and smoke he'd inhaled, and this was not yet his final destination. Another train ride, short and doubtless just as blasted uncomfortable, awaited him before the day was done.

The town's long, crooked main street stretched out beyond the depot. Two-and three-storied wood and stone buildings lined both sides— businesses and professional offices on one, rows of saloons and Chinese washhouses on the other—and the street was packed with rough-garbed men and a variety of conveyances. Behind the saloons, hidden by tall cottonwoods, lay the notorious red-light district known as "Back-of-Town." Quincannon happened to know this by hearsay, not personal experience; this was his first visit to the Queen of the Mines. If he were fortunate, he thought irritably, it would also be his last.

Jimtown's reputation as the "rip-snortin'est, most altogether roughest town in the mines" was evidently justified. A mad cacophony of noises bludgeoned his eardrums—whistles, cowbells, raucous shouts, tinny piano music, crowing roosters, braying mules, snorting horses, clanks and rattles and steam hisses in the rail yards, distant dynamite blasts and the constant pound of stamps at the big Ophir and Crystalline mines on the southern outskirts. Those mines, and hundreds more within a ten-mile radius, had produced more than two million dollars of gold the previous year of 1897. Little wonder that the town was wide open and clamorous.

A reception committee of two awaited Quincannon in front of the depot. The middle-aged gent sporting brown muttonchop whiskers introduced himself as Adam Newell, Sierra Railway's chief engineer. The long and lanky one with fierce gray eyes and a moustache to match was James B. Halloran, Jimtown's marshal. The pair ushered Quincannon into a private office inside the depot, where a third man waited—heavy-set, clean-shaven, dressed in a black broadcloth suit spotted with cigar ash and overlain with a gold watch chain as large and ornate as any Quincannon had ever seen. This was C.W. Cromarty, the railroad's division superintendent.

Cromarty's desk was stacked with profiles, cross-sections, and specification sheets for bridges, rails, switches, and other material; arranged behind it was a series of drafting boards containing location and contour maps of the area. All of this, Quincannon later learned, was for the continuation of the road's branch line to Angels Camp. The branch had been completed as far as Tuttletown, where the trouble that had brought him here had taken place three nights ago.

Cromarty said, after they'd shaken hands, "We'll make this conference brief, Mr. Quincannon. A freight is due in from Tuttletown any minute. As soon as it arrives, we'll leave in my private car."

Quincannon produced his stubby briar and pouch of Navy Plug and began thumbing tobacco into the bowl. "Has any new information come to light on the robbery?"

"None so far."

The engineer, Newell, said, "Tuttletown's constable, George Teague, would have sent word if he'd learned anything. He's a good man, Teague, but out of his element in a matter such as this. We'll be relying on you, Mr. Quincannon."

"A well-placed reliance, I assure you."

"Pretty sure of yourself, aren't you?" Halloran said around the stub of a slender cheroot. His voice and his expression both held a faint sneer.

"With just cause."

"That remains to be seen. You may have a fancy-pants reputation as a detective in San Francisco, you and that woman of yours, but you don't cut no ice up here."

Quincannon bristled at this—literally. When his ire was aroused, the hairs in his dark freebooter's beard stiffened and quivered like a porcupine's quills. He fixed Halloran with an eye more fierce than the marshal's own as he said, "Sabina Carpenter is my partner, not 'my woman'—a Pinkerton-trained detective the equal of any man."

"So you say. Me, I never put much stock in a man that'd partner up with a female, trained or not."

"And I put no stock at all in one who blathers about matters he knows nothing about."

Cromarty said, "Here, that'll be enough of that. Marshal, this is a railroad matter, as you well know. The decision to hire Mr. Quincannon has been made and will be abided by."

"I still say I can do a better job than some citified puff-belly."

Quincannon bit back a triple jointed retort. A fee to fatten the bank account of Carpenter and Quincannon, Professional Detective Services, had been requested in his reply to Cromarty's first wire, and agreed upon in his second. It wouldn't do to get into a sparring match with a small-town peacekeeper who had no say in the matter and no jurisdiction outside his own bailiwick.

He made a point of ignoring Halloran while he fired his pipe with a lucifer. When it was drawing to his satisfaction, he said to Cromarty, "Now then, Superintendent—suppose you provide the details of the robbery left out of your wire. What was the contents of the safe that was stolen?"

"Ten thousand dollars in gold dust and bullion from two of the mines near Tuttletown, awaiting shipment here and on to Stockton."

"A considerable sum. Why was it being kept in the express office overnight?"

"The shipment didn't arrive in time for the last train that afternoon. The Tuttletown agent felt no cause for concern."

"Damn fool," Halloran muttered.

"No, I don't blame Booker. We all believed the gold was secure where it was. What we overlooked was the audacity of thieves who would carry off a four-hundred-pound burglarproof safe in the middle of the night."

Quincannon said, "Burglarproof?"

"A brand-new model, guaranteed as such by the manufacturer."

"I've heard such guarantees before."

"This one has been proven to our satisfaction," Cromarty said. "Sierra Railway Express now uses them exclusively."

"What type of safe is it?"

"Cannon Breech, with a circular door made of reinforced steel. The dial and spindle can be removed once the combination is set, and when that has been done, the safe is virtually impenetrable and indestructible. Not even the most accomplished cracksman has been able to breach it."

"And the dial and spindle were removed in this case?"

"Yes. Booker did that before he locked up and took them home with him. He still has them and swears they were never out of his sight."

"Virtually impenetrable and indestructible, you said? Even with explosives? Dynamite or nitroglycerin inserted in the dial hole in the door?"

"Can't be done, according to the safe company," Newell said. "You couldn't open a dial-less one with a pile driver."

Quincannon remained dubious. Ingenuity could be a two-edged sword, as he well knew; if a burglarproof safe could be built, a way to breach it could likewise be found. "Is this fact common knowledge locally?" he asked.

"I wouldn't say common knowledge, but we've made no secret of the fact."

Then why had the thieves—thieves, plural, for it would have taken at least two strong men to carry 400 pounds of gold-filled steel—broken into the express office and made off with the safe? Halfwits who refused to believe the burglarproof claim? Professional yeggs?

A large, heavy wagon would have been required to transport the safe from the Tuttletown depot, but there was no potential clue in that fact; ore and freight wagons plied the area in large numbers. Nor was there any way to tell in which direction the plunder had been taken, or how far. Two main roads crossed at Tuttletown, one running northward to Angels Camp and the other southward toward Stockton, and there were also a number of intermediate roads connecting with other Mother Lode communities. The town had been the hub of mining activity since placer days, surrounded by a cluster of settlements so close that pioneers from Jackass Hill, Mormon Gulch, and half a dozen others on the west side of Table Mountain could walk into Tuttletown to shop.

These facts had made the town a prime target for thieves before. In the 1880s, the notorious poetry-spouting bandit Black Bart had filched three Wells Fargo stage shipments of bullion and dust amounting to five thousand dollars from the nearby Patterson Mine. Quincannon had been with the Secret Service on the east coast at that time—it wasn't until 1891 that he'd been transferred west to the Service's San Francisco office—so he'd had no opportunity to pit his detective skills against Black Bart's criminal wiles. If he had, he'd once confided to Sabina, there was little doubt that he would have been the one to put an end to the bandit's criminal career.

Outside, a distant train whistle sounded. One long, mournful blast, followed closely by a second.

"That's the Tuttletown freight, Mister Quincannon," Cromarty said. "We'll take our departure as soon as the main tracks are clear."

The superintendent's private car waited on a siding at the near end of the rail yards, coupled to a Baldwin 4-4-0 locomotive. Cromarty, Newell, and Quincannon were the only passengers; Halloran left them at the depot to return to his duties as Jimtown's marshal, with a parting remark about cocksure flycops that Quincannon pretended not to hear. When he resolved this stolen safe business, he vowed to himself, he would not leave Jamestown until he looked up James B. Halloran and claimed the last word.

The car appeared ordinary enough on the outside, but the interior was well appointed with comfortable seats and dining and sleeping compartments. It also contained a pair of ceiling fans and a potbelly stove. The comfort, plus a late lunch once they were underway, improved Quincannon's mood considerably.

The Angels extension branched off Sierra's main line in front of the Nevills Hotel, bridged a creek at the north end of town, then climbed a steep grade to a cut high on Table Mountain. Over on the mountain's west side, the tracks swept down another steep grade and curved around a wide valley and several working mines before swinging northward into Tuttletown. The place was a smaller but no less busy and noise-laden version of Jamestown, its narrow streets, stores, and brace of saloons clogged with off-shift miners and railroad workers from the crews engaged in laying new track and constructing what Cromarty described as a "fifty-foot-high, seventeen-bent wooden trestle" across the Stanislaus River to the north.

A one-man reception committee awaited them here. As soon as the Baldwin hissed to a stop, Quincannon, looking through the window, saw a thin, balding man come out from under the platform roof and hurry over to the car. He was waiting when the three men stepped down, mopping his face with a bandana. Despite the fact that the day was cool and overcast, he was sweating profusely.

Cromarty said, "Hello, Booker," which marked him as the Tuttletown express agent, Howard Booker. "This is John Quincannon, the detective I sent for. Where's Marshal Teague?"

Booker said excitedly, "I got news, Mister Cromarty. Big news. The safe's been found."

"Found, you say? When? Where?"

"About an hour ago. In a field on Icehouse Road. Teague's out there now with the rancher who found it."

"Bully! Abandoned by the thieves, eh?"

"Abandoned, all right, but the news ain't bully."

"What do you mean?"

"Turns out that burglarproof safe's no such thing," Booker said. "She's been opened somehow and she's empty. The gold's gone."

Icehouse Road, obviously named after the stone building with ICE painted on its front wall that squatted alongside a wide creek, serpentined away from town into the hilly countryside. The buggy that Booker had had waiting for them bounced through chuckholes and over thick-grassed hummocks. A grim-visaged C.W. Cromarty sat up front with the express agent, Quincannon on the back-seat with Newell. All four kept their own counsel on the quarter-mile ride.

Around a bend, a broad meadow opened up near where the road forked ahead. Oak and manzanita, and outcroppings of rock, spotted the high grass. A buckboard and a saddled chestnut partially blocked the road, and under one of the large oaks twenty rods away, a group of three men stood waiting. One of the men, a leaned-down gent with a handlebar moustache, detached himself from the others and hurried out to meet the rig. The star pinned to his vest identified him as the local constable, George Teague.

He said to Cromarty, "Damnedest thing you ever saw, Mister Cromarty. Just the damnedest thing. I couldn't hardly believe my eyes."

"Who found the safe?"

"Sam Higgins. He's a dairy rancher lives farther out this way."

Quincannon asked, "Have you discovered anything else here?"

"Just a line of trampled grass. Looks like the safe was carried in from the road." Teague paused. "You the detective from San Francisco?"

Cromarty answered the question and introduced them. Then he said in pained tones, "Very well. Let's have a look at it."

The safe lay tilted on its side in the oak's shade, one corner dug deep into the grassy earth. The black circular door, bearing the words Sierra Railway Express in gold leaf, was open and partially detached, hanging by a single bolt from a bent hinge. Cromarty and Newell stood staring down at it, mouths pinched tight. Quincannon stepped past them, lowered himself to one knee for a closer study.

"She wasn't blowed open," Teague said behind him. "You can see that plain enough."

Quincannon could. There were no powder marks on the door or other evidence that explosives had been used, nor did the center hole for the dial and spindle show any damage. Yet the door had clearly been forced somehow; the bolts were badly twisted. There were marks along the bottom edges of the door, the sort a wedge or chisel struck by sledgehammers would make, but a safe of this construction could not have been ripped open in that fashion, by brute force.

A whitish residue adhered to the steel along where the wedge marks were located. Quincannon scraped it with a thumbnail. Hard and flaky—dried putty, from the look and feel of it.

Another substance had dried on the safe, on one of the outer sides—brownish smears of what was certainly blood. Teague said, "One of 'em must've gashed hisself when they busted into the express office. There's blood on the door and the floor inside, too."

Quincannon said nothing. Something else had drawn his attention—a piece of straw caught on one of the skewed bolts. He plucked it loose. Ordinary straw, clean and damp.

He leaned forward to peer inside the safe. Completely empty—not a gram of gold dust or speck of the other variety remained. He ran fingertips over the smooth walls and floor, found the metal to be cold and faintly moist.

When he straightened, Cromarty asked him, "Have you any idea how it was done?"

"Not as yet."

"If I weren't seeing it for myself, I wouldn't believe it. It just doesn't seem possible."

Again Quincannon had no comment. Actions and events that didn't seem possible were his meat. There was nothing he liked better than feasting on crimes that baffled and flummoxed average men and average detectives.

"Leave the safe here, Mister Cromarty, or take it back to town?" Teague asked.

"Leave it for now. We'll send some men out for it later. Unless you'd rather have it brought in for further examination, Quincannon?"

"Not necessary. I've seen enough of it."

The rancher, Higgins, had no additional information to impart. Nor did the place where the safe had been dumped, or the section of meadow between the oak and the road, or the road itself. The ground was too hard to retain more than vague impressions.

The men rode back into Tuttletown. At the depot, Quincannon asked to have a look at the scene of the robbery both inside and out. Teague and Booker accompanied him to the rear of the building that housed the baggage and express office.

A trio of poplars grew close together near the door on that side; at night a wagon could be drawn up under them and be well hidden in their shadows. The jumbled tracks of men, wagons, and horses told him nothing. He stepped up to look at the door. Its bolt lock had been forced with a pinch bar or similar instrument.

Booker said, "There's a wood crossbar on the door inside, but they got it free somehow. It was on the floor when I come in in the morning."

There was no mystery in how that had been accomplished. Once the bolt had been snapped, the thieves had pried a gap between the door edge and jamb just wide enough to slip a thin length of metal through and lift the crossbar free. He tried the door, found it secure; Booker had replaced the crossbar. Quincannon asked him to go inside and remove it.

While the station agent was obliging, Quincannon studied the broken lock, the gouged wood, the crusty brown stains on the door edge. A fair amount of blood had been lost during the robbery; there were splatters on the platform as well. And more on the rough wood floor inside, he saw when Booker opened up for him.

A dusty square in one corner outlined where the safe had stood. It had been bolted to the floor, the bolts pried loose with the same instrument that had been used on the door. Still more dried blood stained the boards here.

"You know, I looked the place over pretty good myself," Teague said. His patience seemed to be wearing thin. "Thieves didn't leave nothing of theirselves behind, else I'd've found it."

Except for the blood, Quincannon thought but didn't say.

"If you ask me," Booker said, "the ones that done it are long gone by now. And the gold with 'em."

"Possibly. And possibly not."

"Well, they dumped the empty safe, didn't they? What reason would they have for sticking around?"

"Strong ties to the community, mayhap."

"You think they're locals, then?"

"If so, the gold is still here as well."

"That don't put us any closer to finding out who they are."

"Or how they got that safe open," Teague said. "Dynamite wasn't used and they couldn't've done it with hammers and chisels."

"Nor a pile driver," Quincannon said wryly, echoing Newell's words in Jamestown.

"Then how the devil did they do it?"

"The *how* and the *who* may well be linked. The answer to one question will provide the answer to the other."

'Well now, Mister Quincannon," Teague said, "that sounds like double-talk to me. Ain't no shame in admitting you're as fuddled as the rest of us."

No shame in it if it were true, but it wasn't. For one thing, he prided himself that he was never fuddled and only occasionally puzzled. For another, he had already discovered a number of clues which his canny brain was busily piecing together.

Teague mistook his silence for tacit agreement. "So then how you going to go about finding the answers?"

"A detective never reveals his methods until his investigation is complete," Quincannon told him. And sometimes, he added silently, not even then.

Cromarty had invited him to spend the night in his private car, but Quincannon preferred a solitary environment and his own company when he was in the midst of a case. He took a room at Tuttletown's only hostelry, the Cremer House—the best room the hotel had to offer, which turned out to be cramped, spartan, and stuffy. He stayed in it just long enough to deposit his bag. Downstairs again, he asked the pudgy desk clerk if Tuttletown had a doctor.

"Sure have. Doc Goodfellow."

"Where would his office be?"

"Upstairs above the drugstore, one block east."

Quincannon found the doctor in and not busy with a patient. Goodfellow was a tall, saturnine gent who bore a superficial resemblance to Honest Abe. He was evidently aware of the resemblance and proud of it; even the beard he cultivated was Lincolnesque.

Quincannon identified himself and stated his mission in Tuttletown. He asked then, "Have you treated anyone for a severe gash or cut on the hand, wrist, or forearm in the past three days?"

"I have, yes. Two men and a boy."

"Who would the men be?"

"A miner named Jacobsen was the most badly injured," Goodfellow said. "Consequences of a fall at the Rappahanock. Gashed his arm and broke his wrist in two places. I had a difficult time setting the bones—"

"And the other man, Doctor?"

"One of the Schneider brothers—Wilhem. Deep cut on the back of his left hand."

"Miners also, the Schneiders?"

"No, sir. They own the icehouse."

"Ah. Big men, are they? Brawny?"

"Yes, of course. Men who make their living cutting and hauling ice can hardly be puny."

"Have they been in Tuttletown long?"

"Not long. They bought the business about three years ago."

"Where did they come from?"

"I've heard that they owned a similar business down in Bishop," Goodfellow said, "but I don't know for certain. They're a close-mouthed pair when it comes to themselves."

"Peaceable men, law-abiding?"

"Well, the younger, Bodo, has a reputation for rowdiness when he's had too much to drink. But so do half the men who live and work in these parts."

"Do the Schneiders live at or near the icehouse?"

"No. In a cabin on Table Mountain." The doctor frowned. "Do you suspect them of stealing the safe from the express office?"

"At this point," Quincannon said, "I suspect everyone and no one." Which wasn't quite the truth, but it permitted him to take his leave without further questions.

He returned to his room at the hotel, where he stretched out on what passed for a bed—it felt more like an uneven pile of bricks—and tucked his nose into Walt Whitman's *Leaves of Grass*. Poetry was one of his two favorite forms of reading material, the other being intemperate temperance tracts. It soothed and relaxed him and allowed for proper brain-cudgeling.

Some time later, just past nightfall, he laid the book aside and left the room and the hotel wearing what Sabina referred to as his John-is-pleased-with-John smile. A thickening layer of clouds deepened the night's blackness, he noted with satisfaction as he stepped outside. The lamplight that shone within some of the business establishments on Main Street seemed pale by contrast; electric lights had been installed in Jamestown, but not here as yet.

He made his way through the town center, whistling one of his favorite temperance tunes, and turned down the side street that led to Icehouse Road. Here, he had the night to himself. The darkness was unbroken except for distant flickers that marked the locations of mines and cabins at the higher elevations. Under the tall cottonwoods that lined the road and nearby creek the shadows were as black as India ink.

It was a brisk five-minute walk to the icehouse. The building sat creekside a short distance off the road, connected to it by a graveled lane—a low, bulky shape silhouetted against the restless sky. Set apart from it on the near side was a shedlike structure, lamplight making a pale rectangle of its single window. One or both of the Schneider brothers working late in what was probably their office.

Quincannon strolled on past, getting the lay of the place. The wagon entrance was at the far end, barred by a set of wide doors. A livery barn and rough-fenced corral occupied a grassy section between the road and the creek. No conveyances or animals were visible. The wagon and dray horses used for delivering ice would have been put away inside the barn for the night.

When he'd seen enough, he walked at a leisurely pace back to Main Street. The stone-housed general store near the hotel, Swerer's by name, was still open for business. Inside, as he paid for his purchases, the garrulous young fellow behind the counter took considerable pride in informing him that the writer Bret Harte had once clerked there. Quincannon was more impressed by the outlandish prices charged for one dark lantern, one small tin of lamp oil, and a plug of Navy Cut tobacco. Not that the outlay bothered him; the amounts would be added to the expense account he would present to the Sierra Railway Company along with his bill for services rendered.

Hunger prodded him into Miner's Rest Café, where he ate a bowl of mulligan stew and sampled a Mother Lode country favorite, a pie made with vinegar and raisins. The dessert turned out to be more appetizing than its name, fly pie.

Once more in his room at Cremer House. he stripped to his long johns and again made an effort to settle himself on the mound of bricks. He set his internal clock, a mechanism so unfailing that he never used one of the alarm variety. He was asleep within minutes.

At three A.M. Quincannon slipped out of the hotel's side entrance carrying the dark lantern, its wick already lit and the shutter tightly closed. Main Street was all but deserted at this hour: even the saloons had closed. He avoided the one man he saw, a lurcher under the influence, and in less than ten minutes he was hurrying through the deep shadows on Icehouse Road.

No lamplight showed now in the shedlike office next to the icehouse. Darkness shrouded building and outbuildings alike, as well as the road in both directions. Quincannon paused under one of the trees to listen. A night bird's cry, a faint sound from the direction of the corral that was likely the restless movement of a horse. Otherwise, silence.

He picked his way through dew-wet grass to the rear of the icehouse. As he'd expected, the pair of heavy wooden entrance doors were locked. He opened the lantern's shutter a crack, shielding the light with his body, and quickly examined the iron hasp and padlock. Well and good. The padlock was large and looked new, but it was of inferior manufacture.

He closed the shutter, set the lantern down. The set of lock picks he carried, an unintentional gift from a burglar he'd once snaffled, were the best money could buy, and over the years he had learned how to manipulate them as dexterously as any housebreaker. The absence of light hampered his efforts here; it took him three times longer, working by feel, than it would have under normal circumstances to free the padlock's staple. Not a sound disturbed the stillness the entire time.

He removed the lock, hung it from the hasp, and opened one door half just wide enough to ease his body through. The temperature inside was several degrees colder. When he opened the lantern, he saw that he was in a narrow space that sloped downward and was blocked on the inner side by a second set of doors. These, fortunately, were not locked.

The interior of the icehouse was colder still, as frigid as a politician's heart. Quincannon put on the gloves he'd brought with him, then widened the lantern's eye to its fullest and shined the light around. The stone walls, he judged, were at least two feet thick and the wooden floor set six feet or so below ground level. Large and small blocks of ice lined both walls, cut from the creek or hauled from the Stanislaus River during the winter months. Thick layers of straw covered the floor and was packed around the ice; the low ceiling would likewise be insulated with straw to keep the sun's heat from penetrating. A trap door in the middle of the floor would doubtless give access to a stone- or brick-walled pit that would also be ice-filled, a solid mass ready to be broken by axe and chisel into smaller chunks as needed.

He played the light around more slowly, looking for a likely hiding place. None presented itself. The cold had begun to penetrate his clothing; he hurried to the far end and began his search, stamping his feet to maintain circulation.

By the time he had covered three-quarters of the space, finding nothing but ice and straw, he was chilled to the marrow. But his high good humor remained intact; so did his confidence. The stolen gold was hidden somewhere in here. Logic dictated that it couldn't be anywhere else.

Five minutes later, his faith in himself and his deductions was rewarded.

At one wall not far from the entrance, he uncovered a cavelike space formed by ice blocks and a thick pile of straw. The bullion and sacks of dust were piled under the straw—the entire booty, from the look of it.

A satisfied smile creased his pirate's beard. He pocketed one of the sacks, heaped straw over the rest of the gold. Quickly, then, he made his exit, making sure before he stepped outside that the night was still untenanted. He replaced the padlock without closing the staple, then hastened back into town to locate Constable Teague.

Shortly past dawn, in C.W. Cromarty's private car, Quincannon prepared to hold court.

He and Teague, accompanied by a group of deputized citizens that included the express agent, Booker, had taken the Schneider brothers by surprise at their cabin and arrested them without incident. The two thieves were now ensconced in the Tuttletown jail. The gold had been removed from the icehouse and turned over to Booker for safekeeping. With Teague in tow, Quincannon had then come here to tell the superintendent and his chief engineer the good news.

Cromarty was effusive in his praise. "Splendid, Mister Quincannon," he said. "Bully! And the job done in less than twenty-four hours. You're something of a wizard, I must say."

"I prefer the term artiste," Quincannon said. Humility was not one of his virtues, if in fact it was a virtue. Why shouldn't a man at the zenith of his profession be boastful of the fact? "You might say that I am the Rembrandt of crime solvers."

Teague said, "Who's Rembrandt?" but no one answered him.

"Tell us how you deduced the identity of the thieves and the location of the gold," Newell urged.

"And how they got the safe open." The constable appealed to the two railroad men. "He wouldn't tell me before, just said he'd explain everything when we come here."

Quincannon took his time loading and lighting his briar, drawing out the moment. This was the time he liked best, the explanations that demonstrated the breadth and scope of his prowess. He admitted to a dramatic streak in his nature; if he hadn't become a detective, he might have gone on the stage and become a fine dramatic actor. "Ham, you mean," Sabina had said when he mentioned this to her once, but he'd forgiven her.

The others waited expectantly while he got the pipe drawing to his satisfaction. Then he fluffed his beard and said, "Very well, gentlemen. I'll begin by noting clues that led me to the solution. When I examined the safe on Icehouse Road, I found two items—a hard residue of putty where the wedge marks were located on the door, and a piece of straw caught on one of the bolts. Straw, as you all know, is used to pack blocks and chunks of ice to slow the melting process. Also, the walls of the safe were cold, too cold for the night and morning air to have been responsible."

"Pretty flimsy evidence," Teague observed. "And what's putty got to do with it?"

Quincannon addressed the constable's statement, ignoring his question for the moment. "On the contrary, the evidence was not at all flimsy when combined with other factors. Such as where the damaged safe was discarded—less than a mile from the icehouse. The thieves saw no need and had no desire, as heavy and cumbersome as it is, to transport it any farther than that meadow. They were foolishly certain no one would suspect them of the crime."

"How did you know the gold would be hidden in the icehouse?" Cromarty asked. "They might just as well have hidden it elsewhere."

"Might have, yes, but it would have required additional risk. The weight of the gold and the necessity of finding another hiding place also argued against it having been moved elsewhere. As far as they were concerned, it was perfectly secure inside the icehouse until it could be disposed of piecemeal."

"Are you saying that the icehouse was where the safe was opened?"

"I am. It's the only place it could have been managed in this region at this time of year." Quincannon shifted his gaze to Teague. "Do you recall my stating yesterday that the *how* and the *who* of the crime were linked?"

"I do."

"And so they are. Once I determined that the Schneiders were guilty, it was a simple matter of cognitive reasoning to deduce the *how*."

"Fancy talk," Teague said. "Say it in plain English, man. How'd they break into that safe?"

"Strictly speaking, they didn't. The safe was opened from the inside."

"From the *inside?* What the devil are you talking about?"

"The application of a simple law of physics," Quincannon said. "After the safe had been allowed to chill inside the icehouse, the Schneiders turned it on its back and hammered a wedge into the crack of the door along the bottom edge, the purpose being to widen the crack through to the inside, similar to their objective with the express-office door. Then, using a bucket and a funnel, they poured water into the safe until it was full. The final steps were to seal the crack with hard-drying putty"—he glanced meaningly at the constable as he spoke—"and then pack ice around the safe and cover the whole with straw. The object being to completely freeze the water inside."

Newell, the engineer, clapped his hands. "Of course! Water expands as much as one-seventh of its volume when it freezes."

"Exactly. When the water in the safe froze, the intense pressure from the ice caused the door's hinges to give way. It was a simple matter, then, for them to chip out the ice and remove the gold. Whatever residue remained in the safe melted after they carried it away to the field."

Quincannon stood basking in the further approbation that followed these explanations. It was only fitting, of course, for once again he had solved the seemingly insoluble. Superior detective work was a combination of intelligence, observation, deductive reasoning, and supreme self-confidence. These qualities, which he possessed in abundance, made him the most celebrated sleuth west of the Mississippi River. Any man who didn't agree with that assessment was a dunderhead.

Marshal James B. Halloran of Jamestown, for instance.

Quincannon chuckled evilly to himself. Halloran, all unwittingly, had provided him with one other clue to the solution of this case—one he hadn't mentioned in his summation. He was saving it to use as part of his gloat when he sought out that dunderhead marshal before leaving the Queen of the Mines.

"You may be a fancy-pants detective in San Francisco," Halloran had said in Cromarty's office, "but you don't cut no ice up here." Ah, but he had—figuratively if not literally. He'd cut more ice in Tuttletown last night, by godfrey, than the Schneiders had inside that so-called burglarproof safe!

THE GUNNY

The old man sat smoking his pipe in the shade in front of Fletcher's Mercantile, one of the rows of neat frame buildings that made up the town of Bitter Springs. It was mid-afternoon, the sun brassy hot in the hard summer sky, and he was the only citizen in sight when the lanky stranger rode into town from the west.

Horse and rider were dust-spattered, and the lean Appaloosa blew heavily and walked with weary slowness, as if ridden long and hard. But the stranger sat the saddle tall and erect, shoulders pulled back, eyes moving left and right over the empty main street. He was young and leaned-down, with sharp features and a dusty black mustache that bracketed lips as thin as a razor slash. Hanging low on his right hip was a Colt double-action in a Mexican loop holster thong-tied to his thigh.

The old man watched him approach without moving. Smoke from his clay pipe haloed his white-maned head, seeming hardly to drift in the overheated air. He had a frail, dried-out appearance, like leather left too long to cure in the sun; but his eyes were alert, sharply watchful.

As the stranger neared Fletcher's Mercantile, he seemed to take notice of the old man sitting there in the shade. He turned the Appaloosa in that direction, drew rein, and swung easily out of the saddle.

"Hidy, grandpop," he said as he looped the reins around a tie rack. He stepped up onto the boardwalk.

"Hidy yourself."

"Hot, ain't it?"

"Some."

"I been riding three days in this heat and I got me a hell of a thirst. You know what I mean?"

"Don't look senile, do I?"

The stranger laughed. "No, you sure don't."

"Saloon up the street, if a beer's what you're after."

"It is, but not just yet. Got me a little business to attend to first."

"That a fact?" the old man asked conversationally.

"Where can I find Sheriff Ben Chadwick?"

"Most days you could find him at the jailhouse, down at the end of Main here. But he don't happen to be there today."

"No? Where is he?"

"Rode out to the Adams' place, west of town. Somebody's been running off their stock."

"When's he due back?"

"Don't rightly know. What kind of business you got with the sheriff, son?"

"Killin' business."

"So? Who's been killed?"

The young stranger laughed again, without humor. "Nobody yet. Ben Chadwick ain't here, like you said."

The old man took the pipe from his mouth and stared up at the youth. Downstreet somewhere, a dog barked once and was still. The only other sound, until the old man spoke after several seconds, was the faint muffled beat of the hurdy-gurdy in the Oasis Saloon.

"You aim to kill Ben Chadwick, that what you're saying?"

"That's what I'm sayin', grandpop."

"Why?"

"He shot up a couple of men on the trail to Three Forks two weeks ago. I was in Arizona Territory when I heard about it. Else, I'd of been here long before this."

"What's them two fellas to you?"

"One of 'em, Ike Gerard, was my cousin."

"Well, now," the old man said dryly, "looky what we got here. Johnny Goheen, ain't you?"

"That's right, grandpop. Johnny Goheen."

"Your cousin and his sidekick robbed the bank in Three Forks. Killed a deputy. But I reckon that don't cut no ice with the likes of you."

"No, it don't."

"A damn gunny," the old man said, and spat on the worn boards alongside his chair. "Quick on the shoot, are you?"

"Quick as any there ever was."

"Huh. How many men you shot dead, Goheen?"

"Four. All in self-defense."

"Oh sure—self-defense." The old man spat again. "You kill Ben Chadwick, it'll be murder."

"Will it?"

"They'll hang you, Goheen."

"No warrant out on me. Ben Chadwick draws first, sheriff or no sheriff, it's self-defense."

"And you aim to make him draw first."

"That's right."

"Suppose he don't?"

"He will. Yessir, he will."

"Maybe he's faster than you."

"He ain't," Goheen said.

"He's got friends in this town, Ben Chadwick has. They won't let you get away with it."

"You one of 'em? You figure you can stop me?"

The old man said nothing.

Goheen laughed his mirthless laugh. "Tell you what, grandpop. You sit right here in the shade and rest your old bones. No use gettin' all worked up on such a hot day."

Again the old man was silent.

"Nice talkin' to you," Goheen said. He tipped his hat, turned, went upstreet to the Oasis, and pushed in through the batwings without a backward glance.

The old man sat for a minute or so, staring downstreet to the east—the direction Ben Chadwick had ridden out earlier in the day. The road and the flats in that direction seemed empty, motionless except for the heat haze, unmarked by the billows of dust that foretold the arrival of a rider or wagon. Then he knocked the dottle from his pipe, stowed the briar inside his shirt, and got to his feet. He shuffled down to the mercantile's entrance.

Howard Fletcher, an elderly, balding man in shirtsleeves and suspendered trousers, looked up from behind the counter at the far end of the room and smiled. "Well, Jeb, you get tired of setting out there and decide to come in for a game of cribbage?"

The old man didn't return the smile. "I come in to ask a favor, Howard. I need the use of a six-gun."

The curve of Fletcher's mouth turned down the other way. "Now what would you be wanting with a gun, Jeb?"

"I got my reasons."

"Mind my asking what they are?"

"Howard, you and me been friends for a long time and I ain't never asked you for much. I'm asking you for a six-gun now. I'll get it elsewhere if you got objections."

"No objections," Fletcher said. "I just don't understand what's got your hackles up."

"You will soon enough. Colt Peacemaker, if you got one in stock."

"I have."

Fletcher went to a locked window case, opened it with a key attached to his watch chain, and took a new Colt Peacemaker and a box of cartridges from inside. He brought them to where the old man stood, laid them on the counter. His eyes were troubled, but he held his peace.

The old man opened the box of cartridges, removed six, and fitted them into the Peacemaker. Then he spun the cylinder, hefted the weapon in his hand. "Pay you for the cartridges later, Howard, if I use any."

"Just as you say, Jeb," Fletcher said.

The old man nodded, turned, and went outside again. The street and the road and desert flats to the east were still empty under the hard sunglare. He hesitated for a moment, then walked slowly upstreet toward the saloon with the Peacemaker pointed muzzle-downward along his right thigh.

But when he was two buildings away from the saloon, he veered off at an angle, stepped onto the boardwalk, and took up a leaning position against the wall of Henderson's Feed Company. He spat onto the planking at his feet, watching the entrance to the saloon with narrowed eyes. Goheen might do all his waiting inside there, but then again he might not. It would be better if he made up his mind to come outside again. If the old man had to go in after him, some citizen might get hurt.

Five minutes he stood there. Ten. Frank Harper drove by, his wagon loaded with fresh-cut lumber. He waved, but the old man didn't wave back.

Another five minutes vanished. And then the saloon's batwings popped open and Goheen appeared, rubbing the back of one thin arm across his mouth and squinting against the bright sunlight. He moved down off the boardwalk, past the hitchrails into the dusty street.

"Hey, boy!" the old man called sharply. "Come over here, boy!"

Goheen's head jerked up and around; he stopped in midstride with his hand poised over the handle of his revolver. His face registered surprise when he realized who had spoken to him.

"Grandpop, you better not take that tone of voice with me again. What you want?"

The old man pushed away from Henderson's wall, bringing the Peacemaker up in a level point. When Goheen saw it his expression turned to one of slack-jawed amazement.

"What I want," the old man said, "is for you to unbuckle your gunbelt, slowlike, and drop it."

"You gone crazy?"

"Not hardly. I'm making a citizen's arrest and putting you in jail."

"The hell you are. On what charge?"

"Threatening an officer of the law. Disturbing the peace."

"You can't make charges like that stick!"

"Circuit judge is a hard man. He don't like a gunny any more'n I do. You'll do time, boy."

"You ain't arrestin' me," Goheen said. "Be damned if you are. Now put that iron away, grandpop, or—"

"Or what? You'll draw on me?"

"That's right. And I'll kill you dead, too."

"Welcome to try, if that's how you want it." The old man lowered the Peacemaker, slowly, until he was holding it as he had been before, muzzle pointed downward. "Well, boy?"

Seconds passed—long, dragging, tense. Goheen's gaze didn't waver; neither did the old man's. Then, swiftly, Goheen's hand darted down, came up again filled with his weapon—but when he pulled the trigger it was only in belated reflex. The Peacemaker roared first and a bullet kicked up dust from the front of his shirt, drove him half around; his slug went straight down into the dust. His legs buckled and he dropped to his knees. The impact jarred the double-action from his grip; he made no move to pick it up. His face bore the same expression of slack jawed amazement it had minutes earlier, tempered now by shock and pain.

The old man jumped off the boardwalk and kicked Goheen's gun to one side. Men were spilling out of buildings along the street, and from behind him the old man could hear Howard Fletcher calling anxiously, but he kept his eyes fixed on the fallen youth at his feet.

Goheen tried to stand, couldn't, and toppled sideways clutching at his bloody chest. Groaning, he twisted his head to look up at the old man. "Damn you, grandpop, you hurt me bad. Why? I didn't figure you for no . . . no hero."

"I ain't one," the old man said. "I'm just a retired gunsmith that knows how to shoot."

"Then why? Why?"

"Sheriff's got a bad arm, Goheen. Hurt it when his horse shied at a rattler three days ago. I couldn't stand by and let you kill him in cold blood. I'd lay my own life down, and gladly, before I'd let that happen."

"What're you talkin' about?"

"My name's Chadwick, too," the old man said. "Sheriff Ben Chadwick's my son."

FYFE AND THE DRUMMERS

Old-time drummers was a peculiar bunch. It's a fact. I been tending bar here for near forty years—F. X. Fyfe, at your service—and I seen all sorts of folks come through New Appia and the New Appia Hotel, good and bad and some strange. But drummers back before the century turned. . . well, there just weren't none like them peckerwoods. Whisky drummers, cigar drummers, lightning-rod drummers, windmill drummers . . . they was *all* a caution.

You take their general appearance. Not one of them salesmen ever set out to dress like other folks. No, sir. They all wore fancy suits that might've been made of horse blankets, they was that flashy. And waistcoats in different colors than the suits, some decorated with flower patterns that set you in mind of window drapery. And stiff shirts and four-in-hand ties and stickpins with big fake jewels in 'em. And patent-leather shoes shined bright enough so's you could shave and comb your hair looking into the gloss. Most of 'em wore waxed mustaches, too, sometimes dyed pure black, with the ends so stiff and pointy you could've used one to pick your teeth.

Then there was what come out when them boys opened their mouths. Talk? Lordy, old-time drummers could talk a miser out of his gold, a girl out of her drawers, and a politician out of three bought votes. Charm by the carload, that's what they had, and weren't none of it any deeper than a skin of ice after the first hard freeze. Them peckerwoods didn't have to work at being salesmen; they was just natural-born liars and flim-flammers.

You think cowboys is hard drinkers? Why, they're pikers compared to drummers. More times than I can count I threw one out, put another to bed, and served 'em Fyfe's Own Hangover Cure on the morning after. You think Frenchmen is great lovers? I never seen a drummer that wasn't hell-on-wheels with the ladies—or thought he was, or pretended he was. You think minstrel-show and vaudeville comedians know a passel of comical stories? Why, drummers could tell stories for a week straight and never run out. Most of their jokes was bawdy, some was even funny, and danged if they couldn't make you laugh now and then at one that *wasn't* funny.

Yes, sir, all them old-timers was a caution. But I reckon the patent medicine peddlers was the most cockeyed of the lot. How so? Well, I'll give you a first-class example.

This here happened back in the early 'Nineties. Late January, it was. Cold, raw night, mostly wind with a little sleet in it. Wasn't many guests registered at the hotel—never is, that time of year—and there was only half a dozen or so steady customers in the bar parlor when Charley Tuggle walked in.

Charley Tuggle had been a patent medicine drummer for half his forty years—to hear him tell it, anyhow. I knew him tolerable well on account of he'd been coming through New Appia twice a year for the previous seven, always stopped here at the hotel, and always come into the bar parlor to drink hot whisky with sugar water and chew my ear. He wore loud checked suits and fancy flannel waistcoats—I recollect the one on this night was tan, with orange nasturtiums embroidered on it—and he had muttonchop whiskers to go with his pointy mustache. He talked faster than most drummers, which is some fast, and told better dirty stories, too.

Now Tuggle sold all sorts of drugs and medicines—everything from hair tonic to laxatives, from Turkish Pile Ointment to Lydia Pinkham's Vegetable Compound for Ladies. But what he sold best of all was a snake-oil product called Cherokee's Magical Herb Bitters. Likely most medicine drummers never touched a drop of what they peddled, but Tuggle swore up and down that he drank a full bottle of Cherokee's Magical Herb Bitters every week. I believed him, too, as passionate as he was on the subject. He was in the peak of health and says he owed it all to them bitters. Says it to anybody who'll listen. Says it to me every time he bellied up to my bar.

He come in after supper, this night I'm telling about. Carrying a tolerable load (which was nothing unusual), on account of he'd been imbibing spirits most of the day with his best customer, Chet Iams, over to the drugstore. He ordered a hot whisky with sugar water, made some small talk about the weather, and then commenced to bending my ear about them magical bitters of his. Not talking soft, neither. The other patrons sidled off, lest he include them in his pitch, but there wasn't nowhere for me to go. So I listened some as if I'd never heard it all before. Part of my job is to listen, even if it ain't always the best part.

Tuggle started out by saying that Cherokee's Magical Herb Bitters was just the tonic a man needed to stay fit in inclement weather like we was having, for it was the greatest blood and nerve medicine ever manufactured by human beings. Then he says: "Mister Fyfe, this miracle tonic cures all bilious derangements and drives out the foul corruption that contaminates the blood and causes decay. It stimulates and enlivens the vital functions, being as it is a pure vegetable compound and free from all mineral poisons. It promotes energy and strength, restores and preserves health, and infuses new life and vigor throughout the entire system." And so on and so forth.

He was just getting warmed up, old Tuggle was, when this young whippersnapper named Peckham come waltzing in. Now Peckham was also a patent medicine drummer—a newcomer to our fair town, one of them freelancers that work for different manufacturers and don't have a set territory. Full of piss and vinegar, was young Peckham. Full of corn whisky, too, this night, on account of bending elbows all day long with a customer *he* was trying to impress. Weren't usual for two snake-oil peddlers to come through town at the same time, and this Peckham was new on the road, so him and Tuggle wasn't acquainted. Not yet, they wasn't.

Well, here come Peckham into the bar parlor, weaving some and toting his sample case, just as Tuggle declaims that Cherokee's Magical Herb Bitters is the purest, safest, and most effectual medicine known to mankind, and that there ain't no sore it won't heal, no pain it won't subdue, and no disease it won't cure.

Peckham stopped dead in his tracks, listening to this with a scowl. Then he twisted one of his sandy mustaches, and, when Tuggle paused to draw a breath, he says loud and clear: "Bunkum."

That got everybody's attention, including Tuggle's. Old Charley come around, looked the youngster up and down with one squinty eye, and asks him soft and chilly to repeat himself.

"Bunkum," Peckham says again, just as loud. "Pure bunkum."

"Is that so, my brash young fellow?" Tuggle says. "And just what do you know about such matters?"

"Everything I need to know," Peckham counters. "Why, whatever puny concoction you're hawking can't hold a candle to Doctor Wallmann's Celebrated Nerve and Brain Tonic."

"Doctor Wallmann's what?" Tuggle says, haughty. "I have never heard of it."

"You will," the boy says. "You surely will. It is brand spanking new . . . the finest, purest blood, nerve, and brain medicine ever made for the benefit of mankind. Bar none."

"Bunkum," Tuggle says.

Well, it got Sunday-sermon quiet in there. The two of 'em looked each other over like a couple of fancy fighting cocks. Then Peckham strutted up to the bar, opened his sample case, took out a brown bottle of this Dr. Wallmann's Celebrated Nerve and Brain Tonic, and smacked it down with a flourish. "Behold," he says. "The new wonder oil . . . the discovery of the ages."

Tuggle didn't even glance at the bottle. He reached inside his loud, checked coat, produced a brown bottle of Cherokee's Magical Herb Bitters, and smacked that down with an even grander flourish. "Behold," he says. "The old wonder oil . . . the *true* discovery of the ages."

The pair of 'em glared at each other. Then Peckham says by way of a challenge: "Doctor Wallmann's Celebrated Nerve and Brain Tonic cures any affliction you can name, and more afflictions and derangements than any other product on the face of the globe."

"Oh it does, does it?" Tuggle says. "Womb complaints and uterine affections, mayhap?"

"Of course."

"Formation of gas in the bowels?"

"Naturally."

"Sciatica and neuralgia?"

"Most assuredly."

"Chronic rheumatism, pleurisy, gout?"

"With ease, sir. With ease."

"Well, so does Cherokee's Magical Herb Bitters," Tuggle says like a senator to a rube, "and with even *greater* ease. My wonder bitters also cures dyspepsia, costiveness, bad breath, palpitations of the heart, the old Sunday sick headache, persistent and obstinate constipation, fever and ague, and salt rheum."

"So does my celebrated tonic," Peckham says. "Not to mention eczema, erysipelas, tetter, cankers, and water brash."

"But not ulcerated kidneys," Tuggle says.

"Ulcerated kidneys and inflamed kidneys."

"Highly colored urine?"

"*And* greasy froth in the urine."

"Asthma, bronchitis, epilepsy?"

"*And* purulent ulcers, scrofula, and deafness."

By this time Tuggle was red in the face—so red I couldn't help but wonder if Cherokee's Magical Herb Bitters also cured apoplexy. He all but shouts at the young upstart: "Belching of wind and food after eating?"

"With only two teaspoons."

"Lusterless eyeballs?"

"Three tablespoons."

"Catarrh of the bladder?"

"Half a bottle, no more."

"Lost manhood?"

"Guaranteed after the ingestion of but a single bottle."

"Liar!" Tuggle yells. "Charlatan! Only Cherokee's Magical Herb Bitters can stiffen a flaccid man's resolve!"

That got the boy's back up. He moved close to Tuggle and says right in his face: "How dare you call me a liar? I demand an apology, sir."

"To hell with your apology," Tuggle says. "And to hell with Doctor Pipsqueak's Celebrated Nerve and Brain Tonic!"

"Oh, yes?" Peckham says, sparking some himself. "Well, to hell with Quack's Magical damned Bitters!"

I leaned over the bar along in here and says—"Now, gents, settle down, let's keep matters peaceable."—but neither of 'em paid me any mind. They was nose to nose, glaring and growling.

"Diarrhea!"

"Lumbago!"

"Weak lungs!"

"Milk leg!"

"Chilblains and bunions!"

"Distressing heat flashes!"

"Diseased glands!"

"Carbuncles and cutaneous eruptions!"

"Dandruff and falling of the hair!"

"Pressure on top of the head!"

"I'll give you pressure on top of the head!" Tuggle roars, and danged if he don't fetch young Peckham a hellacious thump smack on the cranium.

Well, the blow knocked Peckham to his knees, but not for long. The youngster bounced back up like a jack-in-the-box, bellowing and snarling, and give old Charley a jolt over the heart. Next thing I knew, the two of 'em was mixing it up like a couple of crapulous prize fighters at the county fair—all flailing arms and patent-leather shoes and cuss words, some of which even I was amazed to hear.

By the time I got my bung starter and come over the bar, they was down on the floor, rolling around and punching, gouging and kicking each other. Everybody else had scattered out of harm's way. I leaned in and give Peckham a clout on the shoulder with the bung starter, on account of he'd picked up a spittoon and was aiming to brain Tuggle with it. Wasn't my best clout, though, for he did manage to land that spittoon alongside Tuggle's jaw with some weight behind it. Tuggle let out a bleat, and his eyes rolled up and out he went like a candle in a windstorm. Wasn't nothing I could do then but let Peckham have another whack with my bung starter, this one of the back of his noggin, which put *him* out cold, too, athwart Tuggle.

The other patrons crowded up, and we all looked down at them two sorry specimens. What a sight they was, lying there all bloody and bruised, fancy clothes in tatters, with not a lick of dignity left to either one. And all on account of some danged patent medicines that likely couldn't cure one in fifty of the ills and afflictions they was supposed to.

Including and especially loss of manhood.

Harry Weems, the night clerk back then, was gawping in from the hotel lobby, and I hollered to him to run and fetch the sheriff. Then I went back around the bar for a swallow of something to settle my nerves. Not hardly Cherokee's Magical Herb Bitters and not hardly Dr. Wallmann's Celebrated Nerve and Brain Tonic. No sir—good old bourbon whisky.

Now, while we all waited for the sheriff, one of the regular customers picked up them two brown bottles that was setting side by side on the bar top and looked close at the labels. Then he let out a whoop and handed the bottles to me. And when I had a close look myself, what do you think I saw?

Why, both snake oils was manufactured by the John C. Delacroix Company of Chicago, Illinois. The same danged company! And neither of them peckerwoods had a clue until they woke up in jail together and the sheriff informed 'em.

Didn't I tell you old-time drummers was a caution?

WOODEN INDIAN

I was laying a fire in the cast-iron stove when Henry Bandelier, who owns the Elk Basin General Merchandise Store, came rushing into my office. Usually Bandelier is the unflappable sort, but he was in a dither this cold October morning; he was so flappable, in fact, with his feet moving and his arms sawing up and down, he looked like a scrawny pink crow about to take flight.

"Sheriff, I been robbed!"

That brought me right up to attention. I didn't much care for Bandelier—he was a loudmouth, and no more honest than he had to be—but you don't have to care for a man to do your duty by him.

"The hell you say. When did it happen?"

"Middle of the night," he said.

"How much is missing?"

"How much? *All* of it, of course!"

"All the money in your cashbox?"

"Money? Who said anything about money?"

"Well, you did . . . didn't you?"

"No! Wasn't money that was stolen. It was my Indian."

". . . Come again?"

"You heard me, Sheriff. My prize wooden Indian's been pilfered."

"Now who in tarnation would steal that monstrous—" I stopped, cleared my throat, and started over. "That Indian's been setting out in front of your store six or seven years now. Weighs two hundred pounds if it weighs an ounce. Who'd want to go and steal it?"

"Tom Black Wolf, that's who."

"Oh, now . . ."

"It's a fact," Bandelier said. "You can't go sticking up for that boy this time, Lucas Monk. Him and that cousin of his, Charlie Walks Far, stole my Indian in the dead of night and that's the plain truth."

"How do you know it was them?"

"Lloyd Cooper told me so, that's how I know. He was awake at three A.M., using his chamberpot, and he heard a wagon rattling by the hotel and looked out and it was Tom Black Wolf and Charlie Walks Far making off with my Indian."

"How could Lloyd tell who was on the wagon, at that distance?"

"There was a moon last night," Bandelier said. "You know that as well as I do. A big fat harvest moon. Lloyd saw them plain. Saw something eight feet long in the bed, too, under a piece of canvas. Said it looked like a body. Ain't anything eight feet long that looks like a covered-up corpse, by God, except my Indian."

That was open to debate, but trying to argue with a fractious Henry Bandelier was like trying to argue with a mean-spirited bull in rutting season. I said, "All right, Mr. Bandelier. You just simmer down. I'll drive out to the reservation and have a talk with Tom Black Wolf."

"Talk with him, hell. You arrest him, Sheriff, you hear me? You arrest him and bring back my Indian or I'll know the reason why!" He turned on his heel and stalked out.

I stood puzzling for a time in the cold office. *The reason why*. Well, that was the question uppermost in my mind, even if it wasn't uppermost in Henry Bandelier's.

What would a couple of Indians want with an eight-foot, two-hundred pound wooden Indian?

The damn Model T wouldn't start without I spent twenty minutes at the crank, aggravating my bursitis with every turn. Contraption never failed to give me trouble as soon as the weather turned frosty. Come the winter snows, I'd lock it in my barn again and leave it there until the thaw. Progress is all well and good, and in 1915 a county sheriff's got to have a modern conveyance or folks don't think he's serious about his job; but if you ask me, a good horse is a better asset to a man than any motor car ever manufactured. Horses don't freeze up in the winter, for one thing. And you don't have to crank one until your arm pretty near falls off to get it started on cold mornings.

I pedaled the flivver into low gear and drove on down Main Street, with the exhaust farting smoke and sparks all the way. The front of Henry Bandelier's store looked some better without that wooden indian rearing up next to the entrance. Most folks in Elk Basin would agree with that, too; Bandelier had had more than one complaint about it over the years. But he was right paternal about that Indian, which was ironical because he didn't like real Indians at all; he'd trade with the ones on the reservation but he made them come around to the rear so as not to "offend" his white customers. He claimed the wooden Indian had been a gift from the Cuba Libre Cigar Company of Cleveland, Ohio, in honor of the fact that he sold more Cuba Libre crooks and panatelas than any other merchant in the state. More likely, he'd made some kind of deal with the Cuba Libre people to display that Indian, which had their name written across the chest in bold red letters, in exchange for a fatter discount. Either way, it was an eyesore. And not just on account of its size. It was rough-carved of some tobacco-spit brown wood, the limbs and head were all out of proportion to the body, a piece of the nose had been shot off by a drunken cowboy one Fourth of July, and the "cigars" it was clutching were so big and phallic-looking they'd caused more than one woman to blush when Bandelier first unveiled it.

Officially, though, that wooden Indian might have been the Mona Lisa: it was stolen property, its theft a felony offense. The law's the law and I'm sworn to uphold it. But it sure would pain me to have to arrest Tom Black Wolf and Charlie Walks Far for the crime. Especially young Tom.

He was twenty-two, smart as a whip, and down-deep honest. You could trust him with your money and likely your life, which is a hell of a lot more than I'd say for most white men in Elk Basin. He'd whizzed through agency school, and at the urging of Abe Fetters, the Indian agent, and Doc Cranston and me and a couple of others, he'd come in to attend high school right here in town. Graduated at the top of his class, too. He wanted to be an agronomist. I had to go look that up. It means somebody who specializes in field-crop production and soil management, which is to say somebody who can make crops grow on poor land. He'd applied to the state university and been accepted and would have enrolled last semester—he'd been working two jobs off the reservation to save up enough for his tuition—except that his grandfather, old Chief Victor, had taken mortal sick. Tom idolized Chief Victor, who had once been a great warrior and who was descended from and named after the head chief of the Flatheads during the middle of the last century; and he just wouldn't leave the reservation while the old man was on his death bed. Well, Chief Victor had been on his death bed three months now and was likely to lie there another three before he finally let go. These old warriors die hard.

So that was Tom Black Wolf. And Charlie Walks Far was all right, too. Not as bright as Tom, but a hard-worker and no trouble to anybody. It just didn't make sense that those two, of all the people in the county, red or white, would have swiped Bandelier's damned cigar company Indian. Not even as a prank; they were too sober-sided for that sort of foolishness.

It was a dozen miles out to the reservation, along a road that had been built for wagons, not Model T Fords. The motor car was contrary at the best of times; on such a road as this it kept bucking and lurching, as if it didn't like my company or my hands on its steering wheel. By the time I drove onto reservation land, my backside was sorer than if I'd been sitting a saddle twenty-four hours straight.

The reservation was poor land, rocky and hilly, with almost no decent bottomland. No wonder Tom Black Wolf wanted to be an agronomist; you'd have to have special training, and maybe divine help, to grow worthwhile crops in soil like this. That was the federal government for you: force the Indians onto such land and then expect them to lick your boots in gratitude just because the land was free. It was a hell of a thing to be born with a skin color different than the men who ran the country, particularly when the country had been yours in the first place.

Close to five hundred Indians lived there—Flatheads, mostly, with a few Piegans and Bloods. Their homes were slab-built shacks put up by the government back in the Seventies, most of them scattered around a small, shallow lake. There were some ramshackle barns and livestock pens—the Indians ran sheep, goats, and a few head of cattle—and an agency store and an infirmary where the poorly trained reservation doctor treated ills and disease with such medicines as the Bureau of Indian Affairs doled out. Tweaked my conscience every time I came out here, even though I'd had nothing to do with building the place or with running it. It was squalor, plain and simple, two generations' worth, and no man worth his salt faces squalor with a clear conscience.

A dirt road rimmed the lake, and the flivver made so much noise rattling along it that kids and dogs ran and hid. When I came up to Chief Victor's house—bigger than most, as befitted his station—Tom Black Wolf appeared in the doorway. He watched me shut the motor down and climb off and walk on over to him. Usually he had a smile for me, but today he was all Indian; there wasn't any more expression on his lean face or in his eyes than there was in Henry Bandelier's wooden Indian.

I didn't smile either. I said, "Morning, Tom. Taste of snow in the air, wouldn't you say?"

"Yes. Have you come to see me, Sheriff Lucas?"

"Some questions I'd like to ask you. I don't want to disturb your grandfather, though. We can talk out here."

"Chief Victor has been moved to the infirmary. The doctor requested it two days ago."

"He's bad off, then?"

"Yes. It is almost his time."

"I'm sorry, Tom."

"You shouldn't be," he said. "It is only a passage. Chief Victor has led a long and honorable life and he will find his reward." I nodded, and Tom said then, formal, "Please come inside where it's warm."

We went in. Tom kept the place clean, and mostly neat except for books. He was a reader, Tom was—read anything and everything, on just about any subject you could name. Hungry for knowledge, that was Toni Black Wolf. There were books on the wood-block tables and chairs and scattered in piles over the painted board floor. Some were his, that he'd bought through mail-order; others belonged to the new Elk Basin Lending

Library. Miss Mary Ellen Belknap, the librarian and town historian, let him check out as many as he wanted, despite the few citizens who frowned on such generosity.

I went over and stood by the stove, to thaw myself out. Tom let me warm some before he said, "You have questions, you said?"

"It's a law matter. Seems that wooden Indian sets out in front of Henry Bandelier's store was stolen last night. He thinks you and Charlie Walks Far did the deed."

Tom didn't say anything.

"Did you, son? You and Charlie?"

He just looked at me with his face set and his lips pressed tight together. That gave me another twinge, for it told me he was guilty, all right, and that he wasn't going to own up to it. An Indian who respects you—and I knew Tom respected me—won't lie to your face, the way a white man will. Instead he keeps his mouth shut and lets you think whatever you like.

"Tom," I said, "stealing's a serious crime, you know that. Even if it is of a public eyesore. If you've got that wooden Indian around here somewhere, I'll find it. Go easier on you and Charlie if you tell me where it is and your reason for making off with it."

"You're welcome to search, Sheriff Lucas."

"Is that all you got to say?"

He nodded. Once.

"All right, then," I said. "I'll just go ahead and see what's what around here."

Which I did, and of course I didn't find any sign of that eight-foot hunk of wood. Finding it wasn't going to be *that* easy. When I was done I walked with him to the flivver, and then stopped and turned and said, "You been doing some saw work this morning, Tom?"

It didn't faze him. Takes a better white man than me to surprise an Indian, I guess. He said, bland as you please, "Saw work?"

"Got sawdust all over your shoes." He did, too; I'd noticed it while I was warming up at the stove. "Don't look like cottonwood or jackpine or any other wood grows around here. Matter of fact, it looks like that tobacco-spit brown wood Henry Bandelier's statue is carved out of."

Tom didn't say anything.

"Cut it up for firewood, did you?"

Silence.

"Or maybe it offended you boys somehow. That it?"

Silence.

I sighed, though not so's he could hear me do it, and said, "Reckon I'll be back, Tom," and got into the flivver.

I found Charlie Walks Far tending sheep on the hardscrabble land north of the lake. I had to leave the Ford on the road; if I'd tried to drive up to where Charlie was, I'd have busted an axle or bruised my liver or both. But I was just wasting my time. Charlie was as close-mouthed as Tom. No lies, no admissions; just civility and nothing more.

So then I went to see Abe Fetters, the Indian agent who also ran the reservation store. He didn't know anything about the wooden indian—not that I expected him to—and said he just couldn't believe Tom Black Wolf and Charlie Walks Far would resort to common thievery.

"Particularly not now," Abe went on, "with Chief Victor so sick. Why, it'd be an act of disrespect, and you know how Tom idolizes his grandfather."

"Maybe they had a good reason for it," I said.

"They may have thought so. But what?"

"Well, I don't know. Some ceremonial reason, maybe?"

Abe laughed without much humor. "Take my word for it," he said, "there's no Flathead ceremony involving a wooden Indian."

I asked him to help me comb the village and see what we could find. He said he would. And we did. And that was another big waste of time. Whatever Tom and Charlie had done with the statue, it was well hidden—or its remains were. We didn't find even a speck of sawdust to match the kind on Tom's shoes.

We stopped finally at the infirmary, for I thought it proper to pay my respects—likely my last respects—to Chief Victor. But the old man was asleep and the halfbreed doctor, Joshua Teel, wouldn't let me in to see him. Chief Victor likely wouldn't recognize me anyway, Teel said; the old warrior was mostly delirious now and had been for a couple of days.

So it was a morning of frustrations all around.

Wasn't anything for me to do then but drive on back to Elk Basin. It was well past noon by that time, and I was almost as hungry as I was puzzled. None of it made a lick of sense. Hell, if anything the theft made less sense now than it had before I'd visited the reservation.

Why would two basically honest young Indians steal a worthless wooden Indian? And why in tarnation would they take a saw to it once they had it?

Back in town I put the Model T away in the City Hall barn and then went and hunted up Lloyd Cooper and had a little talk with him. After which I took my sore bones to the Elite Café for a late lunch. But before I could eat it, Henry Bandelier came prancing in; he'd seen me drive through earlier and he'd also seen that I was alone—no Tom Black Wolf, no Charlie Walks Far, and no wooden Indian.

"Well?" he demanded, after he'd sat down uninvited at my table. "Why didn't you arrest those two bucks?"

"I didn't arrest 'em," I said, "on account of I got no evidence they're the guilty parties."

"No evidence? Hogwash! I told you Lloyd Cooper saw them stealing my Indian in the middle of the night."

"That's not exactly what Lloyd saw. I just talked to him myself a few minutes ago. He saw Tom and Charlie, all right, on board a wagon with something in the bed under a piece of canvas, but he didn't see what that something was. Not so much as a glimpse of it."

"It was my Indian. You know it was!"

"I don't know any such thing," I said. "I didn't find that statue of yours out at the reservation, nor anybody who knew anything about it."

Bandelier shaped his lips like a man about to spit. "Just how carefully did you search, Sheriff?"

"Carefully enough." I fixed him with a hard eye. "And I don't like your tone, Mr. Bandelier. You implying that I haven't done my duty?"

"If the shoe fits," he said, prissy.

"Well, it don't fit," I said. "Now suppose you take yourself back behind your store counter and let me eat my lunch in peace and quiet."

"I'm warning you, Sheriff Monk . . ."

"You're doing what?"

He didn't like what he saw in my face. He scraped back his chair, not meeting my eyes now, and said to my left shoulder, "If you won't do anything about those two thieving Flatheads, then I will."

"Such as?"

"That's my business."

"Not if it involves breaking the law. You do anything illegal, like going out to the reservation yourself with mischief in mind, and I'll cloud up and rain all over you. And you can damned well count on that."

I spoke loud, so that the five other citizens in the Elite could also hear my words plain. Bandelier's face got even redder than it already was. But he didn't sling any more words of his own; he put his back to me and walked out all stiff and righteous, like a sinner leaving a tent meeting.

Well, hell, I thought.

Now I'd lost my appetite.

Henry Bandelier was born without the sense God gave a picket-pin gopher: He tried to stir up trouble in spite of my warning. He talked long and fast to anybody who'd listen about the "red heathens out on the reservation," and what lowdown thieves they were, and even though it had been years since we'd had any problems to speak of with the Indians, there were some hotheads who believed him. There'd have been an incident come out of it, too, with white men and red both getting hurt, if I hadn't got wind of a midnight meeting in the back of Bandelier's store. Half a dozen men were there, armed with ax handles and fortified with free liquor, and they were getting ready to ride on out to the reservation to "teach those Indians a lesson," as Bandelier was saying, when I busted in.

I chased the others home and threw Bandelier in jail on a charge of inciting to riot. He squawked long and loud, which was fine with me; he also made some thinly veiled threats, which wasn't fine with me. So I added "threatening a peace officer with bodily harm" to the charges against him.

In the morning Bandelier demanded his lawyer. When Jack Dunlap showed up I talked to him first, after which he consulted with Bandelier in private for the better part of an hour. What he said must have put the fear of God into the storekeeper; Bandelier was some subdued when we all went trooping over to see Judge Cooney. The judge let Bandelier out on bail, and I promised to reduce the charges against him on the proviso that he quit trying to provoke conflict with the Indians and leave the matter of the missing statue in the hands of the law.

That put an end to the trouble. Bandelier had too much self-esteem to suffer a public disgrace lightly; he retreated into his store and his humiliation, and from then on kept his big mouth shut.

I continued to investigate the theft, off and on for two days, but there just wasn't anything to find out. I was considering another drive out to the reservation when Abe Fetters showed up in town with the news that Chief Victor had died.

I talked to Abe over at the train depot, where he was picking up a consignment of supplies from the government. He said the old man had passed on two nights ago, in his sleep. Yesterday there'd been the usual tribal ceremony presided over by the medicine man. Today, though, there'd been something that *wasn't* usual.

"What's that, Abe?" I asked.

"Well, the burial," he said. "They took his remains out to the burial ground before dawn without telling the medicine man. Or me, for that matter. I didn't find out until after it was already done."

"Who did?"

"Tom Black Wolf and members of his family. Funny breach of custom. First time anything like it has happened."

"Tom give you an explanation?"

"No," Abe said. "I asked him and so did the medicine man, but he wouldn't say. He must have had a good reason, though. Indians don't do anything without a good reason."

"You got any idea what it might be?"

"Not a one."

Neither did I, right then.

But I sure did that evening.

The official part of my day ends at six o'clock, when my night deputy, Gus Beemis, comes on. Since I lost my wife Tess two years ago, my evenings tend to be pretty quiet and of a sameness. Usually I have supper at the Elite Café, go on home, do such chores as need doing, turn in, and read myself to sleep. Gets lonely sometimes, especially around the holidays, but a man learns to live with that, same as he learns to live with all the other things, good and bad, that make up his life.

Some evenings after supper I stop by the library before I head home, to pick up and return books. In my early days I wasn't much of a reader; but after Tess passed on I took it up on a regular basis, just as Tom Black Wolf had, and found that I'd been short-changing myself most of my life. Books are more than just tools of knowledge; good books are friends. Better friends, some of them, than the human variety.

This was one of my nights to stop by the library. And I chanced to walk in while Mary Ellen Belknap was having a conversation with Lydia Cranston, Doc Cranston's wife. Indians was what they were talking about—Chief Victor's passing, at first. The library is small, so I couldn't have helped overhearing them if I'd wanted to. And I didn't want to when their talk shifted to Tom Black Wolf.

"I swan," Mary Ellen said, "I'll never understand Indians."

"Why do you say that?" Lydia asked.

"Well, you take Tom Black Wolf. He's always been such a good boy. Smart, well-mannered, and respectful of property. That's why I've let him check out books since he was in high school; he never abused the privilege. But now . . . well, I hope he isn't going to start running wild."

"Why would you think he'd start running wild, for heaven's sake?"

"It's the little things, isn't it?" Mary Ellen said. "That's how it always starts. And now that Chief Victor is gone, the authority figure in Tom's life—"

"*What* little things?"

"The last batch of books he checked out were overdue for almost two weeks. He's never had overdue books before."

"Well, my land, with his grandfather so sick—"

"That's not all," Mary Ellen said. "He also mutilated a book."

"He did what?"

"Mutilated a book. Don't look at me that way, Lydia, it's true. He tore a photograph out of an expensive history book. Oh, he pasted it back in but you can see plainly where it was ripped out—"

I was over at the desk by then. I said, "Mary Ellen, when did you find out about this torn photograph?"

She blinked at me. She's six feet tall and horse-faced and when she blinks she looks like a startled mare. "Why . . . just this afternoon, Sheriff. Tom brought in the books that were overdue. One was the history text—"

"You have that book handy?"

"Yes, it's on my desk."

"Mind letting me see it?"

"Of course not, but what—"

"Just let me see the book, Mary Ellen."

She got it for me. The title and subtitle were stamped in gilt on the front cover: *Sons and Daughters of the Nile. A History of Egypt from Ancient to Modern Times.* I opened it up and found the photograph that had been torn out and pasted back in, and took a good long look at it, and that was when I got my notion. The damnedest notion I'd ever had, but there it was.

I said to Mary Ellen, "I'd like to borrow this book until tomorrow."

"Check it out, you mean? But it needs to be properly repaired—"

"Just until tomorrow, Mary Ellen."

Before she could say anything else I tucked the book under my arm and went on out. I could feel the two women's eyes on my back, and I could hear them start to whisper even before I shut the door.

When I got home I sat in my Morris chair and did some studying on the history book. Then I did some studying without the book, working that notion of mine from different angles. And by golly, all the pieces fit together as pretty as you please:

The missing wooden Indian . . . the sawdust on Tom's shoes the morning after the theft . . . Chief Victor's illness and delirium . . . Tom and his family not letting either the tribal medicine man or Abe Fetters come along to the burial grounds . . . and the torn-out photograph in the Egyptian history book—the photograph of a sarcophagus, one of those stone coffins made in the likeness of the kings and queens and other royalty that were buried inside them.

Suppose Tom and Charlie Walks Far hadn't cut that wooden Indian into pieces; suppose they'd sawed it clean in half, lengthwise, and then hollowed out both halves with hammers and wood chisels. And suppose they'd put Chief Victor's remains inside and buried real Indian and wooden Indian both.

Chief Victor himself would have had to ask for it. And he might have, even if it went smack against tribal custom, if he'd been addled enough in his sickness. Could be he'd got hold of the Egyptian history book—

Tom always had books lying around their shack—and could be he'd seen that photograph of the sarcophagus, and torn it out because it fascinated him, and in his delirium determined that he was royalty, too, descended from the Great Chief Victor, so why shouldn't he have a coffin like the Egyptian royalty did? Tom wouldn't have refused anything his grandfather asked, no matter how daft or heretical; he'd likely have tried to argue against it but in the end he wouldn't have refused. And since there was no time to build a sarcophagus in the old warrior's true likeness, with Chief Victor already knocking at death's door, Tom and Charlie Walks Far had had to make do with what came easy to hand.

But, hell, it was a crazy notion. Pure foolishness, even if all the pieces did fit. Must be some other explanation that made better and saner sense.

And yet . . .

Well, I *could* tell Abe Fetters about it and we could go out to the reservation burial ground and find out for certain. But that struck me as downright sacrilegious. Those poor Indians had enough trials and tribulations without a bunch of white men digging up their sacred burial ground. Besides which, if it did turn out to be true, then the citizens of Elk Basin would have a field day at the Indians' expense and the whole thing would get written up in newspapers around the state and maybe around the country too. And as if that wasn't bad enough, I'd have to arrest Tom and Charlie, and Henry Bandelier would sure as hell press charges against them. There'd be no justice in that. Tom couldn't go to the university and become an agronomist and help his people if he was serving a stretch in the state penitentiary.

No, I decided, the best thing for me to do was to keep that crazy notion of mine to myself. Better yet, dismiss it as a pipe dream and forget all about it.

That's just what I did. And to this day nobody in Elk Basin has ever found out what really happened to Henry Bandelier's wooden Indian. Including me.

Some things, I reckon, folks are just better off not knowing.

THE GAMBLER

For most of his life, he said, nigh on fifty years, he'd been a sporting man.

Faro, that was his game, he said. He'd operated faro banks all over the West, been a mechanic in some of the fanciest gambling houses from one end of the frontier to the other. Poker? Sure, that too. He'd played poker and Brag for big stakes. Three-card monte and twenty-one and Pitch and just about any other card game you could name. His hands weren't much to look at now, all crippled up with arthritis like they were, but once, why he could hold one deck in the palm of his hand while he shuffled up another. That wasn't the least of what he could do, neither. He'd always been a square gambler . . . well, almost always, fella sometimes hit a losing streak and he had to eat then too, didn't he? Not that he'd ever worked any big-time gyps or cons, mind. Just every now and then held out an ace or stacked a deck whilst shuffling or reversed a cut—and done it in the company of men like Dick Clark and Frank Tarbeaux and Luke Short and the Earp brothers, with them watching with their hawk's eyes and never suspecting a thing. That was how good a mechanic he was in his prime.

Those had been wild times, he said, desperate times. But from soda to hock, they'd also been grand times. Oh Lordy, what grand times they had been!

Thing was, he hadn't set out to enter the Life. No, when he'd left Ohio for California that summer of '54, it had been gold mining that was on his mind. Just sixteen that summer, all fixed to help work his brother John's claim in the Mother Lode. But when he got to Columbia, the gem of the southern mines, he'd found poor John a month dead of consumption and his claim sold off to pay debts—and *him* with just two dollars left out of his traveling money. Only job he could get was swamping at the Long Tom.

Hardly a man left now that remembers the Long Tom, he said, but in its day it was the swellest gambling house in Columbia, and Columbia itself the rip-snortin'est town in the whole of the Mother Lode. Thirty saloons, a stadium for bull and bear fights, close to a hundred and fifty faro banks . . . why there hadn't been a town like it since, except maybe Tombstone in the eighties. And that Long Tom, well, that Long Tom was so big it ran from one street clean through to another, with a doorway at either end. Twenty-four tables, twelve on each side of a center aisle wide as a stagecoach runway. Guards on both doors, two armed floormen, and when there was a ruckus those guards would draw their pistols and shoot out the big whale-oil lamps that hung over the aisle and then the doormen would lock the doors and the floormen would shine dark lanterns on the gents that were cheating or otherwise causing trouble and put an end to it, peaceable or unpeaceable. Then the floormen would rig up new lights and the games would commence again just as though nothing had happened.

Well, the Long Tom was owned by the Mitchell brothers, and what they did was, they rented out those twenty-four tables to professional gamblers like Charles Cora, who later on got himself hung for murder by the vigilantes in San Francisco, and Ad Pence and Governor Hobbs and John Milton Strain. Now John Milton Strain was a gold-hunter as well as a gambler, and he didn't mind taking a young buck along with him to do some of the hard labor. Also didn't mind teaching a young buck the ins and outs of the sporting trade. So that was how he'd learned cards, he said—from John Milton Strain, one of the best of the old-time card sharps. (Wasn't any slouch when it came to prospecting, neither, was John Milton. One day he found a gold nugget big as an adobe brick, ten inches wide and five inches thick—all high-grade ore that he melted down into a bar weighing more than thirty pounds. Sleeper's Gold Exchange paid him $7500 for that bar. $7500 for one bar of pure gold!)

He'd worked at the Long Tom three years, he said, learning the gambling trade from John Milton Strain . . . well enough finally so that he'd rented his own faro layout right alongside John Milton's. He might have stayed on longer, except that a fire burned the Long Tom down in '57—burned twelve square blocks of Columbia's business district along with it. The Mitchell brothers put up a new building, but John Milton had had his fill of Columbia by then and he decided he'd had his too. So the two of 'em set out together for greener pastures.

He'd spent nearly ten years touring the mining camps in California and Nevada, about half that time with John Milton Strain for a partner. During those years he learned to hold his own with just about anybody in a "hard cards" game for big stakes. Won more than he lost, consistent, and if it hadn't been for a fondness for hard spirits and the company of fast women, why he'd have been a rich man before he was thirty. Yes sir, a rich man. But money was made to he spent, that was his philosophy. The more he made, the hotter it got sitting there in his pockets; and when it commenced to burn holes, well, what was there to do then but take it out and spend it?

By early '66 he'd had enough of the mining camps; he craved a look at other parts of the frontier, a chance to play with the bigger names in the sporting trade. So he'd drifted east and north, he said, up to Montana and then down to Cheyenne, Wyoming, which was a wide-open town in those days. Plenty of sports there, all right, most of them with the "Hell-on-Wheels" crowd that was following the construction of the Union Pacific Railroad west from Omaha to Promontory Point, Utah.

Now along that Union Pacific route, he said, the railroad set up supply points and campgrounds for track workers and other laborers—impermanent tent-towns for thousands of men. Well, those railroaders played as hard as they worked, so it was only natural that the honky-tonkers would gravitate to the camps to oblige them. In Cheyenne, one of the few real towns along the route, he'd found scores of gamblers, square and sure-thing both, and dozens of small-timers working as ropers, tappers, and steerers. Madams and whores and pimps, too. And saloon operators and confidence men and dips and yeggs—the whole shebang. And what they'd do, every time the railroad moved its base of operations a little farther west, was to pack up their equipment and move right along with 'em. That was how the whole business came to be called Hell-on-Wheels.

He'd joined up with 'em in Cheyenne and stayed on through Fort Saunders and Laramie and Benton City. Crazy wild, those days were, he said. He'd teamed with Ornery Ed Meeker on a brace faro game, and in Fort Saunders he found out Meeker was holding out on him and they'd had it out and one Sunday afternoon he'd shot Meeker dead. Yes sir, one clean shot right in his whiskers. First man he'd ever killed, but not the last. Then he fell in with one of Eleanore Dumont's working girls, to his sorrow, for she stole three thousand dollars he'd won at faro and decamped with the money and a fellow named Peavey, one of Corn-Hole Johnny Gallagher's steerers.

Well, it was just crazy wild. And the wildest place of all was Benton City, which they came into the summer of '68. Hot? Lordy, it was hot that summer! North Platte River was two miles away and the water-haulers charged a dollar a barrel and ten cents a bucket; they had the best graft in town, by a damn sight. He'd worked the Empire Tent there, on account of it was the biggest operation and got the heaviest play and he figured he could make more than he could with his own box. Fellow who ran the Buffalo Hump Corral wanted him in there, too—offered him a piece of the action—but the Buffalo Hump specialized in a game called rondo coolo, which you played with a stick and ivory balls on a billiard table, and what did he know about a game like that? He was a card man, a faro dealer and poker sharp. That was what he knew and that was how he made his living.

He was working the Empire Tent when *he* got shot. Railroad worker accused him of marking cards, which he hadn't been, and hauled out a Colt's six-gun and put a slug in his left arm before he could bring his own weapon to bear. Well, he almost died. Almost lost his left arm and almost died, but if he *had* lost that arm he'd have wished he *had* died, he said, because how could a one-armed gambler expect to make out?

Took him three months to recover, and by then the Hell-onWheels bunch was getting ready to move on to the next stop. They left a hundred dead behind them, their own and railroaders both—a hundred in three months. And him with that busted wing and most of his cash gone for doctoring and what-not. So he'd called it quits, right then and there. Hell-on-Wheels wasn't for him. Killed a man and almost been killed himself . . . no sir, that wasn't for him any more.

So he'd commenced to drifting again, building up stakes and losing 'em and building 'em back up again. Out to Kansas for a spell, Dodge City and the other cowtowns. Shot a man in the Long Branch in Dodge one day but the fellow didn't die; wasn't his fault that time neither, he said. Then, in '73, he'd got wind of a big silver strike in California, down in the Panamint Mountains, and of a new camp that had sprung up there called Panamint City.

Town was wide open when he got there, he said. They called it "a suburb of Hell," which he didn't think it was so far as sin was concerned, not after Hell-on-Wheels—but Lordy, it was hot as hell, up there above the floor of Death Valley like it was. Made the Wyoming plain seem like a cool riverside retreat.

First thing, he'd gone to work as a mechanic for Jim Bruce at the Dempsey and Boultinghouse Saloon. Now Bruce was a hardcase, having ridden the Missouri-Kansas border with Quantrill, and he didn't take kindly to insults and troublemakers. Another dealer, name of Bob McKenny, ran afoul of Bruce and tried to kill him, and what happened was, Jim Bruce blew his fool head off. And what did he do then, straightaway? Why, he took Bob McKenny right out and buried him, that's what he did, on account of Jim Bruce wasn't just a gambler, he was also Panamint City's undertaker!

Well, he said, after a year or so he started dealing for Dave Neagle at Dave's resort, the Oriental, which had a fancy black walnut bar and some of the spiciest paintings of the female form divine that a man ever set eyes on. He stayed on there for four years, and would have stayed longer, likely, for he and Dave Neagle got on fine and he'd taken up with one of the girls at Martha Camp's bawdy house, Sadie her name was, blond and plump like the women in the paintings over the Oriental's black walnut bar. But then a big rainstorm hit the Panamints and a flash flood came boiling down from the heights and swept up more than a hundred buildings as if they were bunches of sticks, the Oriental among 'em, and washed the wreckage all the way down Surprise Canyon and spread it over a mile of the Panamint Valley. Hadn't been for somebody up at one of the stamp mills spotting the flood and raising an alarm, he said, him and most of the other townspeople would have gone sailing down Surprise Canyon too.

From there he'd gone up to Bodie for a while, and then on back to Kansas and the queen of the cowtowns. But Dodge wasn't what she had been a decade earlier, he said, leastways not so far as a sporting man was concerned, and he hadn't stayed long—just long enough to get wind that Dick Clark and Lou Rickabaugh and Bill Harris, who had once owned the Long Branch, had gone into partnership and opened a resort out in Tombstone. Well, he'd never met Dick Clark and wished he had, for Clark was a legend among sporting men, so he'd set out for Arizona Territory. And when he arrived in Tombstone, why Dick Clark was every bit the gentleman he was reputed to be, and his Oriental Saloon and Gambling Hall at Allen and Fifth Streets was by far the grandest gambling house in town. Fancy chandeliers and colored crystals set into the bar, which was finished in white and gilt, and a club room to knock the eye out of a Victorian swell . . . oh, it was grand! He'd never been in a grander place before nor since, he said.

Now Dick Clark, as befitted his station, had some mighty important gents dealing for him. He had Luke Short and Bat Masterson and Wyatt Earp and Doc Holliday, among others, and he paid them twenty-five dollars for a six-hour shift—princely wages for those times. That was where *he* wanted to work, no question about that, so he'd talked to Dick Clark and danged if Dick Clark hadn't hired him. And there he was, he said, dealing at the Oriental Saloon with Luke Short and Wyatt Earp and Doc Holliday and Bat Masterson, all of them swell fellows and don't let anybody tell you different.

Bat Masterson didn't stay long, having fish to fry elsewhere, but Wyatt and Doc, they stayed, and everybody knows what happened with them. Well, sure—they and Wyatt's brothers Virgil and Morgan got into a feud with the Clantons and the McLaury brothers and Curly Bill Brocius and John Ringo, and it all came to a head late in '81 when Morgan Earp got himself ambushed and then Wyatt went out in a vengeful rage and done for Curly Bill and a couple of others in the Clanton crowd. That was when they had the big shootout at the O.K. Corral. He was there that day and he'd seen it all, he said. He'd seen the whole thing from soda to hock.

Nor was that all he'd seen that year, he said. He'd seen Luke Short gun down Charlie Storms, a hardcase who'd been one of the Hell-on-Wheels bunch. Happened right there in the Oriental, right smack in front of *his* table. It was Charlie Storms' doing, he said, no question about that, for he was a mean one and had been in several gunfights in Cheyenne and Deadwood and Leadville, and wanted to add an important name to his list of victims. But he met his match in Luke Short. He goaded little Luke, and goaded him some more, and then when push came to shove, why Luke outdrew him cool as you please and Charlie Storms died a surprised man.

Tombstone in the eighties was a fine place to be, he said, and he'd felt settled there, working for Dick Clark. Now and then he'd develop an itch, same as Dick Clark himself would, and get on a stagecoach and see what Lady Luck had in store in places like Tucson and Phoenix and Prescott and Las Vegas, New Mexico. But he never stayed long in any of those places—particularly not in Las Vegas, where he himself had been goaded into killing his second and last man, this time in a misunderstanding over a woman. He always went back to Tombstone and the Oriental Saloon and Gambling Hall. He was still dealing there, he said, when Dick Clark sold out his interest in '94 and retired from the Life.

He was likewise of retirement age by then, but unlike Dick Clark and some of the other old-timers who'd made their fortunes and bought houses and saloons and other property, or invested their money in stocks and bonds and such, and were comfortably fixed for the rest of their days, *he* was still just a mechanic. Flush some of the time, broke more often. Never saved any of his winnings, never invested any of it or bought any property other than what he could carry in a pair of carpetbags. Sport like him couldn't afford to retire. All he could do, he said, was keep right on dealing cards.

So after Dick Clark sold out his interest in the Oriental, he'd gone on down to Bisbee, which was still a fair hot town in the mid-nineties, and worked for a time in Cobweb Hall. Then he'd moved on to Phoenix and Prescott, and then up to Virginia City, Nevada, and then over to Albuquerque. He was in Albuquerque when the new century came in, he said, sixty-two years old and stony broke in Albuquerque, New Mexico. But then he'd won a stake and moved on to Taos, and then over into Texas—San Antonio and El Paso and Austin and Tascosa—and then back into Arizona Territory, to see if Tombstone was anything like it had been in the old days. But it wasn't. No sir, *none* of the towns were like they'd been in the old days. They were all changed, and still changing so fast you could almost see it happening right before your eyes.

Once, he said, the sporting man had commanded respect. Not just the high-rollers like Dick Clark, no, ordinary sports like himself. Why, you could walk down the street in just about any town and gents would doff their hats and smile and wish you good day. Women would smile, too, some of them, and more than you'd think would do more than smile. Oh, you were somebody in those days, he said. You had a skill few had, and you made big money, and you were somebody and you had respect.

But not after the new century came in. Not after all the people moved west and shrank the land and tamed it. Everything changed then. Men quit smiling and doffing their hats and wishing you good day. Women wouldn't have anything to do with you, none except the whores. They all whispered behind your back and gave you dirty looks and shunned you like you were a common thief. And then the territorial leaders that wanted statehood, they went and put those laws in, all those antigambling laws. Blamed gambling and sporting men for society's ills and took away their livelihood and made them outlaws and outcasts.

It wasn't fair, he said, it wasn't right. What could men like him do, men who'd been in the Life for nigh on fifty years? Where could they go? Some took to running illegal games, sure, but those were the young ones. What about the ones past their prime, old men with hands starting to cripple with arthritis? What about them?

Memories, that was all they left him. Fifty years of memories . . . all the places he'd been, all the things he'd seen and done, all the men and women he'd known. He'd seen it all in those fifty years, by grab. He'd *lived* it all. Been a part of the wildness, and of the slow taming too. But now . . . now the land was too tame, it was like a tiger that had become a pussycat. This wasn't the frontier anymore, a place with growl and howl; this was just a tamed tiger meowing in the sun.

Well, *he* remembered the old days, he said. *He* knew how wild and desperate those times had been. And how grand, too. Oh Lordy, what grand times they had been!

They found him one morning in the dust behind Simpson's Barber Shop, lying crumpled in the dust with his nightshirt pulled up to expose the swollen veins in his pipestem legs. He must have come out during the night to use the outhouse, the town marshal said. Left his room at the rear of the shop, where Simpson had let him live in exchange for sweeping up, and set out for the privy and had a seizure before he got there. He hadn't died right away, though. He'd crawled a ways, ten feet or so toward the privy; the marks were plain in the dust.

That afternoon, the undertaker and his assistant put the corpse in a plain pine box, loaded the box into the mortuary wagon, and drove up the hill to the cemetery. The only other citizen to go along with them was the preacher, but he didn't tarry long. The old man hadn't been religious and had never attended church services; it was only out of common decency that the preacher had decided to speak a few words over the grave. Besides, it was hot that day. Hot as the hinges of hell, the preacher said just before he rode his horse back down the hill.

The undertaker and his assistant made short work of the burying and laid their tools in the wagon. The assistant mopped his sweating face with his handkerchief, spoke then for the first time since their arrival.

"You think he *was* a sporting man?"

"That old coot?" the undertaker said. "Now what makes you ask that?"

"Well, all those stories he would tell . . ."

"Stories, that's all they were. Old man's imaginings. He had nothing when he come here and nothing when he died. No money, no kin, no friends to speak of—nobody, even, to buy him a marker for his final resting place. And him supposed to have been a fancy card sharp rubbing elbows with Wyatt Earp and Bat Masterson? Pshaw!"

The undertaker shook his head, turned to look down the dry brown hill at the dry brown town crouching in the summer heat; at the desert beyond, rolling away like a dead sea toward the horizon.

"Wasn't nobody at all," he said.

FEAR

He sat with his back to the wall, waiting.

Shadows shrouded the big room, thinned by early daylight filtering in through the plate-glass front window. Beyond the glass he could see Boxelder's empty main street, rain spattering the puddled mud that wagon wheels and horses' hoofs had churned into a quagmire. Wind rattled the chain-hung sign on the outer wall: *R. J. Cable, Saddle Maker.*

Familiar shapes surrounded him in the gloom. Workbenches littered with scraps of leather, mallets, cutters, stamping tools. A few saddles, finished and unfinished—not half as many as there used to be. Wall racks hung with bridles and hackamores, saddlebags and other accessories. Once the tools and accomplishments of his trade had given him pleasure, comfort, a measure of peace. Not any more. Even the good odors of new leather and beeswax and harness oil had soured in his nostrils.

It was cold in the shop; he hadn't bothered to lay a fire when he had come in at dawn, after another sleepless night. But he took little notice of the chill. He had been cold for a long while now, the kind of gut cold that no fire can ever thaw.

His hands, twisted together in his lap, were sweating.

He glanced over at the closed door to the storeroom. A seed company calendar was tacked to it—not that he needed a calendar to tell him what day this was. October 26, 1892. The day after Lee Tarbeaux was scheduled to be released from Deer Lodge Prison. The day Tarbeaux would return to Boxelder after eight long years. The day Tarbeaux had vowed to end Reed Cable's life.

His gaze lingered on the storeroom door a few seconds longer. The shotgun was back there—his father's old double-barreled Remington that he'd brought from home yesterday—propped in a corner, waiting as he was. He thought about fetching it, setting it next to his stool. But there was no need yet. It was still early.

He scrubbed his damp palms on his Levi's, then fumbled in a vest pocket for his turnip watch. He flipped the dust-cover, held the dial up close to his eyes. Ten after seven. How long before Tarbeaux came? Noon at the earliest. There were a lot of miles between here and Deer Lodge. If he could work, it would make the time go by more quickly . . . but he couldn't. His hands were too unsteady for leather craft. It would be an effort to keep them steady enough to hold the shotgun when the time came.

A few more hours, he told himself. *Just a few more hours. Then it'll finally be over.* He sat watching the rain-swept street. Waiting.

It was a quarter past twelve when Lee Tarbeaux reached the outskirts of Boxelder. The town had grown substantially since he'd been away—even more than he'd expected. There were more farms and small ranches in the area, too—parcels deeded off to homesteaders where once there had been nothing but rolling Montana grassland. *Everything changes, sooner or later*, he thought as he rode. *Land, towns, and men, too. Some men.*

He passed the cattle pens near the railroad depot, deserted now in the misty rain. He'd spent many a day there when he had worked for Old Man Kendall—and one day in particular that he'd never forget, because it had been the beginning of the end of his freedom for eight long years. Kendall was dead now, died in his sleep in 'eighty-nine. Tarbeaux had been sorry to hear it, weeks after it had happened, on the prison grapevine. He'd held no hard feelings toward the old cowman or his son Bob. The Kendalls were no different from the rest of the people here; they'd believed Cable's lies and that there was a streak of larceny in Tarbeaux's kid-wildness. You couldn't blame them for feeling betrayed. Only one man to blame and that was Reed Cable.

Tarbeaux rode slowly, savoring the chill October air with its foretaste of winter snow. The weather didn't bother him, and it didn't seem to bother the spavined blue roan he'd bought cheap from a hostler in the town of Deer Lodge—something of a surprise, given the animal's age and condition. Just went to show that you couldn't always be sure about anybody or anything, good or bad. Except Reed Cable. Tarbeaux was sure Cable was the same man he'd been eight years ago. Bits and pieces of information that had filtered through the prison walls added weight to his certainty.

Some of the buildings flanking Montana Street were familiar: the Boxelder Hotel, the sprawling bulk of Steinmetz Brewery. Many others were not. It gave him an odd, uncomfortable feeling to know this town and yet not know it—to be home and yet to understand that it could never be home again. He wouldn't stay long. Not even the night. And once he left, he'd never come back. Boxelder, like Deer Lodge, like all his foolish kid plans, were part of a past he had to bury completely if he was to have any kind of future.

A chain-hung shingle, dancing in the wind, appeared in the gray mist ahead: *R. J. Cable, Saddle Maker.* The plate-glass window below the sign showed a rectangle of lamplight, even though there was a *Closed* sign in one corner. Tarbeaux barely glanced at the window as he passed, with no effort to see through the water-pocked glass. There was plenty of time. Patience was just one of the things his stay in the penitentiary had taught him. Besides, he was hungry. It had been hours since his meager trailside breakfast.

He tied the roan to a hitch rail in front of an eatery called the Elite Café. It was one of the new places; no one there knew or recognized him. He ordered hot coffee and a bowl of chili. And, as he ate, he thought about the things that drive a man, that shape and change him for better or worse. Greed was one. Hate was another. He knew all about hate; he'd lived with it a long time. But it wasn't the worst of the ones that ate the guts right out of a man. The worst was fear.

When Cable saw the lone, slicker-clad figure ride by outside, he knew it was Lee Tarbeaux. Even without a clear look at the man's face, shielded by the tilt of a rain hat, he knew. He felt a taut relief. It wouldn't be much longer now.

He extended a hand to the shotgun propped beside his stool. He'd brought it out of the storeroom two hours ago, placed it within easy reach. The sick feeling inside him grew and spread as he rested the weapon across his knees. His damp palms made the metal surfaces feel greasy. He kept his hands on it just the same.

His thoughts drifted as he sat there, went back again, as they so often did these days, to the spring of 'eighty-four. Twenty years old that spring, him and Lee Tarbeaux both. Friendly enough because they'd grown up together, both of them town kids, but not close friends. Too little in common. Too much spirit in Tarbeaux and not enough spirit in him. Lee went places and did things he was too timid to join in on.

When Tarbeaux turned eighteen, he'd gone to work as a hand on Old Man Kendall's K-Bar Ranch. He'd always had a reckless streak, and it had widened out over the following two years, thanks to a similar streak in Old Man Kendall's son Bob. Drinking, whoring, a few saloon fights. No serious trouble to make the law aware of Lee Tarbeaux.

Not a whisper of wildness in Reed Cable, meanwhile. Quiet and steady— that was what everyone said about him. Quiet and steady and honest. He took a position as night clerk at the Boxelder Hotel. Not because he wanted the job, saddle making and leatherwork were what he craved to do with his life. But there were two saddle makers in town already, and neither was interested in hiring an apprentice. He'd have moved to another town except that his ma, who'd supported them since his father's death, had taken sick and was no longer able to work as a seamstress. All up to him, then. And the only decent job he could find was the night clerk's.

Ma'd died in March of that year. One month after Tarbeaux's aunt— the last of his relatives—passed away. And on a day in late April Bob Kendall and Lee Tarbeaux and the rest of the K-Bar crew drove their roundup beeves in to the railroad loading pens. Old Man Kendall wasn't with them; he'd been laid up with gout. Bob Kendall was in charge, but he was a hammerhead as well as half wild: liquor and women and stud poker were all he cared about. Tarbeaux was with him when the cattle buyer from Billings finished his tally and paid off in cash. Seventy-four hundred dollars, all in greenbacks.

It was after bank closing hours by the time the deal was done. Bob Kendall hadn't cared to go hunting banker Weems to take charge of the money. He wanted a running start on his night's fun, so he turned the chore over to Lee. Tarbeaux made a half-hearted attempt to find the banker, and then his own itch got the best of him. He went to the hotel, where his old friend Reed had just come on shift, where the lobby was otherwise deserted, and laid the saddlebags full of money on the counter.

"Reed," he said without explanation, "do me a favor and put these bags in the hotel safe for tonight. I or Bob Kendall'll be back to fetch 'em the first thing in the morning."

It was curiosity that made him open the bags after Tarbeaux left. The sight of all that cash weakened his knees, dried his mouth. He put the saddlebags away in the safe, but he couldn't stop thinking about the money. So many things he could do with it, so many ambitions he could make a reality. A boldness and a recklessness built in him for the first time. The money grew from a lure into a consuming obsession as the hours passed. He might've been able to overcome it if his mother had still been alive, but he was all alone—with no prospects for the future and no one to answer to but himself.

He took the saddlebags from the safe an hour past midnight. Took them out back of the hotel stables and hid them in a clump of buck brush. Afterward he barely remembered doing it, as if it had all happened in a dream.

Bob Kendall came in alone at eight in the morning, hung over and in mean spirits, just as the day clerk arrived to serve as a witness. There was a storm inside Reed Cable, but outwardly he was calm. Saddlebags? He didn't know anything about saddlebags full of money. Tarbeaux hadn't been in last evening, no matter what he claimed. He hadn't seen Lee in more than two weeks.

In a fury Bob Kendall ran straight to the sheriff, and the sheriff arrested Tarbeaux. The hardest part of the whole thing was facing Lee, repeating the lies, and watching the outraged disbelief in Tarbeaux's eyes turn to blind hate. But the money was all he let himself think about. The money, the money, the money. . . .

It was his word against Tarbeaux's, his reputation against Tarbeaux's. The sheriff believed him, the Kendalls believed him, the townspeople believed him—and the judge and jury believed him. The verdict was guilty, the sentence a minimum of eight years at hard labor.

Tarbeaux had made his vow of vengeance as he was being led from the courtroom. "You won't get away with this, Reed!" he yelled. "You'll pay and pay dear. As soon as I get out, I'll come back and make sure you pay!"

The threat had shaken Cable at the time. But neither it nor his conscience had bothered him for long. Tarbeaux's release from Deer Lodge was in the far future; why worry about it? He had the money, he had his plans—and, when one of the town's two saddle makers died suddenly of a stroke, he soon realized the first of his ambitions. . . .

Cable shifted position on the hard stool. That was then and this was now, he thought bitterly. The far future had become the present. Pain moved through his belly and chest; a dry cough racked him. He sleeved sweat from his eyes, peered again through the front window. A few pedestrians hurried by on the wet sidewalk; none was Lee Tarbeaux.

"Come on," he said aloud. "Come on, damn you, and get it over with!"

Tarbeaux finished his meal, took out the makings, and rolled a smoke to savor the final cup of coffee. Food, coffee, tobacco—it all tasted good again, now that he was free. He'd rushed through the first twenty years of his life, taking everything for granted. And he'd struggled and pained his way through the last eight, taking nothing for granted. He'd promised himself that, when he got out, he'd make his remaining years pass as slowly as he could, that he'd take the time to look and feel and learn, and that he'd cherish every minute of every new day.

He paid his bill, crossed the street to Adams Mercantile—another new business run by a stranger—and replenished his supplies of food and tobacco. That left him with just three dollars of his prison savings. He'd have to settle some place soon, at least long enough to take a job and build himself a stake. After that . . . no hurry, wherever he went and whatever he did. No hurry at all.

First things first, though. The time had come to face Reed Cable.

He felt nothing as he walked upstreet to where the chain-hung sign rattled and danced. It had all been worked out in his mind long ago. All that was left was the settlement.

Lamplight still burned behind the saddlery's window. Without looking through the glass, without hesitation, Tarbeaux opened the door and went in under a tinkling bell.

Cable sat on a stool at the back wall, an old double-barreled shotgun across his knees. He didn't move as Tarbeaux shut the door behind him. In the pale lamp glow Cable seemed small and shrunken. His sweat-stained skin was sallow, pinched, and his hands trembled. He'd aged twenty years in the past eight—an old man before his thirtieth birthday.

The shotgun surprised Tarbeaux a little. He hadn't figured on a willingness in Cable to put up a fight. He said as he took off his rain hat: "Expecting me, I see."

"I knew you'd come. You haven't changed much, Lee."

"Sure I have. On the inside. Just the opposite with you."

"You think so?"

"I know so. You fixing to shoot me with the scatter-gun?"

"If you try anything, I will."

"I'm not armed."

"Expect me to believe that?"

Tarbeaux shrugged and glanced slowly around the shadowed room. "Pretty fair leatherwork," he said. "Seems you were cut out to be a saddle maker, like you always claimed."

"Man's got to do something."

"That's a fact. Only thing is, he ought to do it with honest money."

"All right," Cable said.

"You admitting you stole the K-Bar money, Reed? No more lies?"

"Not much point in lying to you."

"How about the sheriff and Bob Kendall? Ready to tell them the truth, too . . . get it all off your chest?"

Cable shook his head. "It's too late for that."

"Why?"

"I couldn't face prison, that's why. I couldn't stand it."

"I stood it for eight years," Tarbeaux said. "It's not so bad, once you get used to it."

"No. I couldn't, not even for a year."

"Man can be in prison even when there's no bars on his windows."

Cable made no reply.

"What I mean, it's been a hard eight years for you, too. Harder, I'll warrant, than the ones I lived through. Isn't that so?"

Still no reply.

"It's so," Tarbeaux said. "You got yourself this shop and you learned to be a saddle maker. But then it all slid downhill from there. Starting with Clara Weems. You always talked about marrying her someday, having three or four kids . . . your other big ambition. But she turned you down when you asked for her hand. Married that storekeeper in Billings, instead."

The words made Cable's hands twitch on the shotgun.

"How'd you know that?"

"I know plenty about you, Reed. You proposed to two other women. They wouldn't have you, either. Then you lost four thousand dollars on bad mining stock. Then one of your horses kicked over a lantern and burned down your barn and half your house. Then you caught consumption and were laid up six months during the winter of 'ninety-one. . . .'"

"That's enough," Cable said, but there was no heat in his voice. Only a kind of desperate weariness.

"No, it's not. Your health's been poor ever since, worsening steadily, and there's nothing much the sawbones can do about it. How much more time do they give you . . . four years? Five?"

"Addled, whoever told you that. I'm healthy enough. I've got a long life ahead of me."

"Four years . . . five, at the most. *I'm* the one with the long life ahead. And I aim to make it a good life. You remember how I could barely read and write? Well, I learned in prison, and now I can do both better than most. I learned a trade, too. Blacksmithing. One of these days I'll have my own shop, same as you, with my name on a sign out front bigger than yours."

"But first you had to stop here and settle with me."

"That's right. First I have to settle with you."

"Kill me, like you swore in court you'd do. Shoot me dead."

"I never swore that."

"Same as."

"You think I still hate you that much?"

"Don't you?"

"No," Tarbeaux said. "Not any more."

"I don't believe that. You're lying."

"You're the liar, Reed, not me."

"You want me dead. Admit it . . . you want me dead."

"You'll be dead in four or five years."

"You can't stand to wait that long. You want me dead here and now."

"No. All I ever wanted was to make sure you paid for what you did to me. Well, you're paying and paying dear. I came here to tell you to your face that I know you are. That's the only reason I came, the only settlement I'm after."

"You bastard, don't fool with me. Draw your gun and get it over with."

"I told you, I'm not armed."

Cable jerked the scatter-gun off his knees, a gesture that was meant to be provoking. But the muzzle wobbled at a point halfway between them, held there. "Make your play!"

Tarbeaux understood, then. There was no fight in Cable; there never had been. There was only fear. He said: "You're trying to *make* me kill you. That's it, isn't it? You want me to put you out of your misery."

It was as if he'd slapped Cable across the face. Cable's head jerked; he lurched to his feet, swinging the Remington until its twin muzzles were like eyes centered on Tarbeaux's face.

Tarbeaux stood motionless. "You can't stand the thought of living another five sick, hurting years, but you don't have the guts to kill yourself. You figured you could goad me into doing it for you."

"No. Make your play or I'll blow your goddamn head off!"

"Not with that scatter-gun. It's not loaded, Reed. We both know that now."

Cable tried to stare him down. The effort lasted no more than a few seconds; his gaze slid down to the useless shotgun. Then, as if the weight of the weapon was too much for his shaking hands, he let it fall to the floor, kicked it clattering under one of the workbenches.

"Why?" he said in a thin, hollow whisper. "Why couldn't you do what you vowed you'd do? Why couldn't you finish it?"

"It is finished," Tarbeaux said.

And it was, in every way. Now he really was free—of Cable and the last of his hate, of the past. Now he could start living again.

He turned and went out into the cold, sweet rain.

Cable slumped again onto his stool. Tarbeaux's last words seemed to hang like a frozen echo in the empty room.

It is finished.

For Tarbeaux, maybe it was. Not for Reed Cable. It wouldn't be finished for him until his dying day.

"Damn you," he said, and then shouted the words. "Damn you!" But they weren't meant for Lee Tarbeaux this time. They were meant for himself.

He kept on sitting there with his back to the wall.

Waiting.

THE CRUEL AND DEADLY WINTER

He felt no pain.

He lay on his side in the snow, and through half-closed eyes he could see blood leaking from the wound in his chest. The echo of the rifle shot that had driven him out of the buckboard was gone now; there was nothing to hear but the wailing of the bitter winter wind.

He tried to move, to lift his body, but the icy cold held him down. He felt strangely hot, fevered, and there was a burning dryness in his mouth and throat. Only his face was cool, fanned by the wind that threatened more snow from the leaden sky.

Flashes of memory came to him as he lay there half-conscious and shivering.

The early years of his youth on the hardscrabble family farm in Ohio and his desire to one day write novels of adventure and romance such as Fenimore Cooper's Leatherstocking tales. His eighteenth birthday six long years ago, the day he joined the Ohio Volunteers and went to fight with the Union army. The things he had seen and done no boy, no man, should ever have to see or do, the roar of cannons and the cries and screams of wounded and dying men.

The aimless wandering after the end of the war in the late fall of 1865, taking work where he could find it—restless, disillusioned, alone and lonely. And then the afternoon in the small Kansas town when it all changed, the afternoon he met Emma.

"Oh, I didn't see you standing there. What are you doing out here by the milliner's?"

"Waiting for you to come out."

"Whatever for?"

"I saw you walking earlier. I wanted to meet you."

"Well, aren't you the fresh one!"

"I apologize if I offended you."

"You didn't offend me. You just … surprised me. You're new to Chandlerville, aren't you? I've never seen you before."

"Nor I you. I just arrived, looking for work."

"Are you thinking of staying on here?"

"Now I am. Tell me your name."

"Why should I?"

"I'd admire to call on you, if you'll allow it."

"My! You don't let a speck of grass grow, do you?"

"Will you allow it?"

"We haven't been properly introduced. I don't even know your name!"

"Clayton Boone. Now will you tell me yours?"

"Emma, Emma Coulter."

Emma. Soft flaxen hair, gentle blue eyes, slender body, the prettiest face he had ever seen. In his thoughts every waking minute after that first meeting. Rekindling his spirit, giving new purpose and meaning to his life.

"Emma, you know I love you. Will you have me for your husband?"

"You know I will."

"Soon?"

"Right away, if it's what you want. Where will we live? There is no room in my folks' house…"

"Nor any future for us, for me as nothing more than a stablehand, here in Chandlerville. We'll move on farther west. Find a place to settle on free land."

Through Kansas and Nebraska into Wyoming, their scant belongings packed in the wagon her father had given them. And near the Wind River range in early spring, the free land they sought—a hilly wooded section a few miles from the settlement of Crossroads, with a stream running through it and a two-room cabin already built and abandoned.

Repairs to the cabin, additions of a lean-to corral to shelter the roan horse and a milch cow bought from the Hansens, their nearest neighbors, and a shed to house the rooster and chicks also supplied by the Hansens. The small vegetable patch tended by Emma. Traps set out for coons, chucks, rabbits. Larger game bagged with his old Hall breech-loading carbine, trout caught in the stream pools.

A good life, a happy life during the spring and summer and early autumn. His desire to write a novel of romance and adventure renewed, the evenings when he wasn't too tired spent with a steel-nib pen and paper at the rough-hewn table, Emma reading each night's work, gently criticizing, praising when she felt praise was due. And to make the time even better—

"I'm pregnant, Clay. I'm going to have our baby."

"A baby!"

"Before year's end."

"Wonderful news. You know how much I've wanted a son."

"You won't be disappointed if it's a girl?"

"How could I be disappointed in anything that was a part of you."

Then all of a sudden, the change that turned their good new life upside down.

Seemingly overnight winter came, late autumn's crisp breezes giving way to howling winds. Day after day of storms, fierce blizzards, ice and snow whitening the land. The Hansens, their only friends, fearing a prolonged siege and fleeing to Laramie to be with kin. He and Emma staying because they had no place else to go. Staying and enduring hardship after hardship—the worst winter he had ever known.

High-piled drifts making it difficult to leave the cabin, once rendering them snowbound for nearly a week. Constant effort to keep the horse and cow alive and healthy. Not enough firewood stacked in before the onslaught. Dwindling supply of staples paid for by the sale of varmint pelts from his trappings, the meager yield from the vegetable patch long gone and game scarce, the few chickens not already eaten by them or by foxes frozen to death. Precious little money left, not nearly enough to buy all the provisions they would need to survive, and no more varmint pelts to sell.

"Clay, what are we going to do? With the baby coming…"

"Try not to fret. We'll manage somehow."

"How? We barely have enough to eat now."

"As soon as possible I'll take the buckboard into Crossroads, buy what I can at the general store and ask Tyndal for credit for the rest."

"What if he refuses?"

"I'll get on my knees and beg if I have to."

The morning of this day. The wind-whipped ride through intermittent snow flurries to Crossroads. Purchase of only a pitiful few necessities with the last of the money, his appeal for credit to the mean-spirited old man who owned the store falling on deaf ears. Tyndal, unsympathetic, unmoved by word of Emma's condition, standing before his well-stocked shelves and telling him that cash and carry was a strict rule with no exceptions. Ordering him to leave, then turning his back and walking away into the storeroom—

The memory flashes winked out.

I shouldn't have done it, he thought. But what other choice did I have?

He could feel pain in his chest now. Deep, throbbing, yet oddly not as terrifying as when the Confederate Minie ball penetrated his leg during the siege at Vicksburg. He felt only sadness, regret, a consuming anxiety for Emma and the child he would never see.

It seemed he had been lying there a long time but it must only have been minutes. He was aware, now, of other sounds above the keening shriek of the wind—the crunch of boots planted, lifted, planted again in the crusty snow. He managed to raise his head as the sounds grew closer. Blinking to clear his vision he saw two men standing a few feet away, one heavily bearded, neither of them familiar. Each carried a rifle, the beardless one holding his weapon leveled from the waist of a long buffalo coat.

"Why'd you shoot him, Russ?" the bearded man said to the clean-shaven one. "He wasn't gonna get away. All you had to do was put one over his head and he would've stopped."

"Yeah, sure, he would've stopped."

"He would, Russ. He don't even have a weapon."

"How'd I know that? Can't take chances with his kind."

"A sack of flour, some sugar and blackstrap, a couple of hams—that's all he stole. A man shouldn't have to be shot for that."

"I say different. I say he got what he deserved, the damn thief."

He drew a thin, shuddery breath. Emma, he thought.

His last breath, his last thought, in the cruel and deadly winter.

"GIVE-A-DAMN" JONES

The most admirable man I've ever known?

Gentlemen, that is a question that should require considerable thought and reflection. In my nearly seven decades of life I have traveled from one end of the country to the other, north and south of our borders and twice across the Atlantic Ocean. I have shaken hands with statesmen, been entertained by royalty, drunk brandy and smoked cigars with two sitting Presidents of these United States. I have known many celebrated and respected newspaper editors and publishers, among them my own father, the redoubtable William Satterlee. And I have spent hours in the company of famous authors, artists, philanthropists, and titans of commerce. The answer to your question should not roll easily off what one member of the fourth estate has seen fit to call "the golden tongue of Senator R. W. Satterlee." But the fact is, my answer requires not five seconds of brain cudgeling.

The most estimable and significant man of my acquaintance was a tramp printer named "Give-a-Damn" Jones.

No, no, I'm not pulling your legs. "Give-a-Damn" was the moniker bestowed upon him by his wandering brethren; his given name was Artemus. Artemus Jones. A tramp printer is what he was, in fact and in spirit, and proud of it.

Most of you are too young to recall the days when itinerant typesetters, a noble and misunderstood breed, were a vital element in the publishing of newspapers large and small. If you have read my resume, you know that I myself was one of that adventurous fraternity in my early youth. Yet the tale of why I chose such a vagabond's trade is not nearly as well known as it should be. Nor, I dare say, is Artemus Jones and the role he played in the destiny of the man who stands before you. I have been remiss in publicly according him the credit he deserves. But no more, gentlemen. No more.

Make yourselves comfortable and I'll tell you why I place a traveling printer above any other man in my life.

It was the summer of 1883, two years after my father purchased the Bear Paw *Banner* and moved our family to that eastern Montana town from Salt Lake City. Bear Paw was generally a peaceful place, but in the spring of that year trouble had sprung up between nearby cattle ranchers and a group of German and Scandinavian farmers who had come west from Wisconsin and settled in the region. The farmers weren't squatters, mind you. The land they claimed was theirs free and clear. The cattlemen, however, had used it for beef graze for a generation and more, and considered the farmers an invasion force bent on using up precious water and destroying prime grassland. Feelings ran high on both sides, with most of Bear Paw siding with the Cattlemen's Association and its leader, Colonel Elijah Greathouse, owner of the sprawling Square G. Fistfights, fence-cutting, arson, two shooting scrapes, and one near lynching came of the disagreement, and there was as much name-calling and finger-pointing that spring and summer as you'll find on the floor of the United States Senate in session.

I was a mere lad of fifteen, but as interested as any full-grown adult in these volatile goings-on. My father, a man of strong opinions and iron will, had taken up the cause of the immigrant farmers and penned several fiery editorials defending their rights and denouncing the injustices perpetrated against them by their Bear Paw neighbors. As a result, the *Banner's* plate-glass front window had been shattered by a rock one night, and the local job printer who had done our typesetting was intimidated by the cattlemen's interests into closing up shop and moving to Helena. William Satterlee had little choice but to set type himself, with my inexperienced help, except on those occasions when a tramp printer happened to stop off in our town.

In the three months before Artemus Jones arrived, an equal number of hand-peggers were hired. None lasted more than three days, and the only one who paid no attention to the uneasy climate was an old man of at least eighty years named Charlie Weems. He was completely toothless, though he chewed tobacco and could ring a spittoon at twenty yards with unerring accuracy; and he had but one eye, claiming to have lost the other in the explosion of a Queen Anne musket not long after the War of 1812. He drank forty-rod whisky from a seemingly bottomless flask, could recite the names and addresses of most houses of ill repute in the Western states and territories, cussed a blue streak while he worked, and set type faster than any man I have seen before or since. He boasted to me that he had never spent more than three days in any town, and he was true to his word where Bear Paw was concerned. There one day, gone the next, riding the rods or the blind baggage or tucked away in a boxcar on the Great Northern's east- or westbound night freight.

Another freight train, the tramp's favored form of transportation, brought Artemus Jones into our midst. I was alone in the *Banner* office when he walked in on a Tuesday morning. He was a lean, wiry man twice my age and a little more, with drooping, tobacco-stained mustaches and eyes a brighter blue than a Kansas cornflower. He wore a disreputable linen duster and carried a bindle wrapped in a bandanna handkerchief. Prepossessing? Not a bit. Yet despite an air of hard-bitten toughness, he was soft-spoken and polite and gave the impression of having more to him than met the eye. I sensed his profession even before he approached with the breed's standard opener: "How's work?" And after only a short while in his company, I sensed, too, that he was no ordinary man.

"Available," I said. "You'll be welcome. We go to press tomorrow night and circulate Thursday morning."

"Standard union wages?"

"Yes, sir. Twenty-five cents a thousand ems."

His blue eyes took my measure. "Young to be the owner of a territorial newspaper, aren't you?"

"William Satterlee is the owner. My father."

"William Satterlee, eh? I believe I've heard the name. And you'd be William, Junior?"

"No, sir. I go by R.W."

He barked a laugh. "You'll go places, then. Men with initials instead of given names always do. My name is Jones, Artemus Jones."

"'Give-a-Damn' Jones?"

"So I've been called. How do you know the name?"

"We had a printer several weeks ago named Charlie Weems. He mentioned you."

"Toothless Charlie's still above ground, is he? I'm glad to hear it, even if he is an unrepentant old liar and sinner."

"He didn't say how you came by the moniker, Mister Jones."

"Nor will I." Short and sharp, as if he were embarrassed by the explanation. "I prefer to be called Artemus. Your father on the premises?"

"Off hunting news. He'll be back before long."

"Well, let's have a look at your shop while we wait."

I took him into the composing room and stood by while he eyed our cranky old hand press, stone table, type frame, and cases. He opened upper- and lower-case drawers and nodded approvingly at the selection of Revier, nonpareil, and agate. Another approving nod followed his examination of the previous week's issue from a leftover bundle.

"This is tolerable good for a jim-crow sheet," he said—jim-crow being printer's slang for small-town. "Your father's been in the game a while, I take it."

"Two years in Bear Paw. Before that five years in Salt Lake, and before that stints in Sacramento and San Francisco, where I was born."

"I like working for a man who knows his business," Jones said. "Heard of the 'Perch of the Devil,' have you, R.W.?"

"Yes, sir!" I said. It was what Butte was called in those days. The copper mines there ran twenty-four hours, and the air was so poisonous thick with sulphur and arsenic fumes and smoke from roasting ores and smelter stacks that no vegetation was left anywhere in or near the town. This fact, plus its location on a steep hillside overlooking a bare butte, plus its reputation as the most wide-open camp in all of Montana had brought it the name. "Is that where you last worked?"

"It is."

"I've heard that on windless days, the smoke is so heavy over Butte it blots the sky and lamps have to be lit at midday."

"True, and then some."

"Which paper were you on? The *Miner* or the *Inter-Mountain?*"

"A. J. Davis's shop. Another man who knows his business."

I was impressed. A. J. Davis was editor and publisher of the *Inter-Mountain*, and reputed to be a stickler for hiring only the best among the typographers and reporters who applied. No "blacksmiths" for him!

"I was there a month," Jones said. "Wages a cut above scale, but that wasn't the reason."

"No. What was?"

"Free beer on tap."

He went on to explain that above the *Inter-Mountain's* offices was a saloon whose beer pipes happened to run through a corner of the composing room. One of the home-guard printers had devised a cleverly hidden plug for the pipe, all unknown to the saloonkeepers. Thus the printers had a constant supply of free suds whenever they felt thirsty.

Jones owned a storehouse of such anecdotes, and, when he was in a proper mood, he would regale me with one after another. He was also a fount of opinions, quotations, professional gossip, place descriptions, and capsule biographies of men and women he had known in his travels. He had been a roadster and gay cat, as young tramp printers were called in that era, since the age of fourteen and had crossed and re-crossed the country half a dozen times. Yet he was reticent about his family background and personal life. He became rude and profane on the few occasions when I attempted to draw him out. And while it was plain that he shared his breed's liking for alcohol and ladies of easy virtue, he did no drinking on the job and was unfailingly courtly to women of every stripe.

He had worked for more than a few of the legends of newspapering, among them Joseph Pulitzer on the St. Louis *Post-Dispatch*, Edward Rosewater, the fighting editor of the Omaha *Bee*, and the beaver-hatted old firebrand, J. West Goodwin, of the Sedalia *Bazoo*. For a time he had traveled with "Hi-Ass" Hull, considered the king of the tramp printers for his union organizing work, whose nickname was derived from a Northwest Indian word meaning "tall man." For another period he'd run with the band of roaming typographers known as the Missouri River Pirates, who frequented the towns along the Missouri River between St. Louis and Sioux City. He had met Jesse James when the outlaw was living in St. Joseph under his Tom Howard alias, two days before the dirty little coward, Bob Ford, fired a .45 slug into Jesse's back. Others whose paths he'd crossed were Bat Masterson, Texas Jack Omahundro, the poet Walt Whitman, himself a tramp printer in New Orleans, and the acid-tongued San Francisco writer, Ambrose Bierce.

Artemus Jones had no formal education, but he was an erudite man. By his own estimate he had read two thousand books, the Bible more than once, and the entire works of Shakespeare. He could quote verbatim passages from the Book and the Bard two and three pages long. Poetry, too, everything from Lord Byron to bawdy limericks. And he conversed knowledgeably on politics, philosophy, art, music, what-have-you.

Now it may seem to you gentlemen that time has clouded my memory, led me to paint you a romanticized picture of this man Jones. You may even be thinking he was a blowhard, a dissembler, or both. I assure you, none of that is the case. My memory of Jones is as clear as spring water. He was exactly as I've described him, and within his province a wholly truthful and honorable man.

Well, then. My father put Jones to work, and an expert typographer he was. He handled planer, mallet, rule, and shooting stick as though he had been born with them in his hand, corrected misspellings without consulting a dictionary, plugged dutchmen in a pair of poorly spaced ads, and generally made the publication of that week's issue an easier task than usual. My father was pleased, and I confess I was in awe. I clung to Jones almost as tightly as his galluses, asking questions, begging more stories, listening with rapt attention to his every word.

William Satterlee's front-page editorial that week was particularly inflammatory—written, in Jones's considered opinion, with a pen dipped in snake venom. There had been another shooting shortly before Jones's arrival, of a farmer who had dared to stray onto Colonel Greathouse's land after a runaway horse. The horse had been shot dead and the settler severely wounded by two Square G fence riders. Sheriff Buckley ruled the shooting justifiable. My father damned Buckley, not for the first time, as an incompetent dullard in the moral, if not actual, pay of the Cattlemen's Association, and he demanded prosecution for murder not only of the two cowhands but of their employer, whom he called, among other things, a cowardly Napoléonic tyrant.

Now Elijah Greathouse was a proud man with a fearsome temper. He had been a brevet colonel with C Company of the Tenth Kansas Volunteers during the War Between the States, and, although he was rumored to have been roundly disliked as a bully by the soldiers under his command, he was boastful of his war record and his military background. The "cowardly Napoléonic tyrant" label infuriated him more than anything else my father had called him in print. The day after the issue appeared, he stormed into the *Banner* office with his foreman, a troublemaker and alleged gun artist named Kinch, and confronted William Satterlee.

"You retract that statement," he bellowed, "or by God you'll suffer the consequences."

My father was unruffled. "I don't respond to threats, Colonel."

"You'd damn well better respond to this one. I mean what I say, editor. Write one more vicious lie about me and you'll pay dear, in one type of coin or another."

"You've made yourself clear. Before witnesses, I might add." Both Jones and I were standing in the composing room doorway, where Greathouse and Kinch could plainly see us. Not that either of them seemed to take much notice. "Now I'll thank you and your cow nurse to get off my property."

Blood-rush turned Kinch's face the color of port wine. He stepped forward and poked my father in the chest with his forefinger. "Cow nurse, am I? Call me that again, you son of a bitch, and you'll find out what else I am."

"I know what else you are," William Satterlee said meaningfully. "Get out before I summon that buffoon of a sheriff and have you arrested for harassment and public profanity."

The two cattlemen left, glaring and grumbling. Jones said to my father: "You've made bad enemies in those two, Mister Satterlee. I've seen their stripe before. Push them too far and one or both will act on their threats."

But my father was a stubborn man, and he had put blinders on where Greathouse and his foreman were concerned. "Humbug," he said. "Knaves, fools, and blowhards, the pair. I've nothing to fear from the likes of them."

Artemus Jones said no more. I held my tongue as well, though I was more than a little worried. No one had ever won an argument with my father when his back was up. Whenever I or anyone else tried, it served only to strengthen his conviction that he was in the right.

The next week passed swiftly. To my considerable pleasure, Jones stayed on in Bear Paw. He had built a stake, he said, working for A.J. Davis in Butte, and after the copper camp's rough and rowdy ways he was content to linger a while in calmer surroundings before moving on. He took a room at Ma Stinson's Travelers' Rest, a combination hotel and boarding house near the Great Northern dépôt that catered to railroad men, drummers, and transients. When he wasn't working, he spent most of his time at the Free and Easy Saloon, which had the best free lunch in Bear Paw. I suspect he also visited Tillie Johnson's parlor house, though I never dared to ask him.

In the composing room I watched his every move while he sat on the tall printer's stool, clad in his leather apron, and picked up the types and assembled them in the composing sticks. He showed great patience in answering the thousand and one questions I asked him about his trade and his travels. Prior to his coming, I had been uncertain of my future goals, though naturally I was tempted to follow my father's ink-stained profession. Before that week was out, I had decided unequivocally that an itinerant printer was what I wanted to be.

Jones neither encouraged nor discouraged me. His was a world of new vistas and high adventure, true, but it was also a lonely life, and a sometimes perilous one. I would have to be willing to take the bad with the good, he said, the hardships along with the ease and freedom of the open road. I allowed as how I could and would, and urged him to take me along when wanderlust claimed him again. He refused. Since his days with the Missouri River Pirates, he had traveled alone and preferred it that way. Besides, neither he nor anyone else could teach me the tricks of his trade—a man learned for himself and by himself. Some weren't cut out for the life and quit sooner or later for tamer, settled pursuits. Why, he had done some reporting here and there and been told by editors that he showed promise, and one day he might just take up that line himself. But when I pressed him, he admitted it was much more likely he'd remain an itinerant typographer until he was too old and infirm to ride the rails. Chances were, he said with a shrug, he would die in a strange town and be buried without a marker in a potter's field grave.

Well, this dissuaded me not at all. If anything, it strengthened my resolve to become a gay cat, to see and do the things and meet the people Jones had. By the end of the week I was making plans to leave Bear Paw on my sixteenth birthday. Plans that I may or may not have carried through, boyish as they were, if the events of that Saturday night had not taken place.

On Wednesday, fuel had been added to the strong feelings between cattlemen and farmers, in the form of a fire of dubious origin that claimed both the barn and house belonging to a homesteading family named Jansen. No one was seriously injured, though Jansen suffered burns in trying to save his livestock. It so happened the farmer's land bordered Colonel Greathouse's south pasture, and there had been a dispute between Jansen and Greathouse over water rights. My father took this to mean that the colonel was guilty of ordering the burnings. His front-page editorial was even more vitriolic than the previous week's, accusing the cattle baron outright and damning him as a savage oppressor who would commit any heinous crime to achieve his purposes.

I was helping Jones with the page lay-outs when William Satterlee came in with the editorial. Jones, while I peered over his shoulder, read it through in silence. Then he said: "Are you sure you want this to run as it stands, Mister Satterlee?"

My father was in an abrasive mood. "Don't ask foolish questions. And don't change so much as a comma when you set it."

"It's certain to provoke Colonel Greathouse."

"That doesn't concern me. What concerns me is his despicable behavior toward the settlers. If I don't take him to task for it, who will?"

"Father," I said, "suppose he does more this time than make idle threats? Suppose he comes after you?"

"He doesn't dare."

"Hadn't you better carry a side arm just in case? Or keep a shotgun by your desk?"

"You know how I feel about weapons and violence. I'll not be reduced to the tactics of men like Greathouse and Kinch, nor will I be intimidated by those tactics. I write the truth, and the truth is the only weapon I want or need." With these noble, if improvident, words, he stalked back into the office.

"Artemus," I said, "I think he's wrong, and I'm afraid for him. If he won't take up a side arm, maybe I should. . . ."

Jones fixed me with a sharp eye. "How much practice have you had with a handgun?"

"Not much, but I know how to shoot one."

"Graveyards are full of men who knew how to shoot guns, or thought they did. Lads your age, too."

"Do you own a pistol?" I asked.

"No."

"But don't you need one on the road, for protection?"

"Some think so. I'm not one of them. I've seen the results of too many gunfights. Your father's right to want to avoid violence if he can."

"But what if he can't? What if he has gone too far this time?"

"There's not much use," Jones said, "in crying fire before you see the flames."

I took his meaning well enough, but I didn't much care for it. I'd expected more of him than a tepid homily. That was all I was to get, however. Twice more I broached the subject that day, and both times he changed it, the last by launching into "The Girl with the Blue Velvet Band" in a rusty baritone. After that, I left him alone and fretted in private.

When the *Banner* appeared on Thursday, it caused the anticipated stir. Men and even a few women flowed in and out of the newspaper office, some to praise my father and more to berate him loudly. None of the visitors was Colonel Elijah Greathouse, his foreman, or anyone else off the Square G. And what few threats were flung at William Satterlee were mild and seemed mostly wind.

Neither Greathouse nor any of his men showed on Friday, or on Saturday. My relief was tempered by the knowledge that the colonel could be a devious cuss. He might well be plotting a more subtle form of revenge, I thought, and I said as much to my father. He scoffed at the notion. William Satterlee was a brave and principled man, but his self-righteousness, his unshakable faith in his beliefs, at times made him his own worst enemy. In this case, as matters soon developed, it nearly cost him his life.

It was his custom to work late at the *Banner* most evenings, even on weekends. He would come home to take supper with my mother and me, then return to the office until eight or nine o'clock. Some evenings I joined him, but my mother did not care for my being out of a Saturday night. It was when cowhands rode in off the nearby ranches to let off steam, the saloons and parlor houses did a boisterous business, and now and then arguments were settled with pistols and knives. Farmers came to town then, too, and, with feelings running as high was they were, there were confrontations virtually every Saturday.

Time passed slowly, and, when my father had yet to come home by nine o'clock, I grew fearful enough to slip out through my bedroom window and hurry the few blocks to Main Street. From the hurdy-gurdy section near the railroad yards I could hear piano music and the shouts and laughter of revelers. But in the business district it was quiet, the street empty. Dark, as well, for the night was cloudy and moonless.

Lamplight shaped the *Banner's* front window. Except for a flickery gas street lamp, it was the only light on the block. Or it was until I neared the building, passing by the alley that ran along its north side. Then, of a sudden, a different kind of light bloomed bright and smoky from the rear, and a faint crackling sound reached my ears.

Fire!

Heedlessly I plunged into the alley. It was our back wall that had been set ablaze, and, as I ran, Artemus Jones's words jolted into my mind: *There's not much use in crying fire until you see the flames.* I opened my mouth to cry it then, thinking to alert my father inside, but the shout was stillborn in my throat. For another cry sounded in that instant—the voice of William Satterlee, already alerted and coming through the rear door.

A scant few seconds later, as I ran clear of the alley, there was the *bang* of a pistol shot.

In the bright fire-glow I saw my father stagger and fall. I saw the other man clearly, too—Kinch, a smoking six-shooter in one hand and a tin of kerosene in the other. An anguished bellow burst from my throat. I stumbled and nearly fell myself. Kinch spun toward me, and, as I regained my balance, I saw his arm raise and his weapon level. I have no doubt he would have shot me dead within another two or three heartbeats. His face was twisted unnaturally, his eyes wild in the firelight.

It was Artemus Jones who saved my life.

He came lunging through the door, his arm upraised, a short, blunt object jutting from his closed fist, and shouted "Kinch! Not the boy, Kinch, *me!*"—in a thunderous voice. No man could have ignored the savage menace in that cry. Kinch swung away from me as Jones charged him. The pistol banged again. Jones's left arm jerked, but the bullet's impact neither stopped nor slowed his rush. He flailed downward with what was clutched in his right hand—a printer's mallet, I realized in the instant before it connected with Kinch's head. The sound of wood colliding with flesh and bone was audible even above the crackling of the flames. The Square G foreman went down all of a piece, with no buckling of his legs—dead before his body settled into the grass.

Jones dropped the mallet and knelt beside my father. "He's still alive!" he called as I started toward him. "Run and fetch a doctor, R.W. Quick!"

I turned and ran. Other men were drawing near on Main Street, summoned by the gunshots. I was aware of lantern light and raised voices as I raced upstreet to Dr. Ferris's house. It took what seemed eons to rouse him from his bed and into his clothes, lead him back to the newspaper building. The flames had been mostly extinguished by then, a dozen men having formed a bucket brigade and others wielding burlap sacks from the feed and grain store. So intent was I on my father's motionless body, it was not until the next day that I learned the fire damage had been confined to a charred wall and a portion of the roof.

Jones was again on one knee beside him, his left arm loose and dripping blood. In spite of his wound he had brought out a cushion to prop up William Satterlee's head and a blanket to cover him. The bullet had entered my father's chest, but its path had missed any vital organs. When I heard Dr. Ferris say,"I don't believe it's a mortal wound," my limbs went jellied with relief.

The rest of that night is a blur in my memory. I recall a long vigil with my mother at the doctor's house, and at some point a brief conversation with Artemus Jones. The damage to his arm was minor, requiring no more than an application of carbolic salve and a bandage. He had no difficulty in using it.

When I thanked him, belatedly, for saving my life, he said in gruff tones: "You shouldn't have been there. And there shouldn't have been any gun play."

". . . What do you mean?"

"Your father was on his way to the privy when he heard Kinch outside . . . he was already through the door before I could react. Else I'd have been the first one out."

"Then you'd have been shot instead."

"Maybe not. I can throw a mallet as well as swing one."

It took a short while for the significance of this to sink in. "You had no reason to be at the office so late tonight," I said then, "unless you were as worried as I was. On guard even if my father wasn't."

Jones shrugged and made no reply.

"But why?" I asked. "It wasn't your trouble."

"I had my reasons."

"You might have been killed. . . ."

"I might have," he said, "but I wasn't. Some chores are worth doing, R.W., for your own sake as well as others'."

I understood that, and something else then, too. I understood why he was called "Give-a-Damn" Jones.

As serious as William Satterlee's wound was, he was conscious and out of danger by sunup. My mother and I went to church to give thanks, and, when we returned to the doctor's, we found a surprise visitor—Colonel Elijah Greathouse. News of the shooting, attempted arson, and Kinch's demise had been delivered to him by another of his cowhands, and he had come to town, he said stiffly, for only one reason. To tell Sheriff Buckley and now my father that Kinch had acted on his own, in this case and in the burning of the Jansen homestead. Despite William Satterlee's public opinion, he neither ordered nor sanctioned senseless violence. Greathouse swore to this with his hand on a Bible he produced from his coat pocket. Afterward, he turned on his heel and walked out.

Admitting to mistakes in judgment was never easy for my father, but no man lying flat on his back with a punctured chest can be as cocksure as when healthy and standing tall. He offered a brief, grudging apology to Jones and me, and, when the sheriff came to see him, he made no attempt to bring charges against Colonel Greathouse. Later, after his recovery, he softened his editorial stance considerably. Still later, when a harsh winter forced an uneasy alliance between ranchers and farmers, he ceased taking sides altogether. There were no more clashes between him and the colonel. They never spoke to each other again.

Artemus Jones did not leave Bear Paw immediately, as I'd been afraid he would. He stayed for three more weeks, while my father slowly mended. To everyone's surprise, Jones volunteered to act as both the *Banner's* editor and typesetter during the convalescence. I was delighted when William Satterlee, a newspaperman above all else, agreed. He seemed to take it for granted that Jones was monentarily motivated, but I knew better.

Jones and I worked tirelessly during those three weeks. In addition to his other duties he wrote most of the news copy and a pair of editorials on brotherhood and Christian charity. If his style was rough-edged, it was also sincere, forthright, and offensive to no one. And for good measure, he made sure that in none of the issues he edited was there a single typographical or grammatical error, unplugged dutchman, pied line, or widow.

By the middle of the third week my father was well enough to return to his desk and pen that week's editorial, in which his praise of Jones was, for him, lavish. Upon reading it, Artemus refused to do the setting and argued in vain against its publication. William Satterlee won the argument, as he always did when hale and hearty, but it was I who set the type. My father also paid Jones, in addition to his printer's wages, a bonus of twenty-five dollars for his editorial work. Jones took the money with no particular reluctance and, in the tramp's typically profligate fashion, spent most, if not all, of it over the next two days at the Free and Easy and Tillie Johnson's.

The day after that, Saturday, he packed his bindle and hopped one of the Great Northern's night freights for parts unknown.

He said nothing to my father or me about moving on. He was not a man for good byes, any more than a man for praise or conceit or sentiment. There one day, gone the next. True to himself, his calling, and his principles in every way.

Well, gentlemen, there you have it, in sum and without embellishment. Why Artemus Jones is the most admirable man I have ever known.

Did we meet again? To my everlasting regret, we did not. I left Bear Paw myself shortly after my sixteenth birthday, and for the next six years I followed the adventurous trail of the itinerant printer across the width and breadth of the country. I encountered men who knew Jones and spoke highly of him, and twice I arrived in cities—Joplin, Missouri, and Spokane, Washington—a few short days after he'd been there and traveled on. But not once, despite my best efforts, did our roaming paths cross.

As many of you know, I left the wanderer's life in 1890, to take the position of police reporter on the Baltimore *Sun*. Newspapering was as much in my blood as printer's ink, but that was not the only reason I settled down. The day of the tramp typographer was drawing to a close. The mechanical age was upon us, and a new-fangled machine in which matrices ran down channels and were assembled to cast a whole line of type at one time—the Linotype, of course—had come into widespread use. Some of the old hand-peggers reluctantly learned the new device and became home-guards in various cities and towns. Others threw out their stick and rule, gave up their union cards, and took the same route as I or embarked on different careers entirely. Only a few hung on to the very end of their days taking catch-as-catch-can typesetting jobs, living hand-to-mouth on the open road.

It is my belief that Artemus Jones was among that last, ever-dwindling group. If he is still above ground, he is an old man, as old as toothless Weems and doubtless as feisty, and still hand-pegging in some backwater shop. More likely he has gone on to his reward, having fulfilled his own prophecy of death in a strange town and burial in an unmarked potter's field grave.

Were it ever in my power to determine his final resting place, I would erect upon it a marble stone engraved with his name and the words: "He gave a damn about his fellowman." That was the credo he lived by, gentlemen—and it is the credo I adopted for myself. Where I have succeeded in following it, the credit is largely his. And where I have failed, the failings are R. W. Satterlee's alone.

RIGHTEOUS GUNS

It was hot.

And quiet—too quiet.

He walked slowly along the dusty street, one hand resting on the Colt Peacemaker pouched at his hip. The harsh midday sun made the false-fronted buildings stand out in sharp relief against a sky more white than blue, like an alkali flat turned upside down. Heat mirage shimmered beyond the livery stable in the next block, half obscuring the road that led up into the foothills west of town.

He paused opposite the Lucky Lady Saloon and Gambling Hall and stood hip-shot, listening to the silence. Nothing moved anywhere ahead of him or around him. There were no horses tied to the hitchrails, no wagons or buckboards, no townspeople making their way along the plank sidewalks. But he could feel eyes watching him from behind closed doors and shuttered windows.

Waiting, all of them—just as he was.

Waiting for the lawmen and their righteous guns.

Sweat worked its way out from under his Stetson; he wiped it away with the back of his left hand, smearing the dust-cake on his lean, sun-weathered face. His mouth tasted dry and dusty, like the street itself, and he thought of pushing in through the saloon's batwings for a beer and a shot of rye. But liquor dulled a man's thoughts, turned his reflexes slow. No liquor today.

From his shirt pocket he took out the makings and rolled a cigarette with his left hand. He scratched a sulfur match into flame on the sole of his boot. His right hand didn't move from the butt of his Peacemaker in its hand-tooled Mexican holster.

How many of them would there be? Close to a dozen, likely, maybe more. Robbing the Cattlemen's and Merchant's Bank as he'd done this morning, shooting down the bank director, Leo Furman, in cold blood when he wouldn't open the safe . . . those were about as serious crimes as there were in the Territory. There'd be plenty in the posse, all right. They'd want him bad, them and their righteous guns.

Not that it mattered much, he thought. A wry smile bent the corners of his mouth. He'd faced lawmen before, in numbers from one to twenty, in towns like this one in half a dozen states and territories throughout the West. This was nothing new. This was just more of the same for a man like him.

It was only a question of time. He'd wait, because there was nothing else for him to do. He hadn't got the money from the bank; Leo Furman had tried for a hideout gun and he'd had to shoot him before Furman could open the safe. So the only thing he could do was wait. Better to face them here, than run and have them chase him down like a dog.

When they came, he'd be ready for them.

He blew smoke into the hot still air and then commenced walking again, thinking about Leo Furman. A bossy, fussy man; like so many bank directors, he'd thought that the money other men entrusted to him gave him power over those men. Demanding, high and mighty, full of contempt—that was Furman. He wasn't sorry he'd killed the bastard. He wasn't sorry at all.

He moved on past Benson's Mercantile, the Elite Café, the Palace Hotel. There was still no sound, nothing stirring in the thick, milky heat. It was as if the town itself was holding its breath now.

On past the Eternal Rest Funeral Home, the blacksmith's shop, the deserted sheriff's office; heading toward the hostler's. He knew just what a menacing figure he cut, moving along that dusty, barren street: big, hard face full of angles and shadows, body leaned down to sinew and bone. Most men stood aside when he passed, avoiding his eyes. So did the women. They were afraid of him, the women; the only way he'd ever had one was by money or by force.

Sometimes, late at night, he would wake up in a strange bed or by the remains of a trailside fire and think of what might have been. An end to the vicious swath he cut through the West; an end to the shooting and the killing of decent men; righteous guns instead of his own desperate ones, or better yet, no guns at all. The love of a good woman, a small ranch on good grazing land . . .

Something moved in the alley between the blacksmith's shop and the livery.

A shadow, then a second shadow.

He tensed, alert to the sudden smell of danger. He slowed to a walk, pitched his cigarette away, let his fingers curl loosely around the butt of his Peacemaker. Squinted through the hard glare of the sunlight.

More movement inside the alley. Over on the far side of the street, too, behind Baldwin's Feed and Grain Store. Furtive sounds reached his ears: the soft sliding of boots in the dust, the faint thump of an arm or hand or leg against wood.

They were here.

Most times they came openly, riding in on their horses, weapons at the ready. Once in a while, though, they came in quiet and slinking like this, to wait in ambush in the shadows. No better than he was, then. In their own way, just as desperate.

Well, it didn't matter.

It was time, and as always, he was ready.

"*Hold it right there, Gaines!*" a voice roared suddenly from the alley. "*We've got you surrounded!*"

He bent his knees and let himself bow slightly at the middle. But he was scowling now. Gaines, the voice had said. How did they know his real name?

"*You can't get away, Gaines! Stand where you are and raise your hands over your head!*"

There was something about that voice, the odd thunderous tone of it, as if it were coming through a megaphone, that made him feel suddenly uneasy. More than uneasy—strange, dizzy. His head began to ache. The sun-baked street, the false-fronted buildings, seemed to shift in and out of focus, to take on new and different dimensions. Sunstroke, he thought. I been standing out here in the heat too long.

But it wasn't sunstroke . . .

One of the shadows in the alley shifted into view—his first clear glimpse of the law. And he stared, for the lawdog wasn't wearing Levi's or broad-brimmed hat or tin star pinned to vest or cotton shirt; wasn't carrying Winchester rifle or Colt sixgun. Strange blue uniform, blue helmet, weapon in one hand like none he'd ever seen before.

He stood blinking, confused. And saw then that the buildings didn't just have false fronts; they had false backs too, and no backs at all on some of them, just a latticework of wooden supports like sets in a play.

Sets in a *movie.*

Movie sets, TV-show sets on the back lot of Mammoth Pictures.

A dozen movies, a hundred TV shows, all starring Roy Gaines in the role of the villain . . . and Leo Furman, the director, always telling him what to do, treating him with contempt, never once letting him be good and decent, never once letting him be the hero . . . wouldn't open his safe, wouldn't give him the money he needed to pay his gambling debts, and so he'd shot Furman dead, just as he would any damned fool who crossed him . . . and then he'd come here, because there was no place else for him to go, a man on the run, killer on the run, here to make still another last stand . . .

"*Gaines! You can't escape! Raise your hands over your head! Don't make us do this the hard way!*"

The hard way, the hard way, the hard way . . .

There was a jolting in his mind; the false-fronted buildings, the sun-blasted street settled back into familiar focus. Then, ahead, he could see four, five, six of the possemen fanning out toward him, keeping to cover.

A grim smile formed on his mouth. He'd done all this before, so many times before. He knew just what to do. He didn't even have to think about it.

"All right," he yelled, "come and get it, boys!" His hand went down, came up again with his desperate gun blazing

And the righteous guns cut him down.

DOC CHRISTMAS, PAINLESS DENTIST

Nothing much happens in an eastern Montana farm and cow town like Bear Paw, even in the good warm days of early summer. So when this gent Doc Christmas and his assistant come rolling into town in their fancy wagon one fine June evening, unexpected and unannounced, it caused quite a commotion.

I was in the sheriff's office, where I conduct most of my civic business, when the hubbub commenced. I hurried out like everybody else to see what it was all about. First thing I saw was the wagon. It was a big, wide John Deere drawn by two bays and painted bright red with a shiny gold curlicue design. Smack in the middle of the design were the words: *DOC CHRISTMAS, PAINLESS DENTIST*. Then I saw up on the seat two of the oddest-looking gents a body was ever likely to set eyes on. The one holding the reins was four or five inches over six foot, beanpole thin, with a head as big as a melon and chin whiskers all the way down the front of his black broadcloth suit coat. The other one, wearing a mustard-yellow outfit, was half as tall, four times as wide, and bald as an egg, and he was strumming an outlandish big banjo and singing "Buffalo Gals" in a voice loud enough to dislodge rocks from Jawbone Hill.

Well, we'd had our fair share of patent medicine drummers in Bear Paw, and once we'd even had a traveling medicine show that had a juggler and twelve trained dogs and sold an herb compound and catarrh cure that give everybody that took it the trots. But we'd never had a painless dentist before.

Fact was, I'd never heard of this Doc Christmas. Turned out nobody else had, neither. He was brand-spanking new on the circuit, and that made him all the more of a curiosity. He drove that gaudy wagon of his straight down Main Street and across the river bridge, with half the townsfolk trailing after him like them German citizens trailed after the Pied Piper. Not just kids—men and women, too. And I ain't ashamed to admit that one of the men was yours truly, Randolph Tucker, sheriff and mayor of Bear Paw.

Doc Christmas parked his wagon on the willow flat along the river, with its hind end aimed out toward the road. It was getting on toward dusk by then, so him and the bald gent, whose name come out to be Homer, lighted pan torches that was tied to the wheels of the wagon. Then they opened up the back end and fiddled around until they had a kind of little stage with a painted curtain behind it. Then they got up on the stage part together, and Homer played more tunes on his banjo while the two of 'em sang the words, all louder than they was melodious. Then Doc Christmas begun setting out a display of dentist's instruments, on a slant-board table so the torchlight gleamed off their polished surfaces, and Homer went around handing out penny candy to the kids and printed leaflets to the adults.

I contrived to lay hands on one of the leaflets. It said that Doc Christmas was Montana Territory's newest and finest painless dentist, thanks be to his recent invention of Doc Christmas's Wonder Pain-Killer, *the most precious boon to mankind yet discovered.* It said he had dedicated his life to dispensing this fantastic new elixir, and to ridding the mouths of every citizen of Montana of loose and decayed teeth so's the rest of their teeth could remain healthy and harmonious. And at the very last it said what his services was going to cost you. Pint bottle of Doc Christmas's Wonder Pain-Killer, *a three months' supply with judicious use*—one dollar. A complete and thorough dental examination in his private clinic—four bits for adults, children under the age of ten free. Pulling of a loose or decayed tooth—one dollar for a simple extraction, three dollars for a difficult extraction that required more than five minutes. There was no other fees, and painless results was guaranteed to all.

As soon as the Doc had his instruments all laid out, Homer played a tune on his banjo to quieten everybody down. After which Doc Christmas began his lecture. It was some impressive. He said pretty much the same things his leaflet said, only in words so eloquent any politician would've been proud to steal 'em for his own.

Then he said he was willing to demonstrate the fabulous power of his pain-killer as a public service without cost to the first suffering citizen who volunteered to have a tooth drawn. Was there any poor soul here who had an aching molar or throbbing bicuspid? Doc Christmas invited him or her to step right up and be relieved.

Well, I figured it might take more than that for the doc to get himself a customer, even one for free. Folks in Bear Paw is just natural reticent when it comes to strangers and newfangled pain-killers, particular after the traveling medicine show's catarrh cure. But I was wrong. His offer was took up then and there by two citizens, not just one.

The first to speak up was Ned Flowers, who owns the feed and grain store. He was standing close in front, and no sooner had the doc finished his invite than Ned shouted: "I volunteer! I've got a side molar that's been giving me conniption fits for near a month."

"Step up here with me, sir," Doc Christmas said, "right up here with Homer and me."

Ned got one foot on the wagon, but not the second. There was a sudden roar, and somebody come barreling through the crowd like a bull on the scent of nine heifers, scattering bodies every which way. I knowed who it was even before I saw him and heard his voice boom out. "No you don't, Flowers! I got me a worse toothache than you or any man in sixteen counties. I'm gettin' my molar yanked first and I'm gettin' it yanked free and I ain't takin' argument from you nor nobody else!"

Elrod Patch. Bear Paw's blacksmith and bully, the meanest gent I ever had the misfortune to know personal. I'd arrested him six times in seven years, on charges from drunk and disorderly to cheating customers to assault and battery to caving in the skull of Abe Coltrane's stud Appaloosa when it kicked him whilst he was trying to shoe it, and I could've arrested him a dozen more times if I'd had enough evidence. He belonged in Deer Lodge Penitentiary, but he'd never been convicted of a felony offense, nor even spent more than a few days in my jail. Offended parties and witnesses had a peculiar way of dropping their complaints and changing their testimony when it come time to face the circuit judge.

Patch charged right up to the doc's wagon and shoved Ned outen the way and knocked him down, even though Ned wasn't fixing to argue. Then he clumb up on the stage, making the boards creak and groan and sag some. He was big, Patch was, muscle and fat both, with a wild tangle of red hair and a red mustache. He stood with his feet planted wide and looked hard at Doc Christmas. He'd been even meaner than usual lately, and now we all knew why.

"All right, sawbones," he said. "Pick up your tools and start yankin'."

"I am not a doctor, sir. I am a painless dentist."

"Same thing to me. Where do I sit?"

The doc fluffed out his whiskers and said: "The other gentleman volunteered first, Mister . . . ?"

"Patch, Elrod Patch, and I don't care if half of Bear Paw volunteered first. I'm here, and I'm the one sufferin' the worst. Get to it. And it damn well better be painless, too."

I could've gone up there and stepped in on Ned Flowers's behalf, but it would've meant trouble, and I wasn't up to any trouble tonight if it could be avoided. Doc Christmas didn't want none, either. He said to Patch—"Very well, sir."—and made a signal to his assistant. Homer went behind the painted curtain, come out again with a chair like a cut-down barber's chair with a long horizontal rod at the top. He plunked the chair down next to the table that held the doc's instruments. Then he lighted the lantern and hooked it on the end of the rod.

Patch squeezed his bulk into the chair. The doc opened up Patch's mouth with one long-fingered hand, poked and prodded some inside, then went out and got a funny-looking tool and poked and prodded with that. He done it real gentle, too. Patch squirmed some, but never made a sound the whole time.

Homer come over with a bottle of Doc Christmas's Wonder Pain-Killer, and the doc held it up to show the crowd whilst he done some more orating on its virtues. After which he unstoppered it and swabbed some thick brown liquid on Patch's jaw, and rubbed more of it inside of Patch's mouth. When he was done, Homer handed him a pair of forceps, which the doc brandished for the assemblage. That painkiller of his sure looked to be doing what it was advertised to do, for Patch was sitting quiet in the chair with a less hostile look on his ugly face.

He wasn't quiet for long, though. All of a sudden Homer took up his banjo and commenced to play and sing "Camptown Races" real loud. And with more strength than I'd figured was in that beanpole frame, Doc Christmas grabbed old Patch around the head with his hand tight over the windpipe, shoved the forceps into his wide-open maw, got him a grip on the offending molar, and started yanking.

It looked to me like Patch must be yelling something fierce. Leastways his legs was kicking and his arms was flapping. But Homer's banjo playing and singing was too loud to hear anything else. The doc yanked, and Patch struggled for what must've been about a minute and a half. Then the doc let go of his windpipe and with a flourish he held up the forceps, at the end of which was Patch's bloody tooth.

Patch tried to get up outen the chair. Doc Christmas shoved him back down, took a big wad of cotton off the table, and poked that into Patch's maw. Right then Homer quit picking and caterwauling. As soon as it was quiet, the doc said to the crowd: "A simple, painless extraction, ladies and gentlemen, accomplished in less time than it takes to peel and core an apple. It was painless, was it not, Mister Patch?"

Patch was on his feet now. He was wobbly, and he seemed a mite dazed. He tried to say something, but with all that cotton in his mouth the words come out garbled and thick, so's you couldn't understand none of 'em. Homer and the doc handed him down off the wagon. The townsfolk parted fast as Patch weaved his way through, giving him plenty of room. He passed close to me on his way out to the road, and he looked some stunned, for a fact. Whatever was in Doc Christmas's Wonder Pain-Killer sure must be a marvel of medical science.

Well, as soon as folks saw that Patch wasn't going to kick up a ruckus, they applauded Doc and Homer and pushed in closer to the wagon. In the next half hour, Doc Christmas pulled Ned Flowers's bad tooth and give a dozen four-bit dental examinations, and Homer sold nineteen bottles of the pain-killer. I bought a pint myself. I figured it was the least I could do in appreciation for the show they'd put on and that stunned look on Patch's face when he passed me by.

I was in my office early next morning, studying on the city council's proposal to buy fireworks from an outfit in Helena for this year's Fourth of July celebration, when Doc Christmas and Homer walked in. Surprised me to see 'em, particular since Homer looked some vexed. Not the doc, though. He'd struck me as the practical and unflappable sort last night, and he struck me the same in the light of day.

"Sheriff," he said, fluffing out his whiskers, "I wish to make a complaint."

"That so? What kind of complaint?"

"One of the citizens of Bear Paw threatened my life not twenty minutes ago. Homer's life, as well."

Uh-oh, I thought. "Wouldn't be Elrod Patch, would it?"

"It would. The man is a philistine."

"Won't get no argument from me on that," I said. "Philistine, troublemaker, and holy terror. What'd he threaten you and Homer for? Body'd think he'd be grateful, after you jerked his bad tooth free of charge."

"He claims it was not the painless extraction I guaranteed."

"Oh, he does."

"Claims to have suffered grievously the whole night long," Doc Christmas said, "and to still be in severe pain this morning. I explained to him that some discomfort is natural after an extraction, and that, if he had paid heed to my lecture, he would have understood the necessity of purchasing an entire bottle of Doc Christmas's Wonder Pain-Killer. Had he done so, he would have slept like an innocent babe and be fit as a fiddle today."

"What'd he say to that?"

"He insisted that I should have supplied a bottle of my Wonder Pain-Killer *gratis*. I informed him again that only the public extraction was *gratis*, but he refused to listen."

"Just one of his many faults."

"He demanded a free bottle then and there. Of course, I did not knuckle under to such blatant extortion."

"That when he threatened your life?"

"In foul and abusive language."

"Uh-huh. Any witnesses?"

"No, sir. We three were alone at the wagon."

"Well, then, sir," I said, "there just ain't much I can do legally. I don't know what to tell you gents, except that so far as I know Patch ain't never killed anybody human. So the chances are he won't follow up on his threat."

"But he would go so far as to damage my wagon and equipment, would he not?"

"He might, if he was riled enough. He threaten to do that, too?"

"He did."

"Hell and damn. I'll have to talk with him, Doc, try to settle him down. But he don't like me, and I don't like him, so I don't expect it'll do much good. How long you and Homer fixing to stay on in Bear Paw?"

"Business was brisk last evening," the doc said. "We anticipate it will be likewise today and tomorrow as well, once word spreads of my dental skill and the stupendous properties of Doc Christmas's Wonder Pain-Killer."

"I don't suppose you'd consider cutting your visit short and moving on elsewhere?"

He drew himself up. "I would not, sir. Doc Christmas flees before the wrath of no man."

"I was afraid of that. Uh, how long you reckon Patch's mouth will hurt without he treats it with more of your Wonder Pain-Killer?"

"The exact length of time varies from patient to patient. A day, two days, perhaps as long as a week."

I sighed. "I was afraid of that, too."

Patch was banging away at a red-hot horseshoe with his five-pound sledge-hammer when I walked into his blacksmith's shop. Doing it with a vengeance, too, as if it was Doc Christmas's head forked there on his anvil. The whole left side of his face was swelled up something wicked.

He glared when he saw me. "What in hell do you want, Tucker?"

"A few peaceable words, is all."

"Got nothin' to say to you. Besides, my mouth hurts too damn much to talk." Then, Patch being Patch, he went ahead and jawed to me anyways. "Look at what that travelin' tooth puller done to me last night. Hurts twice as bad with the tooth out than it done with it in."

"Well, you did rush up and volunteer to have it yanked."

"I didn't volunteer for no swole-up face like I got now. Painless dentist, hell!"

"It's my understanding you threatened him and his assistant with bodily harm."

"Run to you, did he?" Patch said. "Well, it'd serve both of 'em right if I blowed their heads off with my twelve-gauge."

"You'd hang, Patch. High and quick."

He tried to scowl, but it hurt his face, and he winced instead. He give the horseshoe another lick with his hammer, then dropped it into a bucket of water. He watched it steam and sizzle before he said: "There's other ways to skin a cat."

"Meaning?"

"Like I said. They's other ways to skin a cat."

"Patch, you listen to me. You do anything to Doc Christmas or Homer or that wagon of theirs, anything at all, I'll slap you in jail sudden and see that you pay dear."

"I ain't afraid of you, Tucker. You and me's gonna tangle one of these days anyhow."

"Better not, if you know what's good for you."

"I know what's good for me right now, and that's some of that bastard's pain-killer. It's the genuine article, even if he ain't. And I aim to get me a bottle."

"Now, that's the first sensible thing I heard you say. Whyn't you and me mosey on down to the river together so's you can buy one?"

"Buy? I ain't gonna *buy* somethin' I should've got for nothin'!"

"Oh, Lordy, Patch. Doc Christmas never promised you a free bottle of pain-killer. All he promised was to draw your bad tooth, which he done."

"One's free, so's the other," Patch said. "Ain't nobody cheats Elrod Patch outen what's rightfully his and gets away with it. Sure not the flim-flammin' long drink of water that claims to be a painless dentist."

Well, it just wasn't no use. I'd have got more satisfaction trying to talk sense to a cottonwood stump. But I give it one last try before I took myself out of there. I said: "You're warned, mister. Stay away from Doc Christmas and Homer and their wagon or you'll suffer worse'n you are now by half. And that's a promise."

All I got for an answer was a snort. He was on his way to the forge by then, else I reckon he'd have laughed right in my face.

Long about noonday I had an inspiration.

I walked home to Madge Tolliver's boarding house for my noon meal, which I like to do as often as I can on account of Madge being the best cook in town, and afterwards I went upstairs to my room for the bottle of Doc Christmas's Wonder Pain-Killer I'd bought last night. Outside again, I spied the Ames boy, Tommy, rolling his hoop. I gave Tommy a nickel to take the bottle to the blacksmith's shop. I said he should tell Patch it was from Doc Christmas and that it was a peace offering, free of charge. I don't like fibbing or having youngsters fib for me, but in this case I reckoned I was on the side of the angels and it was a pardonable sin. Sometimes the only way you can deal with the devil is by using his own methods.

I waited fifteen minutes for Tommy to come back. When he did, he didn't have the bottle of pain-killer with him, which I took to be a good sign. But it wasn't.

"He took it all right, Mister Tucker," Tommy said. "Then he laughed real nasty and said he suspicioned it was from you, not Doc Christmas."

"Blast him for a sly fox!"

"He said now he had *two* bottles of pain-killer, and his mouth didn't hurt no more, but it didn't make a lick of difference in how he felt toward that blankety-blank tooth puller."

"Two bottles?"

"Got the other one from Mister Flowers, he said."

"By coercion, I'll warrant."

"What's coercion?"

"Never you mind about that. Patch didn't say what he was fixing to do about Doc Christmas, did he?"

"No, sir, he sure didn't."

I left Tommy and stumped on down to the river to see the doc. There was a crowd around his wagon again, not as large today, but still good-sized. Doc had a farmer in the chair and was yanking a tooth while Homer played his banjo and sang "Camptown Races." I waited until they was done and eight more bottles of the Wonder Pain-Killer had been sold. Then I got the Doc off to one side for a confab.

I told him what Patch had said to me and to Tommy Ames. I thought it might scare him some, but it didn't. He drew himself up the way he liked to do, fluffed his whiskers, and said: "Homer and I refuse to be intimidated by the likes of Elrod Patch."

"He can be mean, Doc, and that's a fact. He's as likely as a visit from the Grim Reaper to make trouble for you."

"Be that as it may."

"Doc, I'd take it as a personal favor if you'd pull up stakes and move on right now. By the time you make your circuit back to Bear Paw, Patch'll have forgot his grudge. . . ."

"I'm sorry, Sheriff Tucker, but that would be the cowardly way, and Homer and I are men, not spineless whelps. The law and the Almighty can send us fleeing, but no man can without just cause."

Well, he had a point, and I couldn't argue with it. He was on public land, and he hadn't broken any laws, including the Almighty's. I wished him well and went back to town.

But I was feeling uneasy in my mind and tight in my bones. There was going to be trouble, sure as God made little green apples, and now I couldn't see no smart nor legal way to stop it.

It happened some past midnight, and, depending on how you looked at it, it was plain trouble or trouble with a fitting end and a silver lining.

Most if not all of Bear Paw looked at it the second way. And I'd be a hypocrite if I said I wasn't one of the majority.

I was sound asleep when the knocking commenced on the door to my room at the boarding house. I lighted my lamp before I opened up. It was Doc Christmas, looking as unflappable as ever.

First thing he done was unbutton his frock coat and hand me a pistol, butt first, that had been tucked into his belt. It was an old Root's Patent Model .31 caliber with a side hammer like a musket hammer, a weapon I hadn't seen in many a year. But it looked to be in fine working order, and the barrel was warm.

"Sheriff," he said then, "I wish to report a shooting."

"Who got shot?"

"Elrod Patch."

"Oh, Lordy. Is he dead?"

"As the proverbial doornail."

"You the one who shot him?"

"I am. In self-defense."

He might've been telling me the time of night—he was that calm and matter-of-fact. Practical to a fault, that was the doc. What was done was done, and there wasn't no sense in getting exercised about it.

I asked him: "Where'd it happen?"

"On the willow flat near where my wagon is parked. Homer is waiting there for us. Shall we proceed?"

I got dressed in a hurry, and we hustled on down to the river. Homer was tending to one of the bay horses, both of which seemed unusual skittish. Nearby, between where the horses was picketed and the wagon, Elrod Patch lay sprawled out on his back. In one hand he held a five-pound sledge-hammer, of all things, and there was a bullet hole where he'd once had a right eye.

"It was unavoidable, Sheriff," Homer said as I bent to look at Patch. "He rushed at the doc with that hammer and left him no choice."

"What in tarnation was Patch doing here with a sledge-hammer? Not attempting to murder you gents in your beds, was he?"

"No," Doc Christmas said. "He was attempting to murder our horses."

"Your horses?"

"It was their frightened cries that woke Homer and me. Fortunately we emerged from the wagon before he had time to do more than strike one of the animals a glancing blow."

Well, I knew right then that the Doc and Homer was telling the truth. Patch had caved in the skull of Abe Coltrane's stud Appaloosa with nary a qualm nor regret, and I could see where doing the same to a couple of wagon horses would be just his idea of revenge. Still, I had my duty. I looked close at the sledge-hammer to make sure it was Patch's. It was. His initials was cut into the handle. Then I examined the bay that had been struck and found a bloody mark across his neck and withers. That was enough for me.

"Self-defense and death by misadventure," I said, and I give the doc back his .31 Root's. "Patch had it coming . . . no mistake about that, neither. Too bad you had to be the one to send him to his reward, Doc."

He said,"Yes," but he looked kind of thoughtful when he said it.

Doc Christmas come to see me one more time, late the following afternoon at my office. At first I thought it was just to tell me him and Homer was leaving soon for Sayersville. Then I thought it was to ask if they'd be welcome back when Bear Paw come up on their circuit again next spring, which I said they would be. But them two things was only preambles to the real purpose of his visit.

"Sheriff Tucker," he said, "it is my understanding that you are also the mayor and city treasurer of Bear Paw. Is this correct?"

"It is," I said. "I'm likewise chairman of the annual Fourth of July celebration and head of the burial commission. Folks figured it was better to pay one man a salary for wearing lots of hats than a bunch of men salaries for wearing one hat apiece."

"Then you are empowered to pay out public funds for services to the community."

"I am. What're you getting at, Doc?"

"The fact," he said, "that Bear Paw owes me three dollars."

"Bear Paw does what? What in tarnation for?"

"Services rendered."

"Come again?"

"Services rendered," the doc said. "I am a painless dentist, as you well know . . . the finest and most dedicated painless dentist in Montana Territory. It is my life's work and my duty and my great joy to rid the mouths of my patients of loose and decayed teeth. A town such as Bear Paw, sir, is in many ways like the mouth of one of my patients. It is healthy and harmonious only so long as its citizens . . . its individual teeth, if you will . . . are each and every one healthy and harmonious. One diseased tooth damages the entire mouth. Elrod Patch was such a diseased tooth in the mouth of Bear Paw. I did not extract him willingly from your midst, but the fact remains that I did extract him permanently . . . and with no harm whatsoever to the surrounding teeth. In effect, sir, painlessly.

"For a simple painless extraction I charge one dollar. You will agree, Sheriff Tucker, that the extraction of Elrod Patch was not simple, but difficult. For difficult extractions I charge three dollars. Therefore, the town of Bear Paw owes me three dollars for services rendered, payable on demand."

Did I say the doc was practical to a fault? And then some! He was a caution, he was, with more gall than a trainload of campaigning politicians. If I'd been a lawyer, I reckon I could've come up with a good argument against his claim. But I ain't a lawyer, I'm a public servant. Besides which, when a man's right, he's right.

On behalf of the healthy and harmonious teeth of Bear Paw, I paid Doc Christmas his three dollars.

NOT A LICK OF SENSE

We come down out of the high country some past sunup, Lige driving the wagon too dang fast. Winter had played hob with the track, still had snow on it, deep in places. Every time a wheel jounced into a chuckhole or rut, the big old pine-board outhouse tied onto the bed swayed and creaked and groaned.

I kept hollering at him to slow down. Didn't do no good. When he latches onto some notion, he's like a mule with its teeth in a bale of hay. He don't have a lick of sense, Lige don't. I'm the Hovey born with all the sense; he's the one born with all the stubborn.

"Quit your bellerin'," he said once. "That outhouse ain't gonna bust loose and go flyin'. She's roped in tight."

"That ain't what's worryin' me."

"Won't shake apart, not as solid as we built her."

"Ain't that, neither, and you know it."

"All the more reason to get this here business over with quick. I still ain't sure we ought to be doin' it."

"After all the work we done? Lige, sometimes you're a pure fool."

"Wes," he said, "sometimes you're another."

I breathed some easier when we come to the junction with the county road. Off east was Antelope Valley and the Piegan Indian reservation. Little Creek was four miles to the west, and I had me a wish it was where we was headed right now. After four months up in the high country, we was near out of supplies. And I could scarce recall my last visit to Miss Sally's sporting house behind the Red Rock Saloon.

Lige turned us east. Wasn't near so cold down on the flats, though I could still see the frost of my breath and Lige's and our roan horse Jingalee's. No drifts of snow left on the ground, neither, like up to our place. You could smell things growing again, and about time, too. It'd sure been a long, hard winter.

County road wasn't near as bad off as the mountain track, and Lige commenced to push Jingalee even harder. I hollered at him, but he didn't pay me no mind. Not a lick of sense, by grab. That poor horse was showing lather already, and we still had us a distance left to travel. . . .

"Oh, Lordy Lord!" Lige said, sudden. "Wes, look yonder."

I looked. Man on horseback had just come trotting around a bend ahead. He was all bundled up in a sheepskin greatcoat and a neck muffler, his hat pulled down low, but I knowed him and that steeldust of his right off. So did Lige. Morgan Conagher, sheriff of Little Creek.

"What in tarnation's *he* doin' out here this early?" I said.

"Gonna ask us the same thing." Lige hauled back on the reins some and then give me one of his hot looks, all smoke and sparks. "You and your ideas," he said.

"Ain't nothing wrong with my ideas. You just let me do the talkin', hear?"

He muttered something and slowed us to a rocking stop as Conagher rode up alongside. He was a big 'un, Morgan was, and a holy terror with fists and six-gun, both. Smart, too, for a lawman. Unless a man was plain simple, he walked and talked soft when his path crossed Morgan Conagher's.

"'Morning, boys," he said. "Cold as a gambler's eyeball, ain't it?"

"For a fact. Warmer than up to our place, though."

"Long time since I seen you two. Snowed in most of the winter?"

"Since the first week of December. How come you to be out riding this early, Mister Conagher?"

"Spent the night at Hank Staggs's place in the valley. Little trouble out there yesterday."

"Serious?"

"Not so's you'd notice. Hank figured he had a gripe against a couple of Piegan braves. Turned out to be the other way around." Conagher took his corncob pipe outen a coat pocket and commenced to chewing on the stem. Pipe bowl was black, but I'd never seen him smoke the thing. Gnawing the stem seemed to satisfy him the same as tobacco. "Now that's a curious sight," he said.

"What is?"

"Thing you got tied in your wagon there. Looks like an outhouse."

"Well, that's what she is, all right."

"Can't mistake that half-moon cut in the door."

"No, sir, sure can't."

"Takin' it out for an airing, are you?"

Lige, who don't have no more humor in him than he does sense, just set there. But I laughed before I said: "Be a couple of jugheads if that's what we was doing, wouldn't we, Sheriff? No, the fact is. . . ."

"Fact is," Lige said before I could get anything else out, "we're takin' her over to Charley Hammond's place."

"That so?" Conagher said. "What for?"

Damn Lige for a fool! I give him a sidewise glance and a sharp kick with the toe of my boot, both by way of telling him to put a hitch on his fat lip, but he went right on blabbering.

"She don't set the ground right," he said, "and she's got chinks and warped boards. Wind comes whistlin' through them chinks on a cold night, it like to freeze you where you sit."

"Uh-huh."

"Well, Charley's the best carpenter in the county," Lige said. "So we figured to take her over and let him fix her up."

"Seems like a lot of work for you boys. Been easier to've had Charley bring his tools up to your ranch."

"Sure it would. But he's gettin' on in years, and we're askin' a favor, so we come to the notion of bringin' her down to the valley instead."

Conagher nodded and chewed his pipe stem, and I began to have the hope he'd ride on and leave us be. But then he said: "How come you closed off the bottom end?"

"Sheriff?"

"Bottom end there. Closed it off with canvas, didn't you? Canvas over boards, I'd say."

"Well, now," Lige said, and then he just set there, the big jughead, on account of he couldn't think of no good answer.

"Tell you how it looks to me," Conagher said. "Looks like you boys built yourself a big packing case out of your outhouse. Now why would you go and do a thing like that?"

"Sheriff," I said, "it ain't no use tryin' to fool you. Lige and me done closed off that bottom end, right enough, but it wasn't to make a packing case. No, sir. It was something else entire we made outen that outhouse."

"Such as?"

"A coffin. We built us a coffin."

"Coffin?" Conagher frowned and chewed his pipe stem, and then he said: "Who for?"

"Old Bryce. Our hired man."

"Mean to tell me you got *him* inside there?"

"His poor froze-stiff remains, yes, sir. He up and died two nights ago. Had him the ague and it turned into new-monia, and he up and died on us. Man weighed three hundred pounds, if he weighed an ounce . . . you know how big he was, Sheriff. So there we was with a three-hundred pound, six-foot-and-three-inch-high corpse and no way to give him a proper Christian burial."

"How come no way? Ground still froze at your place?"

"Froze hard as stone," I said. "That's one reason we couldn't plant old Bryce. Other one is, we didn't have no wood left to build a coffin. No lumber a-tall. Winter was so long and cold, we run out of stove wood and had to burn up the last of our lumber to keep warm."

"I thought you boys always took pains to provision yourselves against long winters. Got a reputation for laying in plenty of food, plenty of wood."

"That's just what we do, usual, Mister Conagher. But this winter we got caught short. Had us a lean year, last, and the first blizzard took us unawares, and next thing we knowed, we was snowed in. Why, we was just about ready to chop up that there outhouse and burn *it*. Would have if the weather hadn't finally broke. And then old Bryce up and died on us."

"Uh-huh."

"Big and tall as he was, why, he fits inside there just about snug. Couldn't have hammered up a better coffin from scratch. . . ."

"Where you fixing to bury him?"

"Sheriff?"

"Old Bryce in his outhouse coffin. Where you intend to put him down for his final resting place? Town cemetery's in the other direction."

"Yes, sir, that's right, so it is."

"Well?"

Lige had that hot look in his eyes again; he kicked me down low on the shin where Conagher couldn't see. But I wasn't about to just set there like him. I said: "Potter's fishing hole."

"Bury a dead man in a fishing hole?"

"No, sir, not in Potter's hole. Near it. That was old Bryce's favorite spot in all of Montana. He spent every free chance he had down at Potter's fishing hole, and that's a fact."

"Uh-huh."

"Well, right before he croaked on us, he said as how he'd like to be buried down by Potter's fishing hole. Didn't he, Lige?"

Lige had enough sense to nod his head. Scowl on his ugly face said he was of a mind to gnaw my innards the way Conagher was gnawing his pipe stem.

"Can't deny a man his dying wish," I said. "So me and Lige, we pulled the outhouse down and put old Bryce into her and closed off her bottom and now we're headed down to Potter's to find a shady spot to plant 'em both."

"How you figure on doing the planting?"

"Sheriff?"

"I don't see any tools in that wagon bed."

"Tools?"

"No pick, no shovel. Not even a hoe. Was you boys thinking of digging old Bryce's grave with your bare hands?"

"Lordy Lord," Lige said, disgusted, and spat out onto the road. Done it too close to Jingalee; roan horse hopped forward a couple of steps before Lige hauled him down again. When that happened, the outhouse lurched and swayed some—same as my insides was doing right then.

"Well?"

"Well, now, Mister Conagher, sir. . . ."

"Time you untied those ropes," he said.

"Sheriff?"

"You and your brother. Untie those ropes and we'll have a squint inside that outhouse."

"Ain't nothing to see except old Bryce's froze-stiff corpse. . . ."

"Untie, boys. Now."

Wasn't nothing else we could do. Conagher was wearing his official holy terror look now, and his hand was setting on the butt of his Judge Colt. Lige kicked me again, twice, while we was taking off the ropes; I just let him do it.

"Open up that half-moon door, Wes."

I opened it, and Conagher poked around inside. A smile come to his mouth like a hungry wolf with supper waiting. "Well, well," he said. "Sure don't appear to be old Bryce's remains to me. What's all this look like to you, Lige?"

Lige didn't have nothing to say.

"Wes?"

"Well," I said, "I reckon it's jugs."

"Fifty or more, I'd say. Packed inside there nice and tight, with burlap sacking all around. What's in those glass jugs, Wes?"

I sighed. "Corn likker."

"Uh-huh. Corn likker you boys cooked up over the long winter, using up all your stove wood and spare lumber in the process. You and Lige and old Bryce, who's alive and kicking and tending to his chores this very minute. That about the shape of it?"

"Yes, sir. That's about the shape of it."

"And where were you taking all this corn likker? Wouldn't be over to the reservation to sell to some of the feistier Piegans, would it? Even though it's against the law to sell firewater to Indians?"

"No, sir," I said, "that sure wasn't what we had in mind. We was gonna sell it to the ranchers in Antelope Valley. Charley Hammond and Hank Staggs. . . ."

"Charley Hammond don't drink. He's a Hard Shell Baptist, in case you don't remember. And Hank Staggs don't allow liquor of any kind on his property. And Mort Sutherland's got a bad stomach. You figure to sell more'n fifty jugs of corn to Harvey Ames alone? Don't seem likely. Lot more likely you were headed for the reservation, and I reckon the circuit judge'll see it the same when he comes through next week. Meantime, boys, you'll be guests of the county. Close up the evidence and let's get on to town."

We closed her up. Lige said to Conagher: "You knowed, didn't you, Sheriff? Knowed we wasn't taking her to Charley Hammond's, knowed we didn't have old Bryce's remains inside. Knowed all along she was filled up with jugs of corn."

"Well, I had a pretty fair notion."

"How?"

"Funny thing about that outhouse," Conagher said. "When you first rattled to a stop, and again when your horse frog-hopped, I heard noises inside. Good ears is one thing I can brag on, even in cold weather."

"What noises?"

"Sloshing and gurgling. Never yet heard an empty outhouse that sloshed and gurgled. Nor a man's froze-stiff remains that did, either."

Lige punched me in the chest this time. "You and your gol-dang ideas! You ain't got a lick of sense, Wes Hovey! Ain't got the sense God give a one-eyed grasshopper!"

Well, hell, he didn't neither, did he?

CRUCIFIXION RIVER
(with Marcia Muller)

T.J. MURDOCK

Bad storm making up. And moving in much faster than I'd expected.

You could tell it from the bruised look of the southwestern sky, the black-bellied cloud masses, the raw whip of the November wind. Already the muddy brown water of Twelve-Mile Slough—Crucifixion Slough to the locals—had roughened, creating wavelets that broke high against the muddy banks. The ferry barge, halfway across now, rocked and strained against the bridle looped over the taut guide cable. It took nearly all the strength I possessed to keep the windlass turning. If the storm broke with as much fury as I suspected it would, the crossing would be impassable well before nightfall.

The coming blow was a concern in more ways than one. Annabelle should have returned from River Bend an hour or more past. I hadn't wanted her to go at all, but she had convinced Sophie to let her take the buckboard in for supplies. Seventeen now, no longer a child but not yet old enough to find her own way in the world. Headstrong, impulsive, chafing at the isolation of our lives here at the ferry and roadhouse. The trouble in Chicago was too many years ago for her to remember it clearly, and to her there was no longer any danger or any need for hiding. Perhaps she was right. But neither Sophie nor I believed it. Patrick Bellright had a long memory, and his hate for me would surely continue to burn hotly until the last breath left his body.

On the barge, the Fosters were having difficulty with the nervous mare hitched to their farm wagon. Harlan Foster waved an arm, asking me to hurry, but it couldn't be done. The windlass creaked and groaned as it was, and the cable made sounds like a plucked banjo string as the barge inched along. At the rear of the Fosters' wagon Sophie stood spraddle-legged, against the pitch and sway. It was days like this one that I worried most about her assisting with the ferry work. She was as capable as any man, but cables had been known to snap and ferries to capsize, passengers and crew alike to drown. We could not afford to hire a man for the job, and even if we could, I was loath to take the risk of it. We had been safe here for eight years now, but safety is illusory. People are seldom completely safe no matter where they are. And fugitives from a madman

. . . never.

The barge was nearing the Middle Island shore. Sophie signaled and made her way forward to lower the landing apron and attend to the mooring ropes. At her next signal, I locked the windlass and straightened, flexing the aching muscles across my back and shoulders. As Sophie tied the lines and the Fosters led their skittish mare off the barge, I turned to look up along the levee road. It was still empty, although the Sacramento stage was due from River Bend any time. But the stage was not what I was looking for.

What was keeping Annabelle?

Worry, worry. About the girl, about Sophie, about Patrick Bellright, about strangers, about the weather, about a hundred other things day after day. At times it seemed our lives were nothing but a plague of worry, leavened only occasionally by hopes and pleasures. If it weren't for Sophie and Annabelle, and my writing, my life would be intolerably barren.

The wind gusted sharply, shushing in the cattails and blackberry vines and rattling the branches of the willows lining the slough. I could hear the clatter of the loose shingle on the roadhouse roof. I had been meaning to fix that, just one of the many chores that needed doing. The roadhouse, built of weathered boards reinforced with slabs of sheet metal, stood on solid ground and was solid enough itself, but the puncheon floor inside was warped in places and in need of new boards; there was painting to be done, and a new wood stove was fast becoming a necessity. Outside, the short wharf that extended into the brown water tested rickety and at least two of the pilings should be replaced. The livery barn was in good repair, except for the badly hung door and gaps in the south wall boarding. And now winter was nigh. Another rainy season like the last would keep repair work down to the minimum necessary for reasonable comfort and survival.

This California delta, fifty miles inland from San Francisco where the Sacramento and San Joaquin Rivers merged, was a vast network of waterways and islands linked by ferries and a few levee roads. Its rugged beauty and fertile soil drew farmers, ranchers, fishermen, shanty boaters, Chinese laborers, loners, eccentric groups of one type and another—and not a few fleeing from justice or injustice. But it was a harsh land, too, prone to bad weather and winter flooding. As many people as it attracted, it drove out in defeat and despair. The Crucifixion River sect, for one instance.

I shifted my gaze to the southwest, back along the levee road to where the peninsula extended into the broad reach of the Sacramento River. Stands of swamp oak, sycamores, and willows hid what was left of

Crucifixion River, the settlement that had been built along the tip—more than a dozen board-and-batten shacks and a meeting house, crumbling now after seven years of abandoned neglect. The sect's dream of a self-contained Utopian community that embraced religion and free love had died quickly, destroyed by the harsh elements and the continual harassment of intolerant locals. I held no brief for the sect's beliefs, but I understood all too well their desire to be left alone to live their lives in peace, without fear.

I remembered the day they'd arrived from Sacramento, three score men and women and a handful of children in a procession of wagons. Everyone had been singing, their voices raised high and joyous:

> *We shall gather at the ri-ver,*
> *the beautiful, the beautiful ri-i-ver. . . .*

I remembered the day they had left, too, less than two years later. That day there had been no singing. As I ferried them across the slough, the faces aboard the wagons were bleak and stoic against a cold gray sky. I wondered again, as I had many times, what had happened to them, if they'd found their Utopia elsewhere. I hoped they had.

The Fosters and their wagon were off-loaded now and I could see Sophie waving as they clattered up to the Middle Island levee road. She threw off the mooring lines, raised and secured the apron. Even before she signaled, I had bent again to the windlass. The barge would be waiting here on the eastern shore when the stage arrived.

By the time Sophie and I had it moored tightly to the shore, the first drops of rain had begun to fall. The roiling clouds had moved closer, their underbellies black and swollen, and the wind was a howling thing that lashed the slough water to a muddy swirl. The air had an electric quality, sharp with the smell of ozone.

Sophie rubbed a hand across her thin, weathered face. "What's keeping Annabelle? She should have been home long ago."

"Some sort of delay in River Bend," I said. "No cause for concern."

"The storm is almost here."

"If she hasn't left by now, she knows to wait it out in town."

"She won't. She hates River Bend more than she does this place."

"Then she'll be here before the worst of it."

"If she isn't, how will we know she's safe?"

"The stage is due any time. Pete Dell can tell us if he's seen her."

"And if he hasn't? What then?"

We were both thinking the same. River Bend was more than a dozen miles distant and the levee road would soon enough be a quagmire. If the downpour came fast and heavy and lasted long enough, the levees might give way at some point and render it impassable. More than one traveler had been stranded, more than one conveyance swept away in the turbulent waters.

"Thomas . . . maybe I should saddle Jenny and ride in toward town. . . ."

"No. If she's not back soon, I'll go."

There was more rain now, the drops blown, sharp and stinging, by the wind. I took Sophie's arm and hurried us both to the shelter of the roadhouse.

CAROLINE DEVANE

I heard the rain begin when the coach had traveled only a few miles from River Bend. The threatening storm had been a topic of conversation between the driver and station agent in River Bend, but they had decided to continue on schedule in spite of it. I unbuttoned the side curtain to note that the sky was now dark with heavy, gray clouds. It was cold and damp in the coach. Perhaps we should have remained in town.

When I rebuttoned the curtain, I saw the young man and woman on the seat opposite me looking at each other, their eyes full of concern. "What if the storm prevents us from crossing to Middle Island?" she asked him in a voice barely above a whisper.

"We'll get across." His tone wasn't reassuring, however. He was as tense as the woman, who had clasped her gloved fingers together and held her hands under her chin in an attitude of prayer.

"I wish we could have taken the steamer," she told him.

"You know why we couldn't."

They both lapsed into silence as the wind and rain buffeted the coach, causing it to rock heavily in its thoroughbraces. The storm was now full-born.

I felt some unease myself. Clinging Carrie, my brothers and sisters had called me as a child. But as an adult woman I had sinned, suffered, and lost so much that it would take far more than a storm to unnerve me.

Time passed slowly, it seemed. It was impossible to read or crochet in the jolting coach, so I studied the man and woman on the opposite seat. He was handsome in a raw-boned, strong-featured way; locks of brown hair that matched his mustache crept out from under his hat. She might have been beautiful, with her upswept auburn hair and large blue eyes and full lips, but her face showed lines of strain and dark circles underscored the eyes' loveliness. She had a prosperous look while her companion, although dressed well enough, had the weathered features and work-roughened hands of a ranch hand.

When they'd boarded the coach at the delta town of Isleton, I'd been disappointed that I was to have companions. I had taken the stage from Sacramento, rather than the river steamer, because I wished to be alone. I was starting a new life, and I needed time to prepare myself.

I had overcome my unhappiness at their presence, however, and introduced myself. After some hesitation the woman had said that her name was Rachel Kraft. "And this is my . . . cousin, Mister Hoover."

That hesitation in Rachel Kraft's voice had told me a great deal: the man was not her cousin. But what affair was that of mine? We were merely fellow passengers.

I closed my eyes, trying to picture the ranch in San Joaquin County where my sister Mary lived with her husband and seven children. Mine would be a Spartan existence there, filled with hard work very different from the comfortable life I had enjoyed in Sacramento. But that life with my husband John and my two sons was over now; I was being thrust into exile. I knew neither Mary nor her husband Benjamin wanted me. They were only offering me shelter because I had nowhere else to go.

Fallen woman, divorced woman, shunned woman. Woman deprived of her children. Who would want such a creature?

Hugh had, in the beginning. Hugh Branson, the lover I'd taken in my unhappiness, and cherished, and eventually found wanting. After my husband discovered our affair, the fabric of my life was torn asunder. My children were taken from me in the divorce proceedings, my former friends and acquaintances turned their backs to me, and Hugh—I'd lost Hugh as well. I'd tried to find work—I had some medical training—but word of my transgression had spread and no respectable physician or nurses' service would have me. Life in Sacramento became unbearable. The only solution was to leave. . . .

The coach lurched and slid on the levee road, which by now must have been slicked with mud. Rachel Kraft cried out and clasped her companion's arm. The driver shouted to the horses, a sound barely audible above the voice of the wind, and the stage steadied. Mr. Hoover patted Rachel Kraft's hand and said: "Don't fret. We'll be all right."

"If there's an accident. . . ."

"There won't be an accident."

"The storm's getting worse. What if we can't cross on the ferry . . . ?"

"Hush up." It was a command, not a soothing phrase.

The coach lurched once more, and Rachel Kraft stifled a cry. Her companion comforted her as he had before, then cast an oddly guilty glance at me. There was something wrong with the pair, I thought. She panicked at the slightest provocation, and he wavered between solicitousness and tense distraction.

I closed my eyes again. My fellow passengers' troubles were of no concern to me, as mine were of no concern to them. Except for their sake and that of the driver, I would not have cared if we were cast into the slough and drowned.

Fallen woman, divorced woman, shunned woman. Woman deprived of her children.

It would have been a fitting fate.

JAMES SHOCK

An hour after I was ejected from River Bend, the skies opened wide and it began to rain like billy-be-damned. Well, it had been that type of day. A slip of the hand, an angry citizen crying,"Cheat!", a hard-hearted sheriff, and here I was, out on the lonely road again in the midst of a storm. Instead of a dry livery and a warm meal in that swamp town's only eating house, Nell and I were forced to weather the weather, as it were—where and under what precarious conditions we'd yet to find out. Pity the poor traveling merchant!

The rain came busting down in side-slanting sheets, finding its way inside my slicker and chilling me to the marrow. Late afternoon and the sky was black as sin and the daylight all but blotted out by the deluge. The wagon lurched as Nell slogged on. Careful driving from now on, I reminded myself, to forestall an accidental plunge down the embankment to certain death. On both sides of the levee road, slough water boiled and bubbled up over the banks like soup in a witches' cauldron. If the storm grew much worse, the road would be swamped. It wouldn't do to be stranded out here at the mercy of the elements.

My luck had been running fine until River Bend and the sharp-eyed citizen and that hard-nosed sheriff. There were store boats plying this delta country, but not so many that a wagon seller couldn't make a decent living for himself. Farmers and their wives in need of clasp knives and pocket watches, writing paper and bottles of ink, saddle blankets, good maguey rope, bottles of liniment and cough syrup and female complaint medicine, needles and thread, pots and pans, spices and seasonings, yards of calico and gingham. Town citizens, too, eager to buy when their local mercantiles ran out of the goods I carried in this old red and green, slab-sided wagon with the fresh-painted words on each side:

James Shock—Fine Wares, Patent Medicines,
Knives Sharpened Free of Charge

And here and there, now and then, a few dollars to be promoted by other means. Yes, and a lonely wife or a comely young miss with a yearning for sachets and perfumes and silver Indian jewelry, and an eye for a bold young banjo-strumming traveling man.

Oh, it was a good life most of the time. Freedom. New places and new sights, and seldom the same ones twice. Even a touch of danger, and not only from the elements. For an itinerant merchant was prey to thieves who sought his money and penniless scoundrels who attempted to pilfer his wares. Not that any of them had ever succeeded in relieving Ben Shock's son of what belonged to him, no siree. The nickel-plated revolver I carried under my coat, and the Greener loaded with shells of ounce-and-a-half shot beneath the wagon seat, had seen their share of action since I inherited the wagon from my old man six years ago. And would again, I had no doubt.

The wagon bucked and skidded again, and I drew hard on the reins and braced myself on the rain-slick seat. "Steady, Nell!" I called out to the old dappled gray. She'd been a fine horse in her day, but that day was nearly past. I would have to replace her soon, before she fell over dead in the trace—as the old man had fallen over dead while mixing up a batch of worm medicine that afternoon in Carson City. It was a sad thing to watch animals and folks grow old. I was glad to be young and hale. Yes, and, if I had my druthers, that was how I would die.

But not today, and not from the fury of a gullywasher.

I seemed to recall a roadhouse and a ferry crossing somewhere along this road. But how much distance away escaped my memory. Not too far, else the Sacramento stage would have remained in River Bend instead of pulling out shortly before my own departure. Even now, it couldn't be more than half an hour ahead.

The wind blew up stronger, lashed my face with stinging wet. I ducked my head and wiped my cheeks. Smooth, hairless cheeks they were—I'd yet to need to shave them more than once a week. Baby face. More times than I could count I'd been referred to by that name, and pleased to hear it. A baby face was an asset in both business and romance. Many a customer and many a lass had succumbed to my looks and the shy manner I had learned to adopt.

Thought of lasses past and lasses to come brought a smile and a brightening of my mood. Naturally optimistic fellow, that's me, always looking on the bright side. Survival was a given in any troublesome situation, after all, and this one no different than any other. A minor setback in River Bend, a minor setback on the open road. Never fear! Providence had served me well and would continue to do so.

And it did, not more than twenty minutes later.

By then the downpour was torrential. I could scarcely see more than a few rods past the mare's nose and the road was nearly awash. The wagon slewed around a bend in the road, and there, by grab, was salvation dead ahead.

Roadhouse, livery barn, ferry barge. And beyond the wide slough, all but hidden now by rain and misty cloud, a continuation of the road that would lead, eventually, to Stockton and points south. Ah, but not this night. Not for Nell and me, and not for the driver and passengers in the Concord coach drawn up before the roadhouse. There would be no crossings until the frenzy of the storm abated and the slough waters calmed. I had been on enough delta ferries to determine that from the look of the wind-lashed slough waters and the cable strung above them.

Well, no matter. Sanctuary from the storm was the important thing— a dry stall and hay for Nell, a warm fire and hot food for Ben Shock's son. Heigh-ho! There might even be a dollar or three to be made from the ferryman's family and the stage passengers.

ANNABELLE MURDOCK

I leaned against the buckboard, blinking away angry tears and saying words no young lady should utter.

Lady? I thought bitterly. When had I had an opportunity to learn and polish lady-like skills in this god-forsaken delta? Now it might even be the death of me. At seventeen, before I'd ever have the chance to experience all the good things life had to offer in such places as San Francisco.

I'd tarried late at the River Bend general store, lingering over fancy dress fabrics that I couldn't buy and might never wear, reluctant as always to return to Crucifixion Crossing. The storm had come more quickly than anybody'd expected, and by the time I left town, the rain had started. Now it was pouring down something fierce. And as if that wasn't bad enough, a few minutes ago the front wheel hub had loosened and then jammed and the wheel had nearly come off. The spindle nut was jammed so tightly I couldn't loosen it with the wrench from the toolbox. If no one came along soon, I'd have no choice but to walk home— more than five miles, with the storm worsening by the minute.

I raised my arms to the sky and shouted: "I hate it here! I hate my life!" Maudie, our tired old bay mare, turned her wet head and gave me a sorrowful look. "I hate you, too!" I yelled at her. And then I burst out crying.

I was still sobbing, beating on the nut with the wrench like a demented person, when the man on horseback appeared around the bend behind me. Rescued! I was never so glad to see anybody in my life, even if he was a complete stranger.

He reined up and called out: "Miss? Are you all right?"

"Yes. It's the wheel." I banged on the hub again. "I can't get the spindle nut free to tighten it."

"Let me see what I can do." Quickly he dismounted and came up next to me to have a look. "If you'll let me have that wrench, I think I can do the job."

And he did. In less than ten minutes he had the nut tight again so the wheel no longer wobbled. I smiled at him, my best smile. He was a good-looking man with a bushy mustache and bright blue eyes. And he had nice manners, almost courtly. Old, though. Older than Dad. He must have been at least forty. His name, he said, was Boone Nesbitt.

I told him mine and said: "I can't thank you enough for your help, Mister Nesbitt."

"My pleasure. We're both heading in the same direction, Miss Murdock. Would you mind if I rode along with you? That wheel should hold, but in this weather. . . ."

"I'd be grateful if you would."

He tied his piebald horse to the buckboard and climbed up next to me on the seat. I let him take the reins. Usually I can do anything a man can, even work the ferry winch, but I was wet and miserable, and if he wanted to drive, I was more than willing to let him.

"You live at Twelve-Mile Slough, is that right?" he asked after we were under way.

"How'd you know?"

"The storekeeper in River Bend. He's a talkative gent."

"What else did he tell you?"

"That your father is ferrymaster there. T.J. Murdock."

"That's right."

"The same T.J. Murdock who writes sketches and articles for San Francisco newspapers and magazines?"

"You mean you've read some of them?" I was surprised. My father's little pieces didn't pay very much or bring much attention, but he enjoyed writing them. More than I enjoyed reading them, although I pretended to him that I thought they were wonderful.

"Several," Mr. Nesbitt said. "I remember one in particular, about the religious community that once established itself nearby. Crucifixion River, it was called."

"Yes. People around here call our crossing Crucifixion instead of Twelve-Mile, and I wish they didn't."

"Why is that?"

"We never had anything to do with those people. And now that they're long gone . . . it's really a hateful place."

"Their settlement, you mean?"

"Ghost camp. No one goes there any more."

"How long have you and your family operated the ferry?"

"Oh . . . a long time. I was a little girl when we came to the delta."

"Came from where?"

I remembered Dad's warning about saying too much to anyone about our past. "*Um* . . . Kansas."

"Do you like it here, Miss Murdock?"

"No, I hate it."

"Why is that?"

"I have no friends and there's nothing to do except help with the ferry and read and sew and do chores."

"No school chums?"

"The nearest good school is in Isleton. My mother schooled me at home, but that's done now. I'm grown up. And before long I'm going away to where there are people, gaiety, excitement."

"And where would that be?"

"San Francisco, to begin with."

"I live in San Francisco," he said.

"Do you? Truly? What's it like there?"

"Not as wonderful as you might think."

Well, I didn't believe that. He was old, so his view of the city was bound to be different from mine. "I'll find out for myself one day soon," I said. "Where are you bound, Mister Nesbitt? Stockton?"

"No. Not that far."

"Are you a drummer?"

He laughed, guiding Maudie through a potholed section of the levee road. The rain was really coming down now and I was soaked to the skin. I wondered if I'd ever be warm again.

"No. I have business in the area."

"What kind of business, if you don't mind my asking?"

"I'd rather not say. It's of a personal nature."

"Well, I'm glad you came along when you did. I was just about to start walking and that can be more dangerous than riding. If there's a break in one of the levees . . . but there won't be, not unless the storm gets really bad. The only thing is, I don't think Dad will be able to operate the ferry . . . probably not until morning. You'll have to spend the night with us, Mister Nesbitt. I hope you won't mind."

"No, I won't mind," he said, solemn now for some reason. "I won't mind at all."

JOE HOOVER

When Rachel found it was storming too hard for the ferry to run, I had a hell of a time keeping her calmed down. The ferryman, Murdock, and the stage driver were huddled up under the front overhang of the roadhouse and the Devane woman had gone inside with Mrs. Murdock. Rachel wanted to get out of the coach, but I wouldn't let her do it yet. I was afraid she'd do something wild, maybe go running off like a spooked horse, if I didn't keep her close.

"We can't stay here tonight, Joe. We can't . . . we can't!"

"Nothing else we can do. Keep your head, for God's sake."

"He'll find us. He's out looking by now, you know he is. . . ."

"He won't find us."

"He will. You don't know Luke like I do. It's bad enough for his woman to run off, but the money. . . ."

"Keep still about the money." I could feel the weight of it in the buckskin pouch at my belt—more than $3,000 in greenbacks and gold specie. More money than I'd ever seen or was likely to see in my life. It scared me to have it, but what scared me more was wanting to keep it.

"I shouldn't have taken it," Rachel said.

"No, you shouldn't. If I'd known what you were going to do. . . ."

"I didn't plan it, I just . . . did it, that's all. We wouldn't get far without money and you don't have any of your own."

"Don't throw that in my face. Can I help it if I'm nothing more than a cowhand?"

"I didn't mean it that way, I just meant . . . oh, God, I don't know what I meant. I'm scared, Joe."

"Hold onto your nerve. We'll be all right."

"If he finds us, he'll kill us."

I didn't say anything.

"We shouldn't have left the horses in Isleton, taken the stage. If we'd kept riding, we'd be on Middle Island by now, we'd be on the steamer to San Francisco. . . ."

She broke off, gasping, as the stage door popped open. It was only Murdock. Rachel twisted away from me, but if Murdock noticed how closely we'd been sitting, he didn't let on. All he said was: "Better come inside, folks."

Rachel said with the scare plain in her voice: "Isn't there any way we can cross? If there's a lull . . . ?"

"I'm afraid not. If it keeps storming this hard, you'll likely have to spend the night here."

To stop her from saying anything more, I crowded her off the seat. Murdock helped her down. She let out a little cry when he took her arm—he must've grabbed hold in one of the places she was bruised.

The stage driver called out: "Somebody coming, Murdock!"

He wheeled around. I was out of the coach by then and I peered up at the levee road. It was like trying to look through a thick silver curtain, but I could make out the shape of a big slab-sided wagon with a single horse in the trace.

"That's not Annabelle," Murdock said. He sounded worried.

"Peddler's wagon, looks like," the stage driver said.

I quit paying attention. If Luke Kraft showed, it'd be on horseback, not in a wagon. And if he did come, what then? I guessed I'd find out how much I cared for Rachel and how much I wanted that $3,000—and what kind of man I was when push came to shove.

I took Rachel's arm and we ran across to the roadhouse. It was only a few yards but we were both wet when we got inside. Worst storm I'd seen since I drifted up to the delta from Stockton three years ago. And it couldn't've come at a worse time.

I kept thinking we should've waited, made a plan, instead of running off the way we had. But Rachel couldn't stand any more of Kraft's abuse, and truth was, I hadn't been so sure I'd go through with it if we didn't do it right away. I loved her, right enough, but Luke Kraft was the man I worked for, an important man in this country—big ranch, plenty of influence—and he had a mean streak in him wide as a mother lode. He'd come after us surely, or hire men to do it. Crazy to get myself jammed up this way over a woman. Only I couldn't help it. Once I saw those bruises, once she let me do more than look at them on her body, I was a goner. And now I was in too deep to back out even if I was of a mind to.

We stood just inside the door, dripping. The common room was big and warm, storm shutters up across its front windows. There was a food and liquor buffet on one side, a long trestle table and chairs on the other, and some pieces of horsehide furniture grouped in front of the blaze in a big stone fireplace. There wouldn't be more than a couple of guest bedrooms in back, and those for the women, so this was likely where we'd ride out the storm. Well, I'd spent nights in worse places in my twenty-four years.

The room's heat felt good after the long, cold stage ride. Murdock's wife fetched us towels and mugs of hot coffee. The Devane woman was sitting in one of the chairs, drying herself. I got Rachel down in the chair next to her, close to the fire. She still moved stiffly, sore from Kraft's last beating, and the other two women noticed it. I could see them wondering. The Devane woman had figured out Rachel and me were more than cousins— I'd seen it in her face on the stage. The look she gave me now was sharp enough to cut a fence post in two. I tried to tell her with my eyes and face that she was slicing up the wrong man, but she looked the other way. *Troubles of her own, that one*, I thought.

She wasn't the only one. Mrs. Murdock came in, crossed to the window next to the door, pulled the muslin aside, and looked out. The tight set of her face said she was fretting about something, but it wasn't the same kind of scare that was in Rachel.

Nobody had much to say until the door opened a few minutes later and the wind blew Murdock in. With him was a tall, smiley bird in a black slicker. When he unbuttoned it, I saw that he had a banjo slung underneath. That didn't make me like him any better. If there's one thing I can't abide, it's banjo playing.

Mrs. Murdock had come hurrying over. "Thomas. . . ."

"It's all right," he said. "She's coming. I just spied the wagon."

"Oh, thank God!"

"Our daughter," Murdock said to the rest of us. "Late getting back from River Bend."

His wife threw on oilskins and the two of them hurried out into the storm. The smiley bird moved over by the fire. He had a rake's eye for a pretty face and a well-turned ankle—I could see that in the bold way he sized up Rachel and the Devane woman. I didn't like the way he looked at Rachel. Hell, I hadn't liked the look of him the second I laid eyes on him.

He introduced himself in an oily voice. "James Shock. Fine wares, patent medicines, knives sharpened free of charge."

"Peddler," I said.

"Traveling merchant, brother, if you don't mind. At your service, Mister . . . ?"

"Hoover. Save your pitch. I'm not buying."

"Perhaps one of the ladies . . . ?"

Neither Rachel nor the Devane woman paid him any attention. He shrugged, still smiley. I could feel the weight of that money as I sat down next to Rachel. She laid her hand on my arm and I let her keep it there; the hell with what any of the others thought.

Outside, the wind yammered and rattled boards and metal and whistled in the chimney flue. The rain on the roof made a continuous thundering sound, like a train in a tunnel. I didn't mind it so much now. I figured the longer it kept up like that, the safer we were. Not even that son of a bitch, Luke Kraft, was going anywhere far in a storm like this one.

RACHEL KRAFT

There was a hot fire in the fireplace, but I couldn't get warm. My teeth chattered and I shivered and clutched Joe's arm tighter. Mrs. Murdock had brought a mug of coffee, but there was a roiling in the pit of my stomach that wouldn't permit me to drink it.

The common room was well lighted by oil lamps and candles in wall sconces, but it still seemed full of shadows. Puffs of ash drifted out of the fireplace whenever the wind blew down its chimney. After my outburst to Joe when we arrived, I could barely speak; my throat felt as if it were rusted. I looked around, wishing we were somewhere else far away and wondered what I had gotten myself into. Then I fingered the bruise on my collar bone, another on my arm, and reminded myself of what I was getting *out* of.

I didn't like the way that peddler, Shock, was looking at me, a bold stare that made me feel as though he were picturing what I looked like without my clothing. But then, he was looking at Caroline Devane in the same way. I dismissed him as the type of conceited man who viewed women—all women—as potential conquests.

Outside the wind howled, and from somewhere close by I heard a dripping sound. Probably the roof of this ramshackle old building leaked. Now that we were inside I didn't mind the storm so much, because I hoped—prayed to God—that if Luke was already looking for us, the weather would force him to take shelter, keep him away from here until we could cross to Middle Island. But by now Luke would have discovered that the $3,000 was gone, and, if there was anything that angered him and made him determined to exact revenge, it was having his possessions taken from him. His money and his wife—in that order.

I shifted a little on the chair, and the pain in my ribs made me wince. Out of the corner of my eye I saw that Caroline Devane had noticed. She had a keen eye, had seen that I moved stiffly, and guessed the truth. She'd been giving Joe hard looks, and I wanted to cry out that it wasn't him, it was cold, hard, unyielding Luke Kraft, and if he found us, he would kill us.

Luke. My husband. A monster. Sweet before and after our marriage until two years had passed and I'd produced no son for him. No daughter, either, but that didn't matter. Big Luke Kraft, lord of 2,000 acres of prime delta ranch land, had an infertile wife and no son to inherit his empire.

And in his anger he beat me, once broke my arm, another time tore out a patch of my hair and laughed about it, saying that it was just like scalping a damned Indian.

Thinking of him made me shiver again. Joe didn't notice. He kept his eyes on the fire, thinking Lord knew what. I knew he was angry with me for stealing Luke's money, but I also sensed that he wanted those $3,000. More than he wanted me? Oh, God, not more than me! *Remain calm, Rachel. That's what Joe's always telling you. Remain calm.*

I glanced at him. In profile, he looked strong, his jaw set, his eyes focused. A man who had battled the elements working cattle ranches in Montana before he came to California. A man who was everything Luke was not—strong, gentle, kind. And unafraid of the storm raging outside.

But was he unafraid of the man whose wife he'd run off with? Would he stand up to Luke if he found us?

Of course he would. He loved me. Or kept telling me he did. But did I love him? Or was I with him only because he was my way out of an intolerable situation?

Well, I hadn't had any choice, had I? In time Luke would have killed me, I was sure of that. I couldn't leave by myself, a woman alone with nothing and no one to rely on for protection. I'd been so sheltered as a child in Isleton, and then so isolated on Luke's big ranch, that I knew very little of the world beyond its borders.

The wind gusted, rattling what were probably loose shingles on the roof. With it came another battering downpour and a clap of thunder.

Joe gently removed my hand from his arm, favored me with one of his reassuring smiles, and stood. He moved to the buffet, poured himself a small glass of whiskey, and went to sit alone at the long trestle table.

Dear God, what if he was tiring of me? He'd been so angry with my nervous babbling when we'd first arrived here. "Keep still about the money," he'd told me. *Keep still.* He'd never spoken to me that harshly before.

The door opened, and Sophie Murdock and a young girl of perhaps seventeen wearing mud-spattered oilskins came inside. This must be the daughter she'd been so worried about. Mrs. Murdock clucked over her like a mother hen, helped her out of the sodden rain gear, and then bustled her through the common room to the rear. I felt the dampness on the hem of my traveling skirt, and again I shivered in spite of the stove's heat.

Caroline Devane touched my arm. "There's nothing to be concerned about," she said. "By tomorrow morning we'll be on our way."

"I wish I could believe that."

"What on earth would stop us?"

"That there's nothing to be concerned about, I meant."

After a pause the Devane woman said: "Please don't mind my saying this, but I have the feeling you're fleeing from something. You and your . . . cousin. If you'd care to confide in me. . . ."

". . . I can't."

"Perhaps you wouldn't be so frightened if you did."

I've been afraid for years. Sometimes I think I'll always be afraid.

Caroline Devane put her hand on mine. Normally I don't like to be touched by strangers, but this time I didn't pull away. "We share a common bond," she said softly. "I'm running away, too, you see."

Her words surprised me. There was a quiet strength about her; she didn't seem the type to run from anything.

"Sometimes, Miss Kraft, sharing one's troubles can be a comfort to both parties."

"It's Missus Kraft," I said, and watched knowledge mixed with sorrow come into her eyes. Perhaps her troubles and mine were not so different. Perhaps we did have a common bond, that of sisters who had been badly used by the men they thought they could trust.

BOONE NESBITT

After Murdock's wife took young Annabelle inside the roadhouse, he thanked me again for helping her. I said the pleasure was all mine, and it was true in more than one sense. What she'd told me on the way confirmed my suspicions. Now it was time to prod Murdock and gauge his reaction.

When he offered to put my horse up in the barn, I said: "I'll come along and give you a hand."

"Lot drier and warmer inside, Mister Nesbitt."

"I don't mind helping out."

"Suit yourself."

He climbed up on the buckboard seat and I followed along on foot, leading the piebald I'd hired in Sacramento. Stage or steamer passage would have been more comfortable, but I prefer my own company in situations such as this. There'd be plenty of time for comfort and pleasure later on.

Thunder rumbled, loud, and jagged forks of lightning seemed to split the black sky in two. The time was not much past 4:00 p.m., but daylight was already gone and the wind-whipped rain seemed thick as gumbo. If it weren't for the lightning flares, I wouldn't have been able to see the barn until we were right up to it.

Murdock jumped down, and I helped him get the doors propped open. A pair of hurricane lanterns flickered inside, throwing light and shadow across the Concord coach and the slab-sided peddler's wagon that took up much of the runway between the stalls. There was just enough room for the buckboard. Once he'd drawn it inside, it took both of us to drive the doors shut against the force of the storm.

Cold and damp inside, the combined smells of manure, hay, harness leather, wet animals were strong enough to make a man breathe through his mouth. A bearded oldster was busy unharnessing the stage team, putting the horses into the stalls. He paused long enough to say: "Pete Dell. Wells Fargo driver."

"Boone Nesbitt," I said.

Dell eyed my horse. "Foul weather to be out on horseback."

"That it is."

He shrugged and went on about his business. Murdock began unharnessing the wagon horse. I took my saddlebags off the piebald first, then I removed bridle and bit, uncinched the saddle, and rubbed down the horse with a burlap sack.

Murdock said conversationally: "Don't recall seeing you before, Mister Nesbitt."

"That's because I've never been in the delta before."

"You're seeing it at its worst. It's a good place to live and work most of the year."

"I prefer cities. San Francisco."

"Is that where you're from?"

"No. It's my home at present, but I'm a native of Chicago."

Murdock stiffened. His hand froze on the bay mare's halter.

"Fine city, Chicago. You ever been there, Mister Murdock?"

"No," he said. He finished unharnessing the bay without looking at me, led it into one of the remaining stalls. I ambled over next to Murdock as he measured out a portion of oats. Pete Dell was out of earshot, with the rain beating hard against the roof and walls, but I kept my voice low anyhow.

"Your daughter told me you're the T.J. Murdock who writes sketches for the San Francisco periodicals."

The look he gave me had a mask on it. "Now and then. A hobby."

"I've read some of them. Reminiscent of Ambrose Bierce, but with a distinctive style all your own. Very distinctive, as a matter of fact."

"If you think so, I'm flattered."

"The one in the *Argonaut* about the Crucifixion River sect was particularly good."

"That was several years ago," Murdock said warily.

"Yes, I know. I looked it up after I'd read some of your more recent sketches. You wrote it from first-hand knowledge, I understand."

"That's right. The sect established itself on the peninsula southwest of here."

"Buildings still standing?"

"Mostly."

"Ghosts. The past is full of them."

He had nothing to say to that.

"Funny thing," I said, "how the past can haunt the present. I wonder if the sect members are haunted by their failure here."

"I wouldn't know."

"I'll wager some of them are. Some folks just can't escape their past failures. Or their past sins."

A muscle jumped along his jaw. He seemed about to say something, changed his mind. The mask was back in place, tight as ever. He finished rubbing down the roan, slung a blanket over the animal, and called to Pete Dell: "Going inside now, Pete! Come on in for some hot grub when you're finished."

"I'll be there. Pour me a whiskey to go with it."

"Done. You planning to spend the night in the common room or out here?"

"Out here. Prefer my own company at night, you know that."

"It'll be pretty cold and damp. This barn's drafty."

"Warm enough for me inside the coach."

"Suit yourself." Murdock started toward the doors, glanced back at me long enough to say: "You coming, Mister Nesbitt?"

"Right behind you."

He went on with his shoulders squared, slipped out through one door half, closed it after I followed, and set off in hard strides to the roadhouse. Walking, not running. He was through running, one way or another—we both knew that now.

T.J. Murdock? Not by a damned sight. His true name was Harold P. Baxter and he was a native of Chicago, same as I was. And after eight years, purely by chance, I was the man who'd found him, I was the man who stood to collect the private reward of $10,000 on his head.

ANNABELLE MURDOCK

The common room had never seemed so alive! Two women sitting by the fire, a good-looking man with a banjo slung over his shoulder helping himself at the buffet, another fellow drinking whiskey at the table, and

Mr. Nesbitt and my father and Pete Dell yet to join us. Everyone was subdued by the storm, but as glad to be out of it as I was. This much company was a rare treat; we seldom had more than two or three guests. There were only two guest bedrooms, for ladies only if the company was mixed, and it was seldom that both were occupied for a night.

I'd changed clothes in my bedroom and dried my hair as best I could. Dratted hair—when wet and damp, it curled and tangled and looked like a mare's nest. Yet another reason I hated this backcountry. At least my dress was pretty; I'd put on the blue gingham with the lace collar for our company.

I looked around at the stranded travelers. The women by the fire had their heads together in earnest conversation—stage passengers, surely. The man drinking whiskey at the table looked to be a farm or ranch worker dressed up in his Sunday best. The other man at the buffet, the one with the banjo, had his back to me, but I'd gotten a close look at him when I came in. My, he was handsome in his brown butternut suit. And much nearer to my age than Mr. Nesbitt. Mother came out and placed a basket of fresh-baked bread beside him, and he smiled and nodded his thanks before she returned to the kitchen.

The door opened and Dad came in. His face was tightened up like it got when he'd fought with me or Mother, and he moved in an odd, jerky way. He didn't even look at me as he shucked out of his oilskins and then walked through the room toward the kitchen. It made me cross. I hate to be ignored, and it was particularly annoying after the soaking I'd gotten and the wheel almost coming off the buckboard. Then Mr. Nesbitt came in, and *he* nodded to me as he took off his wet slicker.

I went to the buffet for coffee, and greeted the man with the banjo. Oh, yes, he truly was good-looking—slender, with chestnut brown hair and a nice smile and a rakish gleam in his eyes. And tall—I had to tilt my head to look up at him. I like tall men, probably because I'm short and a man half a head taller makes me feel protected.

He said, smiling: "You must be Miss Murdock."

"Yes. My name is Annabelle."

"James Shock, traveling merchant, at your service."

"Oh, is that right? Where's your wagon?"

"Safe in the barn. It contains all manner of fine merchandise, for ladies as well as men." He raised one eyebrow questioningly.

"Are you trying to sell me something, Mister Shock?"

"An attractive young woman like yourself can always use a new hat, a hair ribbon, sachets, perfume, a bolt of good cloth."

"I've no money for such things . . . not that I wouldn't love to have them."

"My prices are more reasonable than any in town stores."

"They could cost a penny each and I couldn't buy them."

"That's a shame. It truly is."

"I think so, too. May I ask how long you've been a peddler?"

"Traveling merchant, if you please. All my life. My father was in the trade before me and I learned it at his side."

"You must have seen a lot of different places."

"I have, indeed. Traveled far and wide throughout the West."

"Is that so? Have you been to San Francisco?"

"Ah, yes. Many times. I expect I'll be paying another visit before long."

"It's wonderful, isn't it? A wonderful, exciting city."

"That it is, if you know it well. And I do. You've never been there yourself?"

"No, never. The only city I've ever been to is Sacramento, with my folks." I heard myself sigh. "I'd give anything to live in San Francisco. And to visit all the other places you've seen."

He smiled more widely, showing even white teeth. "Why don't you, then?"

"I'm too young. My folks say I am anyway."

"Young, mayhap, but a woman nonetheless. A beautiful young woman."

Well, I couldn't help smiling and preening a little at such flattery. *Lovely woman. Beautiful young woman.* Mr. James Shock was a charmer, he truly was. And so easy to talk to, and to look at. The more I looked into those eyes of his, the more tingly I felt. Why, he all but gave me goosebumps.

"Tell me about your travels," I said. "Tell me about San Francisco."

"With pleasure, Annabelle. I may call you Annabelle?"

"Please do."

"And you'll call me by my given name, if you please. James . . . never Jim."

I laughed. "Will you play a song for me on your banjo, Mister James Never Jim Shock?"

He laughed, too. "That I will," he said. "As many as you like."

"Do you know 'Little Brown Jug'?"

"One of my favorite tunes." He caressed me with his eyes and I felt the goosebumps rise again. "I can see that we're going to be good friends, Annabelle. Yes, indeed. Very good friends."

T.J. MURDOCK

Supper was later than usual because of all the extra mouths to feed. After I finished eating, I donned my slicker and went outside to check on the ferry lashings and the cable. The driving rain had let up some, but the wind remained strong. I had to push my way through it, bent forward at the waist, as if it were something semi-solid.

I thought Boone Nesbitt might follow me, but he didn't. All through the meal I'd felt his eyes on me, dark and implacable in a pokerface. He hadn't said a word to me since the barn, and none to any of the others except for a brief response when someone addressed him directly. I had also remained silent. As had the other stranded travelers, except for the banjo-strumming peddler, Shock, who had kept up a running sales pitch for his various wares and told stories that Annabelle, if no one else, seemed to find entertaining. There was a lost quality to Caroline Devane, a strained tension in Joe Hoover and his companion that seemed more a product of private troubles than the pounding storm. But no one was as tautly wound as I, nor as troubled.

Nesbitt knew my real identity, there was little doubt of that from his questions and comments in the barn. A stranger from San Francisco by way of Sacramento, alone on horseback . . . come upon me so suddenly that I could scarcely think straight. Who was he? What was his game, with his sly talk and watchful eyes? Waiting for the storm to abate, likely, to make his intentions known to me. We both knew there was no escape while the storm raged, and none afterward because of Sophie and Annabelle.

How had he found me, after eight long years? My sketches in the *Argonaut*, *The Overland Monthly*, and other San Francisco publications? He had made a deliberate point of mentioning them and my distinctive writing style. I'd been a fool to submit my writings for publication, even under the Murdock name and in a city far from Chicago. But a writer such as I was and had been for the Chicago *Sentinel* is one who yearns not for fame or money, but to have his words, ideas, insights read by others. And the pittances I was paid augmented the pittance I earned as a ferrymaster, allowing us what few small luxuries we could afford.

I didn't know what to do about Nesbitt. What could I do? Even if it weren't for my family, I would not have run again. The flight from Chicago in 1887, the years of hardship since, were all of a fugitive's life I could bear. If Nesbitt was bent on taking me back to face Patrick Bellright, there seemed little choice but to submit. If he was an assassin hired to finish me here, I would try to defend myself, but I would not take action against him first. I could not premeditate the destruction of a human life, even to save my own. It simply was not in me.

The ferry barge was secure, the cable whipped taut and singing in the wind but showing no indication that it might snap. Crucifixion Slough was a cauldron, frothing near to the tops of the embankments on both shores, inundating the cat-tails and blackberry shrubs that grew on this side. The levee road, as far as I could tell in the darkness, had not been breached close by, but if the storm's fury continued long enough, there were bound to be breaks between here and River Bend and over on the Middle Island roads. In any case, it would be long hours through the night and perhaps into the morning before the ferry could be operated— long, difficult hours of waiting for Nesbitt to reveal himself.

I started back to the house, the wind's might behind me now and forcing me into a lope. Before I got there, however, a pair of shapes materialized, suddenly and astonishingly, on the levee road above. Horse and rider, coming as fast as could be managed through the downpour. I stopped and rubbed wet out of my eyes, blinking. It was no trick of night vision. When the rider reached the muddy embankment lane, he swung in and slid his mount down and across the yard.

He drew rein when he spied me, veered over to where I stood, and dismounted. He wore a heavy poncho and a scarf-tied hat that rendered his face all but invisible. All I could tell about him was that he was big and that his voice was rough-toned, thickened by liquor and an emotion I took to be anger.

"My Lord, what are you doing out on such a night?"

He ignored the question. "Who're you?" he demanded.

"T.J. Murdock, ferrymaster here."

"My name's Kraft. Afternoon stage comes this way, bound for Stockton. You ferry it across before the storm broke?"

"No, it arrived too late for safe passage."

He made a hard, grunting sound. "Passengers still here, then?"

"Yes. Until morning likely."

"Rachel Kraft one of them? Woman, twenty-eight, roan-color hair braided and rolled, pretty face?"

"Yes."

"And a man with short, curly hair and a thick mustache?"

"He's here, too, yes. Is Rachel Kraft related to you?"

"Damn right she is . . . my wife. Where are they?"

"Inside with the others. Mister Kraft, why . . . ?"

He wheeled the horse, spurred it hard toward the house. I hurried after him through the muddy puddles. He jumped down, left the animal where it stood with no thought to its care, and literally ripped at the door latch. I was only a few paces behind him when he bulled his way inside the common room.

The guests were all still at table, lingering over coffee and dried apple pie, Shock picking on his banjo. Rachel Kraft's reaction to sight of her husband was to let loose a keening wail. Joe Hoover stood up fast, nearly upsetting his chair on the near side of the table. Everyone else froze. I shut the door against the rain and wind as Luke Kraft swept his hat back off his head. When I stepped around him, I had a clear look at his face and what I saw stood me dead-still. It was blotched dark red from drink, cold, and the clear mix of fury and hate that brewed inside him.

Rachel Kraft's expression was one of bloodless terror. "Oh, my God . . . Luke!"

"Didn't think I'd find you this fast, did you? You and that son of a bitch you run off with."

Hoover said: "Leave her be, Kraft."

"Like hell I will. You ain't getting away with what you done. She's coming back with me, her and the money both. Right now, storm or no storm."

"You can have the money and welcome, but not Rachel."

"Shut up, Hoover. No damn thieving wife stealer's gonna stand in my way."

"Listen to me. . . ."

Kraft swept the tail of his poncho back, snaked a hand underneath. It came out filled with a long-barreled Colt sidearm. Rachel Kraft cried out again. Nesbitt stood up, doing it slowly, with his hands in plain sight. None of the rest of us moved an inch.

"There's no call for that, Mister Kraft," I said, with as much calm as I could muster. "There are women in here."

"Only woman I'm interested in is my wife. Rachel, get on over here."

"No, Luke, please. . . ."

"I said get over here. Now!"

"She's not going back with you," Hoover said.

"You gonna stop me from taking her? Go ahead and try. I'd just as lief put a bullet in you."

"She's had all the beatings she can stand. I've seen the marks you put on her."

"Yeah, and I know what the two of you was doing when you seen 'em. Rachel! Do what you been told!"

She obeyed this time. Her legs were unsteady as she rose to her feet and started toward him.

Hoover stepped in front her, pushed her behind him, and held her there with one arm. His jaw was set hard. He'd struck me as mild-mannered, but there was plenty of sand and iron in him. The thought crossed my mind that he was more in love with Rachel Kraft than her husband ever could be.

"You can't have her, Kraft."

"I'm taking what's mine, all of it."

She said through her fright: "Luke, Joe didn't steal the money. I did. He didn't know anything about it until after we left. . . ."

"Shut up. I won't tell you again ... get on over here!"

Hoover took a step forward, still holding the woman behind him. "Suppose we keep this between you and me. . . ."

Kraft shot him. Just that quickly.

The sound of the gunshot was nearly deafening in the low-ceilinged room. The bullet struck Hoover in the chest, threw him around, grunting, and down to the floor. Shocked gasps and cries rode the dying echoes of the shot. Rachel Kraft screamed, took one look at the blood streaming from Hoover's chest, and fainted.

The sudden violence, the acrid fog of powder smoke in the air, seemed to have no effect on Nesbitt. He said to Kraft: "You shot an unarmed man, mister. If he dies, that's murder."

"Bastard stole my wife and three thousand dollars out of my safe."

"That's no cause for gun play."

"You saw him start for me. Self-defense, by Christ."

"Everyone here will testify otherwise."

Kraft pointed his weapon at Nesbitt. What he'd done seemed to have had no effect on the rage and hatred that controlled him. "That's enough out of you. You and Murdock pick up my wife and carry her outside and put her on my horse. Tie her down if needs be."

I said: "Be reasonable, man. You can't take her out in this storm. . . ."

"Don't you start in on me, mister, unless you want a bullet, too. We're leaving here as soon as I. . ."

The rest of what he'd been about to say was lost in another report, not as loud but just as sudden and shocking. A bloody hole appeared in Kraft's forehead; he had time for one amazed gasp before his knees buckled and he fell headlong, his weapon coming free of his grasp. I tore my gaze away from his settling body, put it on the shaken, gabbling group around the table.

The peddler, James Shock, said: "That *was* self-defense, brothers and sisters. I trust you'll all testify to the fact."

In his hand, smoke adrift from the muzzle, was a small, nickel-plated revolver.

CAROLINE DEVANE

Mr. Nesbitt and I were the first to move after James Shock's pronouncement. He went to kneel beside the man named Kraft while I hurried to Joe Hoover's side. Young Hoover was alive, barely conscious and moaning, blood pumping from the wound in his chest. As I knelt quickly beside him, I heard Nesbitt say that the drunken rancher was dead. Others were moving about, too, by then, Sophie Murdock attending to Rachel Kraft.

Hoover's wound, fortunately, was high on the left side of his chest, below the collar bone—a location where there were no vital organs. There was considerable blood, but it was not arterial blood. Serious, then, but perhaps not life-threatening if the bullet could be removed, the wound cleaned and properly treated to reduce the threat of infection.

Mr. Murdock said: "How badly hurt he is?"

I told him my prognosis.

"Sounds like you've had nurse's training."

"I have," I said. I looked past him at his wife. "We'll need hot water, clean towels, a sharp, clean knife. Have you any disinfectant?"

"Only rubbing alcohol."

"That'll do. Also sulphur powder, if you have that."

She nodded and hurried away.

Rachel Kraft had recovered from her faint and was sitting up, staring at us with horrified eyes. "Joe," she said. "Oh, God, don't let him die."

"He's not going to die," I said with more conviction than I felt.

She moaned, made an effort to stand, failed, and began to crawl toward us. Nesbitt grasped her arms and drew her to her feet. She cried out in protest, struggled for a moment, and suddenly went limp again. Not the sort of woman one could rely upon in a crisis such as this.

Murdock asked me: "Can he be moved?"

"Yes, I think so."

"We'll take him into one of the guest rooms."

I stood and moved aside as he and Nesbitt lifted the injured man. Nesbitt had helped Rachel Kraft to a chair by the fire; she was conscious again, but inert, and she wore the glazed look of deep shock. James Shock still stood by the table, and, as I followed the men carrying Hoover, I glanced at the peddler. He was smiling faintly, his gaze fixed and thoughtful. He didn't seem particularly affected by the fact that he had just killed a man, and it made me wonder if he had killed before. Whether he had or not, the man's coldness, his unctuousness, his conviction that all women would fall prey to his superficial charm, repelled me.

The men laid young Hoover on the guest room bed. With Murdock's help, I removed the wounded man's coat and shirt. Sophie Murdock came with towels, a bottle of rubbing alcohol, a package of sulfur powder. Laudanum, too, for pain relief afterward. "The water's heating," she said. "It won't be long."

"The knife will have to be sterilized."

"Yes. I have it in another pan on the stove."

I used a towel to sponge blood from the wound. It was as I'd surmised from my cursory examination in the common room—serious but not necessarily life-threatening. Hoover moaned and his eyelids fluttered, then popped open. Pain clouded his eyes, but he managed to focus on me.

"Rachel," he whispered.

"Lie still, Mister Hoover."

"I have to know . . . she all right?"

"Yes. Unharmed."

"Kraft?"

"He's dead," Murdock said. "The peddler, Shock, shot him."

Hoover muttered something, a sound of satisfaction, and his body relaxed and his eyes closed again.

I drew the Murdocks aside. "We'll need a bottle of whiskey," I said. "For anaesthesia. I can't probe into him unless he's partially sedated and held still."

"I'll get it," Murdock said.

"Another lamp, too. More light."

The three of them hurried out, leaving me alone with Hoover. He looked so young and vulnerable, lying there—like one of my own sons. He may have been a thief, as that man Kraft had said, but he was personable and he seemed genuinely to care for Rachel Kraft.

The Murdocks returned with the rest of the items I had requested. I positioned them, one on either side of the bed. Murdock lifted Hoover's head and administered a large dose of whiskey. I sponged more blood from the wound, cleaned it with alcohol—he groaned again but lay still—and then stood staring at the sterilized kitchen knife gleaming on a cloth beside the pan of boiled water. My hand was not steady and perspiration beaded my forehead.

Sophie Murdock looked keenly at me, her tired eyes searching mine. "You've never had cause to do this before, have you?"

"No." My voice was as unsteady as my hand.

"But you have assisted with similar procedures."

"Yes . . . once."

"Then you'll manage. Won't she, Thomas?"

"I have no doubt of it," he said.

I drew several deep breaths. Sophie Murdock was right—I *would* manage to do what was necessary to save this young man's life. I would because I must.

My hand no longer trembled when I reached out for the knife.

JAMES SHOCK

After the wounded wife stealer was carried out, I ambled over for a look at the gent I'd shot. Drilled dead center above the bridge of the nose, by grab. Never knew what hit him. Never expected a banjo-strumming peddler to have a hide-out gun, or in the blink of an eye to draw and fire with perfect aim. He wasn't the first to suffer the consequences of underestimating James Shock, and like as not he wouldn't be the last.

As I turned away, the Murdock girl, Annabelle, came near and caught hold of my arm. Her face was bloodless, but nonetheless attractive for her fright. She wouldn't look at the dead man; her eyes were all for me. "That was a brave thing you did, Mister Shock," she said, all breathless. "Truly it was."

I smiled down at her. Her body was pressed so tightly against my arm I could feel the swell of her breasts. What a sweet little piece she was, all tender and dewy-eyed and ripe for the picking. But not by me, alas. Not in these surroundings and under these circumstances. Underage she was, too. Jail bait. Pity.

"I couldn't let him fire his weapon a second time," I said. "He might've shot someone else . . . even *you*, my dear."

I felt her shiver and squeeze tighter, tight enough to bring a stir to my loins. Seventeen and surely a virgin. I sighed, licking my lips, and reluctantly eased her away from me. No sense in allowing such warm flesh to torment me, eh? Besides, I had more important matters on my mind. Percolating there, you might say.

Murdock and the sharp-eyed gent named Nesbitt returned from wherever they'd carried Hoover. Annabelle stepped farther away from me as Nesbitt approached. Murdock went to the buffet for a bottle of whiskey, then picked up one of the coal-oil lamps. Annabelle said to him, dipping her chin in the direction of the dead man: "Dad, will you please take *that* outside. He . . . it's making me ill."

"I can't right now. Nesbitt?"

"Shock and I will do it."

I shrugged. "For the lady's sake, yes."

"We'll put him in the barn."

"All that distance in this weather? Why not just lay him out front?"

"Cold, aren't you, Shock?"

"Not at all, brother. Practical is the word. After the way he busted in here, a raging threat to all of us, his remains don't deserve consideration."

"The barn. Come on, let's get it done."

Well, I might have argued with him, but I held my tongue. Peace and harmony, now the crisis was ended—that was the ticket. I shrugged and winked at Annabelle and went to put on my rain gear.

And out we went into the storm, my hands full of the dead rancher's scuffed boots, and across a mud field to the barn. The stage driver had gone back out there earlier to sleep in his coach and the storm had prevented him from hearing the gunfire. He woke up quickly when we came staggering in and laid the corpse in one of the empty stalls. Nesbitt gave him a terse explanation of the events inside. Dell said he'd fetch Kraft's horse and went out to do that.

On one knee, Nesbitt ran his hands over Kraft's clothing. Searching for a wallet or purse, mayhap, but he found nothing of the sort. When he stood up again, he said: "You're quite a marksman, aren't you, Shock? For an itinerant peddler."

"A man's profession has little to do with his ability with firearms."

"True enough. Still, it was pretty risky, firing as you did in there. Suppose you'd missed?"

"But I didn't miss."

"But you could have."

"Not at that range, with the element of surprise in my favor," I said. "No, brother, the only danger was that Kraft might have had a notion to fire his weapon again, as drunk and raging as he was. I did what I had to do for all our sakes. You'd have done the same, given the opportunity."

"Would I? Why do you say that?"

"You wear a sidearm. Before I drew and fired, I saw you ease the tail of your coat back."

"Very observant. But I wouldn't have drawn unless Kraft turned his gun in the direction of the table."

"Might've been too late by then. I chose to act immediately. The right choice, eh, brother?"

"As it turned out."

He gave me a long, searching look. As if he were trying to take my measure. It was the scrutiny of a lawman, one I'd seen too many times in my life to mistake. Well, if a lawman was what he was, no matter to me or my plans. I was not wanted anywhere for any sort of crime. A few close calls here and there, that was all. And no one could dispute the fact that I'd plugged the rancher in self-defense; half a dozen witnesses could attest to that. I had nothing to fear from the law. And wouldn't after I left here, if I were careful.

On the walk back to the roadhouse, I thought again of what Luke Kraft had said after shooting down the wife stealer. *Bastard stole my wife and three thousand dollars out of my safe.* $3,000! No one other than the ever-vigilant James Shock seemed to have paid attention to those words. And where were the $3,000 to be found? In the wife's or the cowhand's luggage, possibly, but more likely it was on the cowhand himself. As he'd lain there on the floor, with the Devane woman ministering to him, I'd spied a cowhide pouch fastened to his belt. What better place to keep greenbacks or gold specie or both?

Heigh-ho! And who better to lay claim to those $3,000 than the resourceful Mr. James Shock?

ANNABELLE MURDOCK

After James Never Jim Shock and Mr. Nesbitt took the dead man away, I went over to where Rachel Kraft slumped in a chair in front of the fireplace. Even though the room was warm, she was shaking as if she had the ague and her eyes were unfocused. Well, of course she was in bad way. She'd just seen her husband shoot her lover—*that* had been a surprise, Joe Hoover being her lover, even though the two of them hadn't really acted like cousins—and then her husband shot dead right afterward.

I was still upset myself. All that sudden violence—right here in my home! Oh, we'd had incidents before, drummers imbibing too much whiskey, men cheating at cards and getting into fights. But they'd never been anything that Dad couldn't resolve without any shooting being done. What had happened tonight had been terrible to see. I'd probably have nightmares about it for the rest of my life. If it hadn't been for James Never Jim Shock, that man Kraft might have shot his wife, too, and maybe Dad, or Mother, or even me. It made me shudder again just thinking about it.

"Missus Kraft?" I said.

She didn't answer. Didn't even look at me.

Shaking the way she was, even with the fire, she ought to have a blanket. I hurried to my room, where I stripped away the good heavy woolen one that Mother had ordered for me from a Sears Roebuck catalog last summer. When I came back into the common room, Rachel Kraft hadn't moved. I wrapped the blanket around her and sat down on the chair to her right. And this time when I spoke her name, she turned her head and looked at me with dull eyes.

"Joe," she said, "Mister Hoover. He'll live, won't he?"

I didn't know, but I said: "I think so. Missus Devane and my folks . . . they're doing all they can."

"And my husband? He's dead?"

"Yes. I'm sorry."

She looked back at the fire. "Don't be. He deserved to die. You saw and heard what kind of man he was." After a moment, she added: "A harsh man created by a harsh land. This is no place to make a decent life, especially for a woman."

I nodded. That was exactly how I felt.

"Mister Hoover and I were going away together," she said. "I don't know where, just . . . away. If he dies. . . ."

"He won't die."

"You don't know that he won't."

"I don't know it, but I believe it. You should, too."

"You're so young, so full of optimism. And I'm. . . ."

"Not old," I said quickly. "Not much older than me."

"But I've lived a much harder life. You don't have any idea how hard."

No, I didn't. But I could imagine. From all the things that man Kraft had said before he shot Mr. Hoover, her life with him must have been awful.

"Regardless of what happens to Joe, I'm going far away from here. I hate the delta. I've always hated it."

"So have I."

"Then don't make the mistake I did," Rachel Kraft said. "Don't stay here, don't linger a moment longer than you have to. Leave before it's too late."

As soon as she said that, I thought of James Never Jim Shock. Truth to tell, I hadn't stopped thinking about him since I'd first set eyes on him. Such a handsome man. And he wasn't a mere peddler. He was . . . well, a sort of happy banjo-playing troubadour who'd traveled far and wide, seen wonderful places, and done all manner of exciting things. A free spirit. And a hero, too, the way he'd saved us all from harm tonight.

Did I dare let him be my way out of here?

He seemed as taken with me as I was with him. He'd called me a beautiful woman, and the touch of his hand on mine, the hard muscles I'd felt when I hugged his arm—the memory made me all tingly again, my face feel warm. He was everything I'd ever dreamed of in a man, wasn't he? And he'd be good to me, I was sure of it.

Dad. Mother. The idea of stealing away—they wouldn't let me go voluntarily, not alone and never with a man I'd only just met—and perhaps never seeing them again made me feel sad. I loved them both and their lives had been difficult since that accident in Chicago when I was a child. Mother was so tired, worn down by years of hard work, and lonely except for my company. Dad worked hard, too, his writing his only escape. It put a hollow feeling in my chest, thinking of what would become of them when I left. But I had to think of myself first, didn't I? Don't you always have to think of yourself first when you're young and trapped?

I glanced over at Mrs. Kraft. She was staring into the flames, her mouth bent down, eyes blank again. No, I wasn't going to turn out like her—beaten, broken, and, despite what she claimed, probably trapped here in the delta for the rest of her life. She wasn't a strong woman, not like my mother, not like me. If Joe Hoover didn't live, she'd be completely alone, with nowhere to go.

I went back to my room, where I lay down on my bed in the dark, pulling the quilt around me. Mrs. Kraft was right. This was no place to make a decent life. I couldn't linger here; I had to leave before it was too late. The only question was whether I should wait and make my way alone or leave right away with James Never Jim Shock.

BOONE NESBITT

I spent most of the long night sprawled in one of the overstuffed chairs near the hearth. Now and then I dozed, but I was too keyed up to sleep. Mostly I tended to the fire, listened to the wind and rain, and let my thoughts wander.

The shootings had put me on edge. Sudden violence always has that effect on me, whether I'm directly involved or not. I'd shot two men in my time, been fired upon by them and by two others, drawn sidearm and rifle on half a dozen more, and I was weary of gun play. Weary, too, of drunken fools like Luke Kraft and cold-blooded types like James Shock. No simple peddler, Shock. I'd seen his breed before: sly, deadly connivers hiding behind bright smiles and drummers' casual patter. Kraft wasn't the first man he'd killed with that hide-out weapon of his; the swift draw, the dead-aim bullet placed squarely between the rancher's eyes at forty paces, proved that. He was a dangerous man, capable of any act to feather his nest, and he knew that I knew it. Knew what I was, just as I knew what he was. He'd been as watchful of me as I'd been of him since we'd had our conversation out in the barn.

Be more to my liking if I was here after Shock instead of Harold P. Baxter, alias T.J. Murdock. Shock was the sort I'd always enjoyed tracking down and snaffling—a proper match for my skills and my dislike of criminals. Murdock, on the other hand, seemed to be a decent family man. Likable. Intelligent. Non-violent. His only sin was an incident eight years ago in Chicago, unavoidable and accidental by all accounts except one. If any man other than Patrick Bellright had been affected, Murdock and his wife and daughter wouldn't have had to flee for their lives, or to spend eight years hiding in a California backwater like this one.

Yes, and if any man other than Patrick Bellright had been affected, I wouldn't be here ready and willing to tear their patchwork lives to shreds for a $10,000 reward.

Pure luck that I'd found him. Murdock might've lived the rest of his life at Twelve-Mile Crossing if Bellright hadn't employed the Pinkerton agency; if I hadn't been transferred from the Chicago to the San Francisco office; if I hadn't had a penchant for back-checking old, unsolved cases; if Murdock hadn't risked publishing sketches in San Francisco newspapers and magazines and I hadn't spotted the similarities to Harold P. Baxter's writings for the Chicago *Sentinel*. Circumstances had conspired against him, and in my favor. Bellright's favor, too. Patrick Bellright—financier and philanthropist, with a deserved reputation as a hater and seeker of vengeance and brass-balled son of a bitch.

There wasn't much doubt what he'd do when I brought Harold P. Baxter back to Chicago to face him. He'd pay me my blood money and dismiss me, and a short time later Baxter would either turn up dead in a trumped-up accident or disappear never to be heard from again. An eye for an eye, that was Bellright's philosophy. Hell, he was capable of killing Baxter himself and laughing while he did it.

But that wasn't my look-out now, was it? I'd made my living for twenty years as a manhunter, and I'd been responsible for the deaths of several fugitives, by my own hand and by state execution. One more didn't matter. That was what I'd told myself when I set out from San Francisco two days ago. A stroke of good fortune like no other I could ever expect in my life. $10,000. An end to twenty years of hard, violent detective work and hand-to-mouth living, a piece of land in the Valley of the Moon, maybe a woman to share it with one day. I was entitled, wasn't I?

Sure I was. Sure.

The only trouble was, now that I was here, now that I'd met Harold P. Baxter and his family, doubts had begun to creep in. He was a fugitive, yes, but not from the law and likely not in the eyes of God. All the men I'd tracked and sent to their deaths before had been guilty of serious crimes, but Baxter was an innocent victim of fate and one man's lust for revenge. Send him to a certain death and I would no longer be on the side of the righteous; I'd be a paid conspirator in a man's murder.

$10,000. Thirty pieces of silver.

In San Francisco I'd convinced myself I'd have no trouble going through with it. Now I wasn't so certain.

I dozed for a time, woke to add another log to the fire, dozed again. When I awakened that time, I saw that James Shock was no longer asleep on the nearby sofa. A visit to the privy out back? Or was he up to something? The way he'd been making up to Annabelle hadn't set well with me; she seemed smitten with him. I wouldn't put it past him to sneak into her room. . . .

No, it was all right. Just as I was about to get up for a look around, Shock came gliding back into the common room, paused to glance my way, and then laid down again on the sofa. Wherever he'd gone, it hadn't been to answer a call of Nature. He hadn't put on his rain gear and he was still in his stocking feet.

I sat watching the fire, listening to the rain slacken until it was only a soft patter on the roof. The storm seemed finally to be blowing itself out. I flipped open the cover on my stem-winder, and leaned over close to the fire to read the time. Some past 5:00 a.m. Be dawn soon.

And before another nightfall I'd have to make up my mind about Harold P. Baxter, one way or the other.

RACHEL KRAFT

I was still sitting in front of the fireplace, my mind mostly blank as it always used to be after one of Luke's beatings, when Sophie Murdock came through the door from the bedrooms. At sight of her, I sat up straight, an icy fear spreading through me.

"Joe? He's not . . . ?"

"No. Resting peaceably," she said. "Missus Devane removed the bullet and dressed his wound. You can see him now."

I stood haltingly, a sharp ache in my ribs where two days ago Luke had twice kicked me after knocking me to the floor, and followed the ferryman's wife to a small guest room. Joe lay on a narrow bed, his eyes closed; Caroline Devane was pulling a quilt over him. She straightened, putting a hand to the small of her back as if it ached, and turned toward me.

While Mrs. Murdock gathered up some bloody towels and a basin of pink-tinged water, Caroline said: "He'll sleep for some time, and I think he'll be all right when he wakes."

"I'm grateful for you helping him."

"I'm glad I was able to."

"Would it be all right if I sat with him?"

"Of course. I'll be in the next room. Rouse me if he wakes."

"Yes, I will."

The women left the room, and I moved toward the bed. Joe's brow was damp, his hair disheveled. In sleep, he looked more like a little boy than a grown man who had thrust himself between me and Luke's long-barreled Colt. I took my handkerchief from my skirt pocket, wiped his brow, and then drew over a rocker from the other side of the room and sat close to the bed, studying his face.

It was a good face, strong if not particularly handsome, weathered by his work on the range. He'd taken me away from the ranch, forgiven me for stealing Luke's money, and given me hope for a new and better life. But did I love him? I'd wondered before if he were merely a way out for me. Now that I no longer needed him to defend me from Luke's abuse. . . .

With a sense of shock, I realized what I hadn't allowed myself to think before. I was now a wealthy widow. I didn't have to remain in the delta; all that rich ranch land would bring a handsome price, and I'd be able to go anywhere, do anything.

Of course Joe would go with me. He'd want to, wouldn't he? Surely he would. And after all he'd done for me, I couldn't abandon him.

But Joe had ranching in his blood. It was all he knew, all he cared about. He'd spoken often enough of owning a place of his own, perhaps in the cattle country of eastern Montana. Was that what I wanted for myself, life with another rancher and in another hard and lonely place?

When I'd married Luke, all I wanted was love, a family to nurture, an untroubled life. Joe could offer me all of that. I'd told Annabelle Murdock that the delta was a harsh place that had bred a harsh man, but not everyone here was like Luke. His father had been a hard man who frequently beat him. Maybe it wasn't the delta but the lack of love that had turned him cruel and bitter and led him to take out his frustrations on me.

Seeing Joe lying there so helpless, having put his life on the line for me—not for the money, for me—I thought that perhaps I had enough love to make a new life with him no matter where it was. And it would be a good life, an untroubled life, with a good and gentle man.

I moved the rocker closer to the bed, slipped my hand under the quilt, and entwined my fingers with his rough, calloused ones. And soon dozed. . . .

"Missus Kraft?"

The man's voice seemed to come from far away. I moved my head from side to side against the rocker's high back, slowly opened my eyes. The first person I saw was Joe, still resting easily. Then, when I twisted around, I found myself looking at the peddler, James Shock.

"I didn't mean to startle you, sister," he said softly. His expression was grave, with no hint of the lustful gleam that had been in his bold stare earlier. "How is he?"

"He'll recover. Missus Devane saved his life."

"He'll have a doctor to look at him tomorrow. I'll see to that." He paused. "I'm sorry about your husband. But he left me no choice."

"I know that, Mister Shock."

He peered keenly at my face. "You look tired. How long have you been sitting here?"

I truly didn't know and I told him so.

"How would it be if I sat with him while you rest?"

I didn't want to leave Joe, but my body, bruised as it was, ached from sitting in the hard chair. Perhaps I should lie down for a while. It seemed days since I'd last slept. "Thank you, Mister Shock. If you wouldn't mind."

"Not at all."

"You'll call me if he wakes? I'll be in the next room."

"Immediately, sister. Immediately."

I stood and, after brushing my hand across Joe's forehead which was cool and dry now—I left the room.

The roadhouse was quiet, everyone in bed or asleep in the common room. Sometime while I'd dozed, the storm had slackened; the sound of the rain was a light pattering now. I opened the door to the second guest room. The lamp was still lit and I saw that Caroline Devane was still awake, sitting up on one of the two beds, crocheting an antimacassar of intricate design.

"Mister Hoover?" she asked.

"Still asleep. Mister Shock offered to sit with him so I can rest a bit."

"The accommodating Mister Shock."

"You don't care for him, do you?"

"Not very much, no."

"He saved our lives."

"It was his life he was interested in saving, not anyone else's."

"Perhaps. Does it really matter?" I lay down on the second bed and drew the counterpane over me. "Can't you sleep, Missus Devane?"

"No. As tired as I am, I have decisions to rethink. What has happened here tonight is sufficient to make one reconsider the wisdom of the course she's undertaken."

"I'm not sure I know what you mean."

She hesitated before speaking, the crochet needles clicking in the silence. Then, as if needing to unburden herself, she said: "Two years ago I had an affair with a friend of my husband. My marriage wasn't a brutal one like yours, it was simply . . . empty. I seldom saw John. He was in state government and constantly traveling from Sacramento to San

Francisco. When he was at home, he ignored the children and me. I needed someone, and Hugh . . . well, he was everything John wasn't . . . kind, attentive, ardent. And so we became lovers. Our affair lasted six months."

"What happened then?"

"John found out about us."

"What did he do?"

"Immediately began divorce proceedings. The court awarded him custody of David and William, with virtually no visitation rights allowed me. Life in Sacramento soon became intolerable for me. You must be aware how society treats a divorcee, particularly one of an important man."

"Caroline, I'm so sorry. Did Hugh stand by you?"

"For a time. But he's a successful lawyer and the scandal was damaging to him, too. I no longer blame him for ending our relationship. He really had no choice."

"What will you do now?"

"The only member of my family who hasn't turned on me is my sister Mary. She and her husband have invited me to live with them on their farm in San Joaquin County. But I suspect they only want me as extra help with the chores and their seven children. It would be a hard life for me."

"Then why go there?" I said. "With your nurse's training. . . ."

"That's what I've been considering. No one in Sacramento would allow me to practice. But this is a large country, and John's influence and the web of rumor only extend so far. If I could establish myself in a new city, rebuild my respectability, then perhaps once my children are old enough. . . ." She sighed. "But it takes time and means to accomplish that. I have a great deal of the former, but none of the latter."

I was silent.

"Well, I've burdened you enough with my troubles," Caroline said. "You have far too many of your own, and you must be very tired. I'll let you sleep now. Perhaps I can, too."

But I didn't sleep right away. Joe was alive because of Caroline's ministrations; I owed her a debt of gratitude for that. I found myself thinking of the $3,000 I'd taken from Luke's safe. I no longer needed it now that Luke was dead and I was a wealthy widow. The money meant little to me, but it would mean a great deal to Caroline Devane. She was so desperately unhappy, just as I had been before Joe came into my life. My fortunes had changed, and it was in my power to change hers, too.

She wouldn't take the full amount if I tried to give it to her; she was too proud to accept money as a gift. But she might be persuaded if I offered part of it as a loan. I determined to speak to her about it in the morning, and not to take no for an answer.

T.J. MURDOCK

Traces of light began to seep in around the shutters on the bedroom window. Almost dawn. Sophie stirred beside me; I knew she'd also been awake for some time, even though she'd lain still and silent.

"Stopped raining," she said now.

"About an hour ago. Wind's died down, too."

"I heard you get up earlier."

"Checking on Joe Hoover. Missus Devane was there with him."

"How is he?"

"Alive and resting easy. No fever."

"She's a good nurse and a strong woman, troubled or not."

"Yes, but he still needs a doctor's attention. He can't travel . . . we'll have to keep him here until the peddler can send Doc Kiley out from River Bend."

"That's right. Shock offered to return there this morning."

"Not for any selfless reasons, I suspect. He knows he has to report shooting Kraft to the sheriff, even with witnesses to back him up, before he can move on."

"Do you think the slough's passable yet?"

"Water seemed to be settling when I looked out earlier, but it's still running high and there's a lot of debris. I'll know better when it's light. We'll ferry the stage across as soon as it's safe."

She lay quietly again for a time. Then: "Nesbitt?"

"Too many people here now for him to do much except bide his time."

"If he doesn't speak to you right away, bring it out into the open yourself. We have to know what his intentions are."

"I will."

Blackbirds cried noisily somewhere outside—a sure sign that the weather had improved. When it was quiet again, Sophie said: "I'm not leaving you alone with him."

"You have to. If Nesbitt's bent on using that sidearm of his. . . ."

"No. We'll put Annabelle on the stage in Pete's care, but I'm staying here. No matter what happens. I won't run again, Thomas, any more than you will."

I made no reply. I had told her about Boone Nesbitt last night, when we were alone in bed, and she'd said the same thing then no more running and hiding, for either of us. There was no point in trying to argue with her when her mind was made up. Whatever happened with Nesbitt, we would face it together.

Eight years. Eight long, difficult years. We'd sought to convince ourselves that after so much time, this day might never come. And yet we'd never quite believed it. Patrick Bellright was a relentless, bitter, vengeful man with unlimited funds; he would never stop hunting me until his dying day. There would be a reward on my head, a large one, and it would carry no stipulations or caveats. Wanted—dead or alive.

It was a monstrous miscarriage of justice, the result of an accident that was not my fault, that I could not have avoided. A Sunday afternoon drive through Jackson Park in a rented carriage, a small child chasing a ball out of a line of shrubs and yelling loudly enough to frighten the horse. Thrashing hoofs, a scream, a crushed form sprawled in the roadway. We had rushed the child to the nearest doctor, even though Sophie and I were sure there was no life left in her. Marissa Bellright. Seven years old, and Patrick Bellright's only child.

The rest was nightmare. Dire threats, a murderous assault by one of his hirelings that I'd barely escaped. And then flight, again by bare escape, and arduous travel across country to this isolated backwater and a new, hardscrabble life as ferrymaster and innkeeper—labors as far removed from my former position as newspaper reporter and columnist as Chicago was from Twelve-Mile Crossing.

I had been a fool to submit my sketches for publication in San Francisco. Yet of all the possible ways I might be found by Bellright's hirelings, my pseudonymous writings had seemed the most remote. There was no way I could have anticipated a man like Nesbitt, whoever he was, making the connection between Harold P. Baxter and T.J. Murdock. But it had happened, and now it was too late. For me, but not, I vowed, for Annabelle or Sophie.

The dawn light was brightening. Sophie and I both rose, washed up, and dressed. She went to the kitchen to make coffee and get breakfast started, and I went to check on Hoover again. Caroline Devane and Rachel Kraft were both with him now; the two women seemed to have developed a comradeship. There was no change in Hoover's condition.

Nesbitt was alone in the common room, stoking up the fire as he must have done throughout the night because the room was still warm. There was no sign of the peddler, Shock. As I crossed to the front door, Nesbitt stood up.

"We need to have a talk, Murdock," he said.

"Yes, but not right this second. I have work to attend to."

"Soon, though."

"I'll be around," I said. "I'm not going anywhere."

"I didn't suppose you were."

Outside, the yard was rain-puddled and littered with leaves and branches. The levee roads on both sides of the slough seemed to have survived intact, so far as I could see, although down toward where the slough bent to the south, the water level was only a couple of feet below the surface of the Middle Island road. Both embankments appeared to have held without crumbling. The slough waters were chocolate brown, frothy, still running fast and bobbing with tree limbs and other detritus from the storm.

I slogged through the mud to the landing. The barge was as I'd left it, moored fast, and the strung cable and windlass had come through undamaged. As I finished my examination, Pete Dell appeared from the direction of the barn. I went to meet him.

"How's she look out there, Murdock?"

"It should be safe enough for the stage to cross in another couple of hours."

"Good enough. I'm so far behind schedule now, couple more hours won't make any difference. Some wild night, eh?"

"In more ways than one."

"That peddler, Shock, is over in the barn hitching up his wagon."

"Already? He must be eager for an early start to River Bend."

"So he says. I don't much like that fella, tell you the truth."

"I would have said the same before he put an end to Luke Kraft's terrorism last night."

"Even so. But then, I never much liked Kraft, neither. His death's likely to cause a stir up Isleton way, even if he did deserve what he got." Pete stretched and blew on his hands. "Coffee ready?"

"Should be. Breakfast, too, just about."

We went on into the house. Two hours, I was thinking bleakly, and part of another for the stage to cross. And then Nesbitt. And then, one way or another, an end to my freedom.

JAMES SHOCK

I finished harnessing Nell to my wagon, hauled the Murdocks' buckboard to one side of the runway, opened the doors, and led Nell out of the barn. Bitter cold this morning, but I scarcely felt the bite. The $3,000, nestled inside my coat, provided warmth aplenty.

As I drove across the muddy yard, the ferrymaster stepped out of the roadhouse and hailed me. I drew to a stop, arranging my face in an expression of gravity. "I was about to stop in," I lied, "to ask after Mister

Hoover."

"He's awake and taking nourishment. He passed a comfortable night."

"Well, he'll soon enough have the attention of a doctor."

"Good of you to make the trip to River Bend, Mister Shock."

"Not at all. I know my duty."

"Will you have breakfast before you go? Or at least a cup of hot coffee?"

"Thank you, no. I've no real appetite this morning, and I'd just as lief make tracks while the weather is dry. How much do I owe for the night's lodging?"

"Not a cent, under the circumstances."

"Christian of you, brother, but I insist on paying for your hospitality."

"As you please. Two dollars, then."

I leaned down to pay him. He thanked me and wished me Godspeed, and I touched my hat and gigged Nell up the muddy embankment. The wagon's wheels slipped a bit, but the old plug held her footing and soon enough we were on the levee road, headed in the direction of River Bend. I cast no backward glance.

Even if the money were missed, no one at the ferry crossing could be sure that I'd taken it; not even Nesbitt, if he was a lawman, would have cause or impetus to chase after me. I had only to pass through River Bend and I was safe. Sheriff, doctor? Hah! I wouldn't tarry in the town long enough to wave at a passer-by. Straight on through and back to Sacramento as quickly as I could get there.

I felt a song welling up in me and began to hum and then to sing softly. Later, when the day warmed a bit, I would bring out my banjo to celebrate properly my good fortune. $3,000, more than I'd ever had at one time. What a man could do with that much money! Why, I might just board Nell in a livery, put the wagon in storage, and take passage on one of the river packets to San Francisco. Yes, that was just what I'd do. A room in the city's best hotel, fine food, champagne, a pretty lass for company and bed. Heigh-ho! Life's bounties in abundance.

After a mile or so I passed a weed-infested side road that meandered off onto a long peninsula. Ahead was a sharp bend, both sides of the levee road shaded by sycamores. The road's surface was less slick here and we were clomping along at a right pert pace when we reached the bend and started through.

I didn't spy the downed tree until we were almost upon it. It lay blocking the road from one side to the other, its root-torn bole jutting high and its upper branches drooping down into the slough. I yanked back hard on the reins. Nell shied and the wagon slewed sideways, and, when that happened, just before we slid to a halt a few feet from the sycamore, something shifted and clattered inside. I could scarcely believe what I heard then the startled, pained cry of a woman.

I set the brake, jumped down, ran to the rear of the wagon, and pulled open the doors. And lo, there she was, asprawl on the floor among a small litter of items dislodged from their hooks and cubbies, the hem of her traveling dress twisted up to reveal her drawers.

Annabelle Murdock.

"What the devil are you doing in my wagon?"

"Please don't be mad at me, James Never Jim Shock. Please!"

"Answer me, girl."

"I had to get away. I couldn't stay any longer. You'll let me come with you, won't you? I'll do anything you say. . . ."

"How did you get in there? The doors were locked."

"No, they weren't. I slipped out of the house and into the barn while it was still dark and the doors weren't locked, and I found a place to hide. . . ."

Damnation! I must have neglected to lock them when I brought out my banjo last night. Fury rose, hot and thick, in my chest and throat. Everything proceeding so well, and then the downed tree across the road and now this stupid priss of a girl. I wheeled away and stomped ahead to look at the sycamore. Blocking the road for fair, and a thick-trunked bugger it was. It would take a crew of men with axes and saws to cut it up and clear away the debris. The fury rose higher; my head commenced to throb with it, my hands to palsy some.

Annabelle had come out of the wagon and was standing, small and fearful, next to Nell. And fearful she should be, the little bitch. As if the blocked road wasn't enough of a trial, now I had this rattlebrain to contend with.

"You won't send me back?" she said. "Please say you won't send me back."

Send her back? Hell, no, I wouldn't. It was only a mile or so to the roadhouse, a short and easy walk, but once she arrived, there was no telling what she might say or the Murdocks might think. She may already have been missed. They might believe I'd enticed her away or, worse, kidnapped her. It was a risk I couldn't afford to take.

"James Never Jim Shock? Say you. . . ."

"Don't call me that, you little bitch. Shut your damn mouth and let me think."

A stifled gasp, and she was still.

Take her with me? I couldn't do that, either, even if the road were free for passage. She was a tender morsel, right enough, but under the age of legal consent. If I were caught with her, it would mean prison.

Turn the wagon around, drive it back to the crossing, take the ferry to Middle Island and points south? That was the logical choice, except for the $3,000. The money might already have been discovered missing, or the discovery made before I could make the crossing. Murdock, Dell, Nesbitt a damned lawman, I was sure of it—and all of them armed. No, returning to the roadhouse was a fool's choice.

Nell. Unhitch her, ride her bareback over the obstruction, and into River Bend where I could secure better transportation. But she was old, slow, and anything but sure-footed, and the sycamore would have to be jumped rather than stepped across. And abandoning the wagon with all my wares and possessions was a galling prospect.

In my mouth was a foul taste, as if I'd been force-fed a plate of cowshit soup. What the bloody hell was I going to do?

"Mister Shock?" Timid now. I'd almost forgotten she was there.

"Didn't I tell you to keep your lip buttoned?"

"Are you going to send me back?"

No, I thought, *I'm going to put a bullet in your silly head and dump your body in the slough. Be rid of one problem, at the least.* I'd never killed a woman before, but there's a first time for everything, and she was a burden I couldn't bear. I eased back the tail of my coat.

"If you take me with you," she said, "I'll tell you how we can go on."

"Go on? With this blasted tree blocking the road?"

"There's a way around, another road that intersects with this one about a mile farther south."

"What road? You mean the one we passed a ways back?"

"Yes. It leads out to Crucifixion River."

"What's that?"

"It's . . . a kind of ghost camp."

"Nobody lives there?"

"Nobody."

"And the side road continues through it and back to the south of here?"

"No. There's another road in the camp, a track the people who lived there used."

"Easy to spot, this track?"

"It's overgrown. But I know where it is . . . I can show you."

"You're not lying to me?"

"No! I swear it."

I stared at her, long and hard. Her blue eyes were guileless. Some of my rage began to ease and I let the coattail fall closed. Her death sentence had been reprieved—for however long it took us to reach Crucifixion River.

CAROLINE DEVANE

Rachel was standing at Joe Hoover's bedside when I went in to check on him. From her expression it was plain that she was upset and trying to hide it, but the reason was not her lover's condition. He was conscious, although not fully alert, and his color was good and his eyes clear. And his pulse, when I checked it, was strong.

The dressing on his wound needed changing. I removed the old one and was relieved to find no sign of infection. He would be all right until the doctor came from River Bend, and eventually, I thought, he would mend good as new. I put on more sulphur powder and a fresh bandage. His grimace prompted me to ask if he was in pain.

"Some," he said weakly, "but it's tolerable."

I gave him a spoonful of laudanum anyway, to help him sleep. He needed to rebuild his strength, and rest was the best remedy.

When I was done, Rachel squeezed his hand and whispered something to him that I deliberately did not listen to. Then she plucked at my sleeve and gestured toward the door. Whatever was upsetting her, she didn't wish to discuss it in front of Hoover. As soon as we were in the hallway, with the door closed, she said: "It's gone, Caroline."

"What is?"

"The money. The three thousand dollars I took from my husband's safe. Joe had it in his belt pouch and now the pouch is empty."

I vaguely remembered seeing the pouch when Mr. Murdock and I had taken off Joe Hoover's jacket and shirt, but in my urgent need to extract the bullet and clean and dress the wound, I'd thought no more about it. "When did you learn this?"

"A few minutes ago, just before he woke up."

"Perhaps the Murdocks removed it for safekeeping."

"I don't think so. They'd have said something to me."

Yes, they would have. In the chaotic aftermath of Luke Kraft's sudden intrusion, I had forgotten his mention of the $3,000 and I suspected the Murdocks and the others had as well. All except one . . . and there was only one person among us that could be.

Rachel realized it at the same time. "James Shock," she said. "He took it last night."

Of course. Shock had slipped into the room, late, and talked her into leaving him there alone. Out of the goodness of his heart? Hardly. He was a cold-blooded opportunist, perfectly capable of taking note of the rancher's words and Hoover's belt pouch, and conniving to steal the money.

"Yes," I said, "but it's too late to confront him. Mister Murdock told me he drove off early to summon the doctor from River Bend."

"The money's gone for good, then. He won't stop in River Bend."

"Mister Murdock and Mister Nesbitt might be able to catch him on horseback. . . ."

"Why should they bother? It's not their place."

Footsteps, coming quickly from the family's quarters. Sophie Murdock appeared, her mouth set in grim lines.

"Have either of you seen my daughter?"

"Not at all this morning," I said, and Rachel shook her head. "She's not in her room?"

"No, and some of her things are missing. Clothing and her carpetbag."

"Oh, Lord. You think she may have run off?"

"I don't know. It's possible. She's young and restless, she dislikes her life here, and after what happened last night. . . ."

I recalled the adoring looks Annabelle had lavished on James Shock. Was it possible that he'd sweet-talked her into leaving with him? Or that she'd decided to join him on her own?

My face must have betrayed what I was thinking. "What is it, Missus Devane?"

Sophie Murdock asked. "Do you have an idea where Annabelle's gone?"

"Yes," I said, "I'm afraid I do."

BOONE NESBITT

I was out in the livery barn, watching Murdock help Pete Dell harness the stage team, when Sophie Murdock came rushing in. The look of her was both frantic and frightened. "Thomas," she said to her husband, "Annabelle's gone."

"What do you mean . . . gone?"

"She's nowhere on the property, and some of her clothes and her carpetbag are missing. But that's not all. Missus Kraft just told me Joe Hoover was carrying three thousand dollars in a belt pouch, the money her husband was shouting about last night, and that's missing, too."

"My God, you don't believe Annabelle stole it?"

"I don't know what to believe."

"She'd never do such a thing. She's not a thief."

Sophie Murdock was looking at the stalls. "The saddle horses . . . they're all here."

"Yes, and she's not foolish enough to go traipsing off on foot."

"Missus Devane thinks she may be with the peddler, Shock."

"What!"

"Missus Devane may be right," I said. "Shock was in a hurry to pull out this morning. Stolen money in his pocket and maybe the girl hidden in his wagon could be the real reason."

"What're you saying, Nesbitt? That he kidnapped my daughter?"

"More likely she went of her own free will, with or without his knowledge."

Murdock said grimly: "Well, I'll find out. It's been less than two hours since Shock drove out and he can't make fast time in that wagon of his. With luck I can catch him on horseback before he reaches River Bend."

"I'll go with you," I said. "Shock's fast with that revolver of his, and a crack shot. Two makes better odds."

"Three makes better still," Pete Dell said.

"Murdock and I can do the job. Best if you stay here with the women."

"You hand out orders real easy, mister. Who put you in charge?"

"Don't argue with him, Pete," Murdock said. "We don't have any time to waste."

He sent his wife into the house for his sidearm and shell belt; I was already wearing mine. I saddled the rented piebald. Murdock didn't own a decent saddle horse, but Luke Kraft's roan gelding was broke enough to let a stranger throw Kraft's old McClellan saddle on his back and climb aboard. We were out of the barn and on the levee road inside of five minutes.

The road was in reasonably good shape after the storm. Rain-puddled and muddy, so we couldn't run the animals even though it chafed Murdock not to. I set the pace at a steady lope that was still some faster than Shock could drive that peddler's wagon of his, and we had no trouble maintaining it.

Mostly we rode in silence, except for one brief exchange. Murdock twisted his head my way and said: "Just who are you, Nesbitt?"

"Does it matter?"

"You talk and act like a lawman. Are you one?"

"In a way. I work for the Pinkertons."

"So that's it. That's how you knew about me."

"We'll talk about that later."

"Does Bellright know yet?"

"Not yet."

"All for yourself, eh? How much are you getting for me, dead or alive? Five thousand? Ten? More?"

"Later, Murdock. Keep your mind on Shock and your daughter for now."

The morning was cold and gray, the debris-choked slough waters on both sides receding and mist rising here and there from the half-drowned cat-tails along the banks. Birds screeched and chattered, frogs croaked long and loud—the only sounds that reached my ears. We had the road to ourselves, but there were fresh wheel and hoof tracks to mark the passage of Shock's wagon.

I slowed as we passed a side road that cut away through a swampy peninsula to the north. There were no tracks at the entrance to the road, but the grass and pig weed farther on seemed to be mashed down in places. I kept us riding ahead because I couldn't think of a reason for Shock to have detoured onto a side road—not until we rounded a bend and came on the fallen sycamore.

"That tree's been down a while," Murdock said. "There's no way Shock could have gotten his wagon around it."

"He didn't," I said. "He doubled back to that side road we passed. Where does it lead?"

"Crucifixion River. What's left of it."

"Any other way out of there?"

"An overgrown track the sect members used. But Shock wouldn't know about that."

"Your daughter does, though, doesn't she?"

"Yes," he said, tight-lipped. "Annabelle knows."

We rode back to the intersection. As we turned onto the Crucifixion River road, I leaned down for a better look at the ground. Up close you could see where Shock had tried to rub out and hide the wagon tracks at the turning. A short ways beyond I spied a pile of horse manure that still steamed in the cold air. We couldn't be far behind them now, I judged.

I said as much to Murdock, and, riding as fast as we dared, we followed the wagon tracks through the wet grass and swampy earth.

ANNABELLE MURDOCK

I sat forward as Crucifixion River came into view ahead. It was an awful, bleak place in the best of weather, and on a dark gray day like this one the look of it made me shiver and hunch up even more inside my black dog coat. Except for marsh birds, the quiet was eerie. You could almost hear the people singing "We Shall Gather at the River", the way they had been the day they arrived and Dad and Mother ferried them across the slough. I was just a little girl then, but I still remembered the singing and it still gave me chills.

There was a big weedy meadow where the road ended, stretching out along the banks of the mud-brown river. At one end were the remnants of the potato and corn and vegetable patches the sect people had started, and at the other was a church or meeting house and about a dozen cabins built back among willows and swamp oaks. There wasn't much left of the buildings now. After the people moved away, shanty boaters had come in and carted off everything that was left behind. Even doors, window coverings, floorboards. They were all just hollow shells now, some of them with collapsed walls and roofs. Dead things waiting for the swampland and the river to swallow them up.

"Now isn't this a pretty spot," James Shock said.

Pretty? It was like visiting a cemetery.

But I didn't say anything. I hadn't looked at him since we left the levee road and I didn't look at him now. I sat away over on the wagon seat, as far away from him as I could get, and hunched and hugged myself and tried not to think what was going to happen.

He wasn't James Never Jim Shock to me any more. He wasn't a handsome, romantic, banjo-playing traveling man; he was just a peddler and a cold-souled, foul-mouthed killer, and I didn't know how I ever could have believed he was a man to run away with and give my favors to. Shame made my face and neck flush hot. I wasn't ready to leave the delta yet, on my own or with anybody. I knew that now. What an addle-pated fool I'd been!

I kept remembering the way he'd talked and the look on his face when he found me in the wagon, as if I were a bratty child instead of a woman— as if he'd like nothing better than to paddle my backside, or do something even worse to me. His eyes—Lord, that cold, ugly, stare! It wasn't anything at all like the way his eyes had been in the common room last night. That James Shock had been a sham, a sweet-talking wolf in sheep's clothing. This was the real James Shock, sitting next to me right now. And I was as purely scared of him as I'd been of anything in my whole life.

"This road just ended," he said. "And I don't see any other."

I gestured without looking at him. "It runs through that motte of swamp oak down along the river, on the far side of the meeting house."

"It better had. And it better lead where you say, back to the levee road."

"Why would I lie to you?"

"Well, that's right, now, isn't it? You wouldn't have any reason to lie."

"None at all. What . . . what are you going to do with me?"

He didn't answer, just snapped the reins and clattered us across the meadow toward the meeting house. We were almost there, angling past the big empty shell, when he shifted around in a way that made me cast a quick glance in his direction. He was holding the reins in his left hand and he'd moved his right down and was pulling the tail of his coat back, reaching inside to his belt.

I don't know how I knew he was about to draw his revolver, and what he intended to do with it, but I did know, all at once, and never mind that I couldn't see any rhyme or reason for him to want to harm me. I just knew, with a certainty that made the hair on my scalp stand straight up, that he was planning to kill me as soon as he was sure of where that other road was.

I'd been scared before. Now I was terrified.

"Annabelle? You sure, now, the road starts in that motte of trees?"

I couldn't have spoken if I'd tried. And I didn't dare sit there next to him a second longer. My only hope was to jump off the wagon and try to get away from him, and that was what I did, quick as a cat.

I landed all right on both feet, but then I lost my balance and sprawled headlong in the wet grass. Shock yelled something, but I didn't listen to it. I rolled over and pulled my legs under me and lifted my skirts and ran as fast as I'd ever run, away from the wagon toward the meeting house.

The open doorway yawned ahead. I was almost there, almost safe. . . . And then—oh, God!—he started shooting at me.

T.J. MURDOCK

The first two shots sounded, faint and echoing in the morning stillness, when we were a few hundred rods from the camp. I pulled back hard on the reins; so did Nesbitt. The ghost buildings weren't within sight yet, hidden behind a screen of trees ahead.

"Small caliber," he said. "Handgun, not a rifle."

"Christ!"

"Can't be Shock. What would he be firing at?"

"Nobody else out here."

"Hunters, shanty boaters?"

"Not this soon after a big storm."

Another shot cracked.

My heart slammed and my mouth turned dry as dust. I kicked Kraft's roan into a run, no longer mindful of the boggy ground. Nesbitt was right behind me. I had stopped caring what happened to me, but Annabelle . . . if anything happened to Annabelle. . . .

JAMES SHOCK

The little bitch had caught me by surprise, jumping off the wagon that way. I yanked Nell to a halt, dragged on the brake with my left hand, and drew the revolver with my right. I had it out quickly enough, while she was still running, but haste threw off my aim. The round missed wide, tearing splinters from the building wall. I steadied my arm and fired again just as she ducked through the doorway inside. I couldn't tell if I'd hit her or not.

Cursing, I hauled the Greener out from under the seat and jumped down and ran over to the tumble-down building. By grab, I'd blow her damned head off when I caught her.

ANNABELLE MURDOCK

Hide!

But there was nowhere to hide in the meeting house. It was just one big room, with no partitions or cubbyholes and a section of the roof gone and a hole in the back wall where the fireplace had collapsed.

I couldn't stay here. I had to get out quick and find some place else. The woods, one of the other cabins, any place where Shock wouldn't find me. I wasn't hurt, but I'd felt the heat of the second bullet on my cheek as it whizzed by. I was so scared I thought I might wet myself.

Enough daylight came in through the holes so that I could see well enough. There wasn't anything on the uneven floor but weeds and animal droppings and pools of rain water. I stumbled across it to the jumble of fireplace stones, clambered and clawed my way over and through them to the opening in the wall. My foot slipped before I reached it and my knee knocked hard on one of the rocks.

And just as that happened, I heard a *thwack* above my head and then the bark of Shock's revolver behind me.

Gasping, sobbing, I crawled over the rest of the stones and flung myself through the hole, tearing a long rip in the sleeve of my coat. My knee burned like fire, but I didn't care as I scrambled to my feet. All I could think was: Run!

Run, run, run!

BOONE NESBITT

Kraft's roan was a better horse than the piebald and Murdock was ten rods ahead when we cleared the trees and Crucifixion River came into view. But I had only a peripheral look at the crumbling ghost camp and Shock's wagon stopped in the open meadow. What caught and held my attention was the girl staggering across open ground between the shell of a large building and a cluster of decaying shacks squatting among the trees.

"Annabelle!"

It was Murdock who yelled her name. We both veered sharply in her direction, guns already filling our hands. She heard us coming, twisted her head in our direction, but she had the sense not to slow up any. Shock was chasing her; in the next second, he came busting through a hole in the sagging back wall of the large building, brandishing a shotgun.

He spied us before he'd taken half a dozen steps. He swung around, crouching, as Murdock bore down on him. I pulled up hard just as Murdock fired—a wild shot, like most from the back of a running horse. Shock didn't even flinch. He let go with one barrel of the Greener, and the spray of buckshot knocked Murdock off the roan's back and sent him rolling through the grass.

I swung out of leather. If the ground hadn't been wet and slick, I would've been able to set myself for a quick, clear shot at Shock. As it was, my boots slid out from under me and I went down hard enough on my backside to jar the Colt loose from my grip. It landed a few feet away, and by the time I located it and started to scrabble toward it, Shock was up and moving my way with that Greener leveled.

I heard him say, "All right, you son of a bitch," as I got my hand on the Colt, and I was cold sure it was too late, I was a dead man.

Only it didn't happen that way.

It was Shock who died in that next second.

Murdock was hurt, but the buckshot hadn't done him enough damage to keep him out of the play. He'd struggled up onto one knee and he put a slug clean through Shock's head at thirty paces. The Greener's second barrel emptied with a roar, but the buckshot went straight down as he was falling. Dead and on his way to hell before he hit the ground.

I got up slowly, went over to him for a quick look to make sure, then holstered my weapon, and went to Murdock's side. He squinted up at me, his jaw clenched tightly. There was blood and buckshot holes on his left arm and shoulder and the side of his neck, but he wasn't torn up as badly as he might've been.

"Dad! Dad!"

Annabelle. She'd seen it happen, and, now that it was finished, she'd come running. She dropped down beside him, weeping, and he hugged her and crooned a little the way a relieved father does when he sees his child is unharmed.

There were some things I wanted to say to Murdock, but this wasn't the time or place. I turned away from them and went to where the peddler's wagon stood in the meadow, to see what I could find to treat Murdock's wounds.

ANNABELLE MURDOCK

I huddled in my bed, the quilt drawn tightly around me. My scrapes and bruises hurt, but not nearly as much as my conscience. For a while after we got back from Crucifixion River in the peddler's wagon, I'd cried and felt sorry for myself, but I wasn't feeling sorry for *me* any more. . . .

A tap on the door and Mother came in. I asked her how Dad was, and she said she and Mrs. Devane had gotten all the buckshot out of his arm and shoulder and she'd given him some laudanum for the pain.

"He's going to be all right, isn't he?"

"Of course he is. He and Mister Hoover both."

I said: "It's all my fault." And then—fool that I am—I started crying again. "If I hadn't fallen for James Shock and hidden in his wagon, Dad wouldn't've been shot. I did an awful thing, and he could have died and so could I."

Mother sat beside me and patted my back, just as she'd done when I was a little girl and had hurt myself. It only made me sob harder. I felt like a child right now. A *bad* one.

She said: "That's true enough. But we've made you live such a sheltered, isolated life, you couldn't possibly know what a wicked man that peddler was. And you've never made a secret of how much you want to leave the delta."

"Maybe it's not so bad here, after all." But I didn't really believe that. Did Mother? I didn't think so, but she'd made the best of the past eight years in this place. So had Dad. The least I could do was the same while I was still living here.

I wasn't crying any more. I wiped my eyes with a corner of the sheet and said: "Someday I may still want to go to San Francisco, have a different kind of life. You'd understand, wouldn't you?"

"Of course we would. But you'll tell us when the time comes, let us help you? You won't try to run away again?"

"No, Mother, I've learned my lesson," I said, and I meant it. "I'll never run away again, not ever."

RACHEL KRAFT

I walked out of the roadhouse as the driver was bringing the stage around from the livery barn. Caroline Devane, wearing a gray serge traveling dress, stood still as a statue looking out over Twelve-Mile Slough, her crocheting bag and reticule beside her; the wind blew wisps of her hair, and her gaze was remote, as if she'd already traveled many miles from here.

I said her name, and she turned and gave me a wan smile. "Have you made a decision about your future?"

"Yes. I'm going on to my sister and her family, because they're expecting me, but I won't stay long. There's a shortage of trained nurses in this state. I ought to be able to find employment in Los Angeles or San Diego."

"Do you have enough money to live until you do?"

"Enough, if I'm fortunate. Before I left Sacramento, I sold my jewelry."

Mr. Nesbitt had returned the $3,000 to me when he and Annabelle and her poor father came back with word of the peddler's death, and, after talking to Joe, I'd put the money into his belt pouch. Now I pressed the pouch into Caroline's hands.

"Perhaps this will help."

She stared down at it, then opened it. Her eyes widened with astonishment when she saw the bills and specie inside.

"It's half the money I took from my husband's safe," I said. "Fifteen hundred dollars."

"I can't accept it." She closed the pouch and thrust it back at me. "Why would you want to give me so much money?"

"You saved Joe's life."

"I only did what I was trained to do."

"Please take it. Joe and I want you to have it."

"No, I wouldn't feel right. . ."

"Please."

Our eyes locked—two stubborn, proud women.

"You're going away," she said, "you'll need it. . . ."

"I'm not going away and I don't need it. Joe and I decided to return to the ranch when he's able to travel. My late husband's affairs have to be put in order and there are other things that need attending to. After that . . . well, we'll see."

"Still, I can't take money from you. . . ."

"It's not a gift, it's a loan. I can have a paper drawn up to that effect if you like."

"But you hardly know me. . . ."

"I know enough. You're good and honest and caring and you've already paid a high price for your sins. You shouldn't have to pay any more."

"I . . . I don't know what to say."

"Say yes. It will make starting your new life so much easier."

She was silent for several seconds. Then, slowly: "Well, if it's to be a loan. . . ."

"From one new friend to another."

I pressed the pouch into her hands again. This time she kept it, her eyes bright with tears.

Two stubborn, proud women, one strong, the other learning how to be.

T.J. MURDOCK

In the darkened bedroom I lay waiting for the pain in my bandaged shoulder to ease. It had been a long, rough ride in Shock's wagon with Nesbitt driving and Annabelle making me as comfortable as she could inside, and the removal of the buckshot and treatment of my wounds had been another ordeal. But all I cared about, then and now, was that Annabelle was safe and unhurt.

"How're you feeling, Murdock?"

Nesbitt. I hadn't even heard him come in. If I'd been more alert, I might have been surprised to see that he wore one of my old, grease-stained dusters, unbuttoned, over a black broadcloth suit.

"Drowsy," I said. "Sophie gave me laudanum."

"You'll have a doctor soon enough. You and Hoover both."

"I won't be in any shape to travel for a few days. You figure on staying here until then?"

Instead of answering, he said: "Pete Dell's ready to travel right now. I told your wife I'd help her and Annabelle winch the stage across to Middle Island."

"That why you're wearing my duster?"

"That's why." There was a little silence and I could feel the pain dulling, my eyelids growing heavy. Then he said: "I owe you thanks for saving my life in Crucifixion River. Another second and Shock would've blown my head off with that Greener."

"I know it."

"You could've waited and let that happen before you shot him. Some men in your position would have, to save their own hides."

"I'm not one of them."

"No," he said, "you're not. Not the kind of man Patrick Bellright thinks you are at all."

"Won't make any difference to him when you hand me over."

"I won't be handing you over."

I wasn't sure I'd heard him right. "Say that again."

"I'm not giving you to Bellright," Nesbitt said. "Seems I made a mistake . . . you're not Harold P. Baxter, you're T.J. Murdock. Soon as the stage is ferried across, I'll be heading to River Bend to talk to the sheriff and send you a doctor, then on back to San Francisco."

"But . . . the reward . . . ?"

"To hell with the reward. I've gotten along well enough on a Pinkerton salary and I'll keep right on getting along. I don't need a piece of land in the Valley of the Moon."

I was too numb to ask what that meant. All I could manage was: "Why?"

"You saved my life, now I'm returning the favor. Simple as that. And you can quit worrying about somebody else like me finding you. It's not likely to happen, and, even if it did, it'd have to be before next summer. After that it won't matter."

"Won't matter? What do you mean?"

"I checked up on Bellright before I came out here. The old bugger's dying of cancer. He'll be gone in six months and his vendetta with him." Nesbitt went to the door, then stopped again long enough to say: "I hope you keep on writing for the *Argonaut* and *The Overland Monthly*, Murdock. I really do enjoy those sketches of yours."

Then he went out and left me to the first real peace I'd known in eight long years.

THE END

Bill Pronzini Bibliography

(1943-)

Crime Fiction:

The Stalker (Random House, 1971)
Panic! (Random House, 1972)
Snowbound (Putnam's, 1974)
Games (Putnam's, 1976)
Masques (Arbor House, 1981)
The Cambodia File (with Jack
  Anderson; Doubleday, 1981;
  mainstream)
Day of the Moon (with Jeffrey
  Wallmann; Robert Hale, 1983)
The Eye (with John Lutz; Mysterious
  Press, 1984)
The Lighthouse (with Marcia Muller;
  St. Martin's, 1987)
With an Extreme Burning (Carroll &
  Graf, 1994; reprinted as *The
  Tormentor*, Leisure, 2000)
Blue Lonesome (Walker, 1995)
A Wasteland of Strangers (Walker,
  1997)
Nothing But the Night (Walker, 1999)
In an Evil Time (Walker, 2001)
Step to the Graveyard Easy (Walker,
  2002)
The Alias Man (Walker, 2004)
The Crimes of Jordan Wise (Walker,
  2006)
The Other Side of Silence (Walker,
  2008)
The Hidden (Walker, 2010)
The Violated (Bloomsbury, 2017)
The Peaceful Valley Crime Wave
  (Tor/Forge, 2019; western mystery)

"Nameless Detective" Series:

The Snatch (Random House, 1972)
The Vanished (Random House, 1973)
Undercurrent (Random House, 1973)
Blowback (Random House, 1977)
Twospot (with Colin Wilcox;
  Putnam's, 1978)
Labyrinth (St. Martin's, 1980)
Hoodwink (St. Martin's, 1981)
Scattershot (St. Martin's, 1982)
Dragonfire (St. Martin's, 1982)
Casefile: The Best of the "Nameless
  Detective" Stories (St. Martin's,
  1983; stories)
Bindlestiff (St. Martin's, 1983)
Quicksilver (St. Martin's, 1984)
Double (with Marcia Muller; St.
  Martin's, 1984)
Nighshades (St. Martin's, 1984)
Bones (St. Martin's, 1985)
Deadfall (St. Martin's, 1986)
Shackles (St. Martin's, 1988)
Jackpot (Delacorte, 1990)
Breakdown (Delacorte, 1991)
Quarry (Delacorte, 1992)
Epitaphs (Delacorte, 1992)
Demons (Delacorte, 1993)
Hardcase (Delacorte, 1995)
Sentinels (Carroll & Graf, 1996)
Spadework: "Nameless Detective"
  Stories (Crippen & Landru, 1996;
  stories)
Illusions (Carroll & Graf, 1997)
Boobytrap (Carroll & Graf, 1998)
Crazybone (Carroll & Graf, 2000)
Bleeders (Carroll & Graf, 2002)
Spook (Carroll & Graf, 2003)
Scenarios: A "Nameless Detective"
  Casebook (Five-Star, 2003; stories)

Nightcrawlers (Tor/Forge, 2005)
Mourners (Tor/Forge, 2006)
Savages (Tor/Forge, 2007)
Fever (Tor/Forge, 2008)
Schemers (Tor/Forge, 2009)
Betrayers (Tor/Forge, 2010)
Camouflage (Tor/Forge, 2011)
Hellbox (Tor/Forge, 2012)
Kinsmen (Cemetery Dance, 2012; novella)
Femme (Cemetery Dance, 2012; novella)
Nemesis (Tor/Forge, 2013)
Strangers (Tor/Forge, 2014)
Vixen (Tor/Forge, 2015)
Zigzag (Tor/Forge, 2016; stories)
Endgame (Tor/Forge, 2017)

Carpenter and Quincannon Series:

Quincannon (Walker, 1985)
Beyond the Grave (with Marcia Muller; Walker, 1986)
Carpenter and Quincannon (Crippen & Landru, 1998; stories)
Burgade's Crossing (Five-Star, 2003)
Quincannon's Game (Five-Star, 2005)
The Bughouse Affair (with Marcia Muller; Tor/Forge, 2013)
The Spook Lights Affair (with Marcia Muller; Tor/Forge, 2013)
The Body Snatchers Affair (with Marcia Muller; Tor/Forge, 2015)
The Plague of Thieves Affair (with Marcia Muller; Tor/Forge, 2016)
The Dangerous Ladies Affair (with Marcia Muller; Tor/Forge, 2017)
The Bags of Tricks Affair (Tor/Forge, 2018)
The Flimflam Affair (Tor/Forge, 2019)
The Stolen Gold Affair (Tor/Forge, 2020)
The Paradise Affair (Tor/Forge, 2021)

As by Robert Hart Davis
The Pillars of Salt Affair (*The Man from U.N.C.L.E. Magazine*, 1967; novella)
Charlie Chan in The Pawns of Death (with Jeffrey Wallmann; *Charlie Chan's Mystery Magazine*, 1974; reprinted as by Bill Pronzini & Jeffrey Wallman, Wildside Press, 2002)

As by Jack Foxx
The Jade Figurine (Bobbs-Merrill, 1972)
Dead Run (Bobbs-Merrill, 1975)
Freebooty (Bobbs-Merrill, 1976)
Wildfire (Bobbs-Merrill, 1978)

As by Alex Saxon
A Run in Diamonds (Pocket, 1973)

In Collaboration with Barry N. Malzberg
The Running of Beasts (Putnam's, 1976)
Acts of Mercy (Putnam's, 1977)
Night Screams (Playboy Press, 1979)
Prose Bowl (St. Martin's, 1980)
Problems Solved (Crippen & Landru, 2003; stories)
On Account of Darkness and Other SF Stories (2004; stories)

Mystery Short-Story Collections:

Graveyard Plots (St. Martin's, 1985)
Small Felonies (St. Martin's, 1988)
Stacked Deck (Pulphouse, 1991)
Carmody's Run (Dark Harvest, 1992)
Duo (with Marcia Muller; Five-Star, 1998)
Sleuths (Five-Star, 1999)
Night Freight (Leisure, 2000)
Oddments (Five-Star, 2000)
More Oddments (Five-Star, 2001)

Dago Red (Ramble House, 2010)
The Cemetery Man (Perfect Crime, 2014)
A Little Red Book of Murder Stories (Borderlands Press, 2016)
Small Felonies 2 (Stark House Press, 2022)

Western Novels:

The Gallows Land (Walker, 1983)
Starvation Camp (Doubleday, 1984)
The Last Days of Horse-Shy Halloran (M. Evans, 1987)
The Hangings (Walker, 1989)
Firewind (M. Evans, 1989)
Give-A-Damn Jones (Tor/Forge, 2018)
As by William Jeffrey
Duel at Gold Buttes (with Jeffrey Wallmann; Tower, 1981)
Border Fever (with Jeffrey Wallmann; Leisure, 1983)

Western Short-Story Collections:

The Best Western Stories of Bill Pronzini (Ohio University Press, 1990)
All the Long Years: Western Stories (Five-Star, 2001)
Coyote and Quarter-Moon (Five-Star, 2006)
Crucifixion River (with Marcia Muller; Five-Star, 2007)

Non-Fiction Books:

Gun in Cheek (Coward McCann, 1982)
1001 Midnights: The Aficionado's Guide to Mystery and Detective Fiction (with Marcia Muller; Arbor House, 1986)
Son of a Gun in Cheek (Mysterious Press, 1987)
Sixgun in Cheek (Crossover Press, 1997)

Made in the USA
Middletown, DE
21 March 2025